# The Three Loves OF CHARLIE DELANEY

## BOOK THREE

### JOEY W. KISER

# CHARLIE DELANEY
## BOOK THREE

iUniverse books may be ordered through booksellers or by contacting:

iUniverse
1663 Liberty Drive
Bloomington, IN 47403
www.iuniverse.com
1-800-Authors (1-800-288-4677)

Because of the dynamic nature of the Internet, any web addresses or links contained in this book may have changed since publication and may no longer be valid. The views expressed in this work are solely those of the author and do not necessarily reflect the views of the publisher, and the publisher hereby disclaims any responsibility for them. Any people depicted in stock imagery provided by Thinkstock are models, and such images are being used for illustrative purposes only. Certain stock imagery © Thinkstock.

ISBN: 978-1-4917-7654-4 (sc)
ISBN: 978-1-4917-8629-1 (hc)
ISBN: 978-1-4917-7653-7 (e)

Library of Congress Control Number: 2015917892

Print information available on the last page.

iUniverse rev. date: 1/08/2016

# CONTENTS

# Chapter 1
## CHARLIE'S THIRD LOVE

Charlie lies in the hospital for the three days before he hears the news about Karen. Mrs. Thomas is there when he wakes up. Charlie's right wrist is wrapped in a bandage. He has several other bandages on his head and other parts of his body. His voice sounds groggy as he asks for some water. Mrs. Thomas kindly hands him a glass.

She stands up and looks down at Charlie with kindness and compassion. Her voice is soft and kind. "Charlie. Hello there, Charlie. How are you feeling?"

"Ma, tell me … Tell me about Karen. Is she all right?"

Mrs. Thomas sits on the bed and gently begins to brush Charlie's hair with her fingers. She looks deep into his eyes, and a single tear runs down her cheek, dropping on Charlie's chest. "Charlie, there is something I must tell you."

Charlie knows something is wrong by the tone in Mrs. Thomas's voice. He quietly lies there as she continues.

"Charlie … you see, Charlie … Karen didn't make it." Her face is filled with compassion as she speaks the words.

"When can I see my bride? You know we still have a honeymoon to go on. She will like—"

Mrs. Thomas turns her head sideways in disbelief and interrupts Charlie. "Charlie, didn't you hear me? I said Karen didn't make it. She died, Charlie. She was buried yesterday."

"No! You are wrong! Don't lie to me! Karen is fine! We just got married. She has to be fine. We are going on our honeymoon. Don't tell me she is …" Charlie begins to cry hysterically. His aching body prevents him from acting wildly. Mrs. Thomas leans over and hugs him as he cries out terribly. She comforts him until he gets control of himself.

She brushes his hair gently as she says, "Everything will be all right, Charlie. We will just have to take care of each other now. Everything will be all right. Okay, Charlie?"

Charlie continues to cry, but silently. After a few minutes, Charlie breaks his silence. "Who hit us? Who hit us?"

Mrs. Thomas looks down at Charlie with compassion. "The police said it was a drunk driver. He was arrested and sent to jail, Charlie."

Hearing this, Charlie becomes furious. "Why, God?" he exclaims. "Why did you let this happen? Why did you allow Karen to be killed?"

Mrs. Thomas gives Charlie a stern look. "Charlie, try to understand something. There are a lot of things that happen in this world that we don't fully understand. We can't blame God for everything bad that happens. My husband died in Vietnam. I don't fully understand why he died. I guess I never will, but I can't blame God for something I don't understand."

Charlie listens to Mrs. Thomas with his complete attention and says sadly, "But I loved Karen. We were going to have a family and—"

Mrs. Thomas interrupts him. "Charlie. She is gone now. You can't keep thinking about what you and she were going to do. You have to think about the future without her now. I know it's going to be difficult, but if you don't let her go, it's going to be even more difficult."

"I just don't understand." Charlie begins to cry again.

The tears running down Charlie's face seem to impact Mrs. Thomas greatly. To see a grown man cry ignites an explosion of despair in her feminine soul. She begins to run her fingers through Charlie's hair again as tears of sorrow drop from her eyes. "I know, Charlie. I know what you are feeling now."

"No, you don't, Ma."

Mrs. Thomas looks surprised. "What makes you say that, Charlie?"

Charlie looks into her confused eyes. "You see, Ma, all my life I have had a battle with depression. Lately, I have been on medication to overcome the pain. But since the wreck I haven't had a chance to take any of the lithium. That's what I take—lithium."

Mrs. Thomas gets up and walks over to her pocketbook. She takes out a prescription bottle and walks back to Charlie's bed. "Is this what you take, Charlie?"

Charlie looks at the bottle and sees his name on it. "Yeah, that's it! Where did you get that?"

"I found it in your suitcase."

"Oh yeah. I was going to tell Karen about it while we were on our honeymoon. Would you please give me a couple and a glass of water?"

Mrs. Thomas doesn't hesitate to do what Charlie asked. Charlie swallows the two pills with ease.

Mrs. Thomas timidly says, "How long does it take before you start to feel it working?"

"For me, it's about three hours. This stuff is a godsend! It is the best thing I have ever experienced in my life. If you knew all the misery I have suffered in my life because of depression, you could understand it better."

Mrs. Thomas smiles. "Did you hear what you just said, Charlie?"

"Huh?"

"You just said, 'This stuff is a godsend.' Lithium. Is that what it is, Charlie?"

"Yes. That's right."

"You see, God sent you something to make your life better. Then you said that if I knew what misery you have suffered because of depression, I could understand it better. Isn't that what you said, Charlie?"

"Yes. What are you getting at, Ma?"

"Just this: we don't understand why these bad things happen to us. But if we did understand, we surely wouldn't blame God. As long as we are confused about what went on, we shouldn't blame God."

Charlie listens intently to Mrs. Thomas.

"Just like that drunk driver who ran into you and Karen. You shouldn't blame God for what he did."

Charlie gets a mean look in his eyes. "What happened to him? Was he hurt too?"

Mrs. Thomas turns her head away from Charlie. "No, Charlie. He wasn't hurt very badly. He went to the hospital but was released in less than an hour."

Infuriated, Charlie bellows, "I'll kill him! When I get out of here, I will kill him!"

Looking disturbed, Mrs. Thomas gets up and begins to walk around the room. "Oh no, you're not, Charlie! You are going to do no such thing!" Mrs. Thomas looks at Charlie with a harsh, disgusted expression, and his attitude changes.

"Ma? That man killed your daughter. Don't you think he should pay for it?"

"Charlie, Charlie, Charlie. Do you think killing him will bring Karen back?"

"No, but that's not the thing. He should pay for what he did!"

"He will pay for what he did. He will have to live with himself for the rest of his life. Killing him would only relieve him of his anguish. Can't you see that, Charlie?"

"Yeah, I guess so. I just hate him for what he did. Don't you hate him too?"

"Charlie …" Mrs. Thomas pauses for a moment before she continues. "Charlie, God doesn't hate the sinner but only the sin he commits. That's the way we should look at it. We should not hate the man that killed Karen but hate the sin of killing her. Hating someone will only make you bitter. It will eat your soul up! Nothing good will come from hating someone, only more hate."

Charlie once again listens quietly to Mrs. Thomas's words.

She walks over and sits back down on Charlie's bed, giving him a warm, compassionate smile. "You see, Charlie, I know what I am talking about. I used to hate the United States Air Force something awful. When Alan was shot down over in South Vietnam, they refused to answer my questions. All they told me was that Alan had been shot down by enemy aircraft. They contradicted themselves several times on the matter. Eventually, they told me to stop bothering them altogether. They were very rude to me, Charlie. I got very resentful at the whole department. They told me there was a war going on, and they didn't want a lot of negative publicity on the matter. All I wanted to know was the truth."

Charlie frowns at Mrs. Thomas. "He didn't die that way, Ma."

There is a long moment of silence in the room. Mrs. Thomas stares at Charlie peculiarly. "What are you talking about, Charlie?"

He feels forced to answer. "I know your husband didn't die that way. He died from friendly fire."

Mrs. Thomas gives Charlie a very stern look, and after another tense pause, she asks, "Charlie, how do you know how he died?"

Charlie looks at Mrs. Thomas seriously. "You see, Ma, before I started dating Karen, I hired a private investigator to find out about her and her family. I just wanted to know something about Karen so I could develop a relationship with her. Please don't be angry with me."

Mrs. Thomas studies his face carefully and with a concerned look says, "Go on, Charlie. Tell me more about Alan."

Charlie motions for her to come closer, and she does. Charlie holds her hand and says, "Ma, the investigator had a buddy up in Washington, DC … He found a report on how Colonel Alan Thomas was shot down. It caused a stir after he made a copy of the report, and—"

Mrs. Thomas excitedly interrupts him. "Charlie! Do you have the report?"

Charlie hesitates for a second. "Yes, I do, but …"

"But nothing. I want to see that report! I want to see that report right now!"

"Now wait a minute! There is something I need to tell you first."

Mrs. Thomas nods impatiently as her facial expression communicates authority and determination.

"You see, Ma, when my investigator's source found that file, he got into a lot of trouble. A general from the United States Air Force paid my PI a visit."

Mrs. Thomas removes her hand from Charlie's. "What was the general's name?"

Charlie looks at Mrs. Thomas with confusion. "I don't know what his name was. Will you let me finish?"

"Okay, Charlie, go ahead."

"This general wanted to know who wanted this information. My PI didn't divulge anything to him, but the general made it clear that you should never find out about it. My PI's buddy up in Washington, DC, got in a lot of trouble over it. My PI said he would get into trouble too if you ever found out about that report."

"Are you finished?"

Charlie, not knowing what to say, replies, "Well, I guess so."

"Fine. You show me that report, or I will break both your legs."

"Yes, ma'am! I will show you it the first chance I get."

Mrs. Thomas smiles at Charlie as a doctor comes into the room.

"How are you feeling today, Mr. Delaney?"

"Physically, I feel like shit, but I believe I'll live."

The doctor looks at Charlie with concern and says, "Good. You should be able to leave the hospital in a couple or three days. There seems to be no internal damage, I'm glad to say. You are very lucky you weren't hurt any worse than you were."

"Yeah right, I'm so lucky I wasn't hurt anymore. My wife has just been taken from me, and I'm supposed to feel lucky. Ha!"

The doctor gives Charlie another concerned look. "I know this is an awful situation, Mr. Delaney, but matters could have been worse. I want you to rest now; later on in the day, I want you to get up and try to walk around a little bit."

Charlie doesn't say anything but looks at the doctor like he doesn't care what the doctor just said.

"Yes, doctor, we will see that he gets out of that bed today."

The doctor smiles at Mrs. Thomas and then looks back over at Charlie. "So let's shoot for Friday, Mr. Delaney. All the test reports should be in by then. If everything goes well, you can go home then."

Charlie nods his head in agreement, and the doctor exits the room.

Mrs. Thomas, anxious to see the reports about Alan, says, "How would you like me to go get you a double cheeseburger right now?"

"That would be great, Ma!"

Mrs. Thomas smiles lovingly at Charlie. She walks over and sits down on his bed and runs her fingers through his hair. She smiles enticingly at him. "Charlie."

"Yes, Ma?"

"Don't you think that calling me 'Ma' is a little outdated now?" Without waiting for a response, Mrs. Thomas kisses Charlie on his forehead. She looks deep into his eyes with a sincere expression. "Charlie, will you promise me something?"

Charlie, overwhelmed by Mrs. Thomas's behavior, says, "Yes, ma'am. What?"

"Promise me you will call me by my first name from now on."

Charlie marvels at the delicate tone with which Mrs. Thomas speaks. He gazes into her alluring eyes as she softly continues.

"I want you to call me Elizabeth from now on. Is that okay with you, Charlie?"

Charlie, mesmerized by her stare, says, "Yes, ma'am. I mean … yes, Elizabeth." After calling Mrs. Thomas by her first name for the first time, he looks at her in a totally different way, enchanted.

She slowly reaches down and lightly kisses his soft, unsuspecting lips. The tender touch of their lips pressing together activates an unusual feeling in both of them. Elizabeth breaks the gentle but long-lasting kiss. She runs her fingers through Charlie's hair and around his ear. They stare at each other with wonder and enjoyment.

Elizabeth breaks the silence with a soft utterance. "I don't have anybody else in the whole world now, Charlie."

"I don't have anybody in the whole world either, Elizabeth."

"I guess we will have to take care of each other from now on."

Charlie smiles as he meets Elizabeth's mysterious gaze. They silently look at each other as Elizabeth continues to gently run her fingers through his hair.

"While I am gone to get you a cheeseburger, I think I will stop by your house and tidy up a bit. I will bring you some clothes so when they say you can leave, you will be ready."

"Thank you, Elizabeth. That will be fine."

"Oh, by the way, since I will be at your house, why don't you tell me where that report is?"

Charlie grins before saying, "In my bedroom closet, on the top shelf, all the way in the back, to the right."

"Thank you, Charlie. I will be back shortly. I want you to get out of this bed today."

"You and I both. I can't wait till I get out of this place. I hate hospitals."

"Well, I'm going to leave now, Charlie. I will see you soon." She gets up from the bed and leaves the room.

Charlie lies back, thinking of Karen, Elizabeth, and that report. He dozes off and sleeps until a nurse comes in and wakes him up. She gets Charlie out of bed, and the two walk up and down the hallway several times before the nurse returns him to his bed. Charlie feels lonely lying there in the quiet, still room. He thinks about what he would have been doing now on his honeymoon if he hadn't been in the car accident. His heart aches with sadness and despair. He is left only with emptiness and sorrow over the loss of his young virgin bride.

Immediately upon leaving the hospital, Elizabeth drives in a mad rush to Charlie's house. She has had all of Charlie's belongings since the automobile accident, including his house keys. She opens the door to Charlie's house and eagerly runs upstairs to his bedroom. She rushes to the closet and looks on the top shelf. She takes down a box from the far back on the right and then sits down on the bed. Elizabeth nervously begins to explore the contents of the box. She finds a large yellow envelope with "Colonel Alan Thomas" written on it. She quickly opens it and dumps the contents on the bed. Picking up the stack of papers, she begins to read the military report on her late husband's death. Tears run down her face in streams as she reads. She doesn't stop until she has finished the entire report.

Back at the hospital, Charlie looks at the clock and sees it is three o'clock. He wonders why Elizabeth hasn't brought him his cheeseburger yet. He begins to feel concerned about her whereabouts. He wonders if he made the right decision by telling her about the report on her late husband. His mind is full of doubt when a doctor walks in.

"Hello, Mr. Delaney. How are you feeling today?"

"Fine, I guess."

"Good, good. I have been told that you have been walking some today. Is that right?"

"Yes. I walked up and down the hall for about fifteen minutes today."

"Good, good. I have some good news you will be glad to hear. You have no internal damages, no broken bones, and it seems everything is mending just fine. I think you can go home by Saturday, maybe even Friday. How does that sound?"

"That sounds just fine. I will be glad to get back home."

"Good, good. I have to run now. It's good to see you are feeling better." The doctor shakes Charlie's hand and departs the room swiftly.

Charlie lies back in the silent room and thinks about going home. The lithium has begun to attack his depression. It feels like a cool breeze blowing on the top of Charlie's brain. It cools the fire that the depression creates. Charlie lies in his bed, content with the outcome of the doctor's report. He then dozes off for a short nap.

When Charlie opens his eyes again, Elizabeth is walking into the room. He smiles a quick grin and asks, "Where have you been? A fellow could starve to death waiting for you to come back."

Elizabeth puts her handbag down on a chair and walks over to Charlie with a sack in her hand. "Didn't they bring you anything to eat, Charlie?"

"Yeah, they brought me something, but I didn't eat it. I want a cheeseburger, a double cheeseburger."

"You do? Well, that's just what I have for you."

Elizabeth pulls the cheeseburger from the sack, and Charlie eagerly takes it from her hand. She watches Charlie eat the sandwich with apparent amusement. She waits until he is finished to bring up the subject of the report.

"Charlie, I want to thank you for letting me read that report. I have always thought Alan died that way, but there was some doubt. Knowing how he died finally gives me some closure. I thank you for finding it out." Teary-eyed, Elizabeth bends down and kisses Charlie on his forehead before sitting down on the bed.

"Guess what?" Charlie says.

"What?" she asks, taking his hand.

"I walked up and down the hallway today."

"That's great, Charlie!"

"The doctor said I could go home by Saturday, maybe Friday."

"Well, Charlie, I am so glad to hear that! That just makes my day complete."

Charlie smiles gladly at Elizabeth, but her happy expression disappears as she looks Charlie in the eye.

"Charlie, there is something I want to tell you."

He looks at her with concern and curiosity and silently waits for her to continue.

"Charlie, you told me about having to take medication for your depression. Well, I have to take medication for something too."

He continues to listen in silence as the atmosphere in the room becomes very intense.

"You see, Charlie, since Alan died, my heart hasn't worked very well. I have been told by my doctor that I have a heart condition. When I am confronted with a great deal of stress and anxiety, it has a negative effect on my heart." Elizabeth pauses, and when she speaks again, her voice is softer. "I just came from my doctor."

"What did he say?"

"He said that I might have to have an operation. He will know more after I go through some tests."

"What kind of tests?"

"I don't know, Charlie, but last night, I was awoken by a very sharp pain in the center of my chest. It only lasted a few seconds, but it scared the hell out of me." Her face is full of worry.

Before Charlie can respond, a nurse enters the room. "Hello, Mr. Delaney. I thought you and I would like to go for a walk."

"No! Not right now. Go away! I am busy right now!"

"Charlie! Don't be rude. She is only doing her job."

"That's right, Mr. Delaney. You want to go home, don't you?"

"Yeah."

"Then we need to get you out of that bed."

"Charlie, I will come and see you tomorrow. You be nice. Okay?"

"Okay, Ma … I mean Elizabeth. It's going to take me a while to get used to calling you by your first name. I will be expecting you tomorrow, and bring me another cheeseburger, okay?"

"Bring you a what?" says the nurse. "You know better than to eat things like that."

"Pay no attention to her, Elizabeth. Bring me one anyway. Okay?"

Looking at him shyly, she says, "Well, we will see, Charlie. Bye now."

As Elizabeth leaves the room, the nurse gives Charlie a stern, ascetic look.

The next day, around noon, Elizabeth enters Charlie's room as he is reading the newspaper. He is excited to see her until he notices she isn't holding a bag.

"Hey! Where's my cheeseburger?"

Elizabeth puts her index finger to her lips. "Not so loud, Charlie. I don't want you to get into any trouble."

"Trouble? All I have is trouble. I'm hungry. I want a cheeseburger."

Elizabeth opens her handbag and pulls out a cheeseburger. She walks over to Charlie's bed and hands it to him. He gladly accepts it.

"Have you been a good boy today, Charlie?"

"No," he says, chuckling. "Yeah, I guess I have. You know that nurse, the one you met yesterday, the one who didn't want me to have a cheeseburger?"

"Yes. What about her?"

"As she was bending over yesterday, after our walk, I reached over and pinched her on her big fat ass. You should have heard her scream," Charlie says, laughing.

"Charlie! Charlie Delaney! You should be ashamed of yourself."

Charlie laughs a little more before he begins to eat his cheeseburger. "She kept on giving me a hard time about eating anything besides what the hospital gives me. Who is she to tell me what I should eat? You should take a look at her large, wide ass. You would think she was a black woman. It stuck out like a turret on a tank."

"Charlie! I have never heard you talk like this."

"I guess being confined to this damn room is making me a little bit edgy." Charlie laughs and takes another bite of his sandwich. "Yeah, when she bent over, I pinched a large chunk of her ass. I pinched hard too! She jumped like a kangaroo, and I laughed as she fussed some more."

"Charlie!"

"The more I laughed, the angrier she got."

"You should apologize to her."

"I probably will. Well … I don't know. It sure was fun to see her jump like that."

Elizabeth sits down on Charlie's bed and watches him as he finishes eating his cheeseburger. He gobbles it down in no time.

"Boy, was that good! I just love cheeseburgers! Thank you, Elizabeth. You see, I am catching on good."

Elizabeth smiles at Charlie upon hearing him use her first name. But her smile diminishes after a moment. "Charlie, I have been reading over the report on Alan's death. There are a few things in it that bother me."

"Go on," Charlie says, giving her his complete attention.

"The part about Alan's radio not working properly—they shot his plane down because they couldn't receive adequate radio contact on the ground. Earlier in the report it states that while on his mission he contacted the other planes he was flying with and told them that his plane wasn't flying properly; as a result he aborted the mission and turned back. You see, Charlie, there is still some doubt about that report."

He looks up at Elizabeth with confusion. "Yeah. I also wondered about that."

"Another thing—if the plane Alan was flying had a malfunction in it, why was he shot down?"

"Yeah, it seems like it would have crashed instead of being shot down."

"And one more thing: part of the report was written by the air force, but the other part, about the plane being shot down, was written by the marines, a Philip Spencer—Corporal Philip Spencer of the United States Marine Corps. This corporal wrote the part about the plane being shot down. Charlie, I know this sounds stupid, but …"

Charlie pays close attention as Elizabeth takes his hand.

"I want to know the truth before I die. Charlie, I want to meet this Corporal Philip Spencer."

Charlie turns his head away as he lets go of her hand. "I don't know, Elizabeth. Trying to locate that corporal will be pretty difficult, maybe impossible."

"I was thinking that maybe that private investigator you hired earlier would help us track this man down."

After a long pause, Charlie turns and looks at Elizabeth. "He told me you were never to see that report. Like I told you before, one of his buddies up in Washington got into a lot of trouble by getting that report for him, and a big-shot general from the air force came down and paid him a visit. Mr. Bowman told me that you were never to see that document. So I don't know if we should pursue the matter anymore."

Elizabeth stands up angrily and bellows, "Well! If you aren't going to help me, I guess I will have to do this on my own!" Elizabeth turns around and storms out of the room, leaving Charlie bewildered and confused.

Charlie notices that she left her pocketbook in the chair. He gets up and walks over to it. Opening it, he finds his bottle of lithium. He takes a couple of capsules out and swallows them with some water and then places the bottle in the drawer beside his bed. Charlie takes the pocketbook and hides it under the sheets of his bed. He thinks, *She will be back. I see where Karen got her temper from now.* He lies back down and waits for Elizabeth to return.

A short while later, Elizabeth quietly walks back into the room for her pocketbook. Charlie pretends not to notice her. He casually reads the newspaper like there is nobody in the room. Elizabeth looks at Charlie with the newspaper in his face.

"Okay, Charlie. What did you do with my pocketbook?"

Charlie lowers the newspaper and says nonchalantly, "Oh, hello there, Elizabeth. When did you come in?"

Elizabeth's timid expression touches Charlie's heart. Charlie motions for her to come over to him. As she walks slowly toward his bed, he says, "I finally see where Karen got her temper."

She gives him a halfhearted smile and says, "Just give me my purse, and I will be on my way."

"In that case I don't think I will ever give it to you."

"I don't have time for this. I have other things I need to—"

Charlie takes her by the hand as he interrupts her. "Hey. If you want to pursue this matter, I want to be right beside you. I don't care what kind of trouble you will get me in. I just want you to know you can count on me all the way."

Tears of joy run down Elizabeth's face. "Charlie, I don't know how to thank you."

"You can thank me by bringing me another double cheeseburger and some fries, tomorrow."

"Okay, Charlie. I'll be glad to do that."

He pulls out her purse from under the bed covers. They stare at each other with intense emotion in their glassy eyes.

When Saturday comes, Charlie leaves the hospital and goes to stay with Mrs. Thomas. He manages to walk around without much trouble. When he arrives, she has already collected some of his things and put them in Karen's room. Little Charlie keeps Charlie occupied while Elizabeth is at work. Charlie guesses that he will be able to go back to his house in a week or so.

When Elizabeth comes home from work on Monday afternoon, she picks up the newspaper and brings it into the house with her. She finds Charlie sitting in the living room playing with Little Charlie.

She throws the paper on the floor. "Fetch, Charlie! Fetch!"

Charlie looks up and happily says, "Which one of us are you talking to?"

"Both of you. I was wondering who would fetch it first."

"Very funny. How was your day at the florist?"

"Oh, pretty good, I guess. How was yours?"

"Excellent. I think I will be able to go home later this week."

Elizabeth frowns slightly but then smiles at Charlie. "Well, I guess all good things must come to an end, sooner or later."

"You sound disappointed."

"I kinda like having someone to cook for. It's not going to be the same when you leave, Charlie. This house is going to be very quiet without someone to yell at. By the way, did you contact that private investigator yet?"

Charlie remains quiet as Elizabeth walks over and sits down beside him. "Well, I thought it would be better if I talked to him in person. I thought I might drive down there, but I don't have anything to drive yet."

Without hesitating for even one second, Elizabeth asks, "How would you like to buy Karen's Mustang? I don't have any need for it. I could sell it to you for whatever you think it's worth."

"Hey! That's a great idea. I sure would like to have it."

"Fine. Do you think two thousand is too much?"

"Elizabeth, it is worth much more than that."

"Okay. It's settled. I will go get the title."

"You sure are eager to sell it."

"No, not really, Charlie. I am just eager for you to pay that private investigator a visit, and besides, you need some type of transportation anyway."

Charlie just smiles as Elizabeth stands up to go get the title. He opens the newspaper and begins to read it over. As he reads, an idea pops into his mind. *Dee! Yeah! I think I will call her up. Yeah! That's just what I will do.* Charlie goes up to his temporary room and finds his little notebook lying on the dresser. He flips through the pages until he finds the number written discreetly in a corner of one of the pages. Charlie dials the number. After ten rings he decides to hang up and call back later. He starts back down the stairs, and Elizabeth looks up at him.

"I was wondering where you got off to. I found the title to the car."

Charlie continues down the stairs. He takes the title from Elizabeth and then wraps his arms around her and gives her a great big hug. He kisses her on her cheek. "You are wonderful. I will get you the money as soon as possible."

"No hurry, Charlie. Just as long as it's by tomorrow. Just kidding. No hurry. Just whenever you can get it will be fine." She doesn't let Charlie go. She wraps her arms around his neck and continues to hug him. She whispers in his ear, "Charlie. I'm scared. I'm scared, Charlie."

Charlie walks her over to the couch, and the two sit down. Charlie takes her by the hand. "Why are you scared, Elizabeth? Please don't be scared."

"I'm scared about my heart. I think I will have to have that operation soon, Charlie. I'm just scared to death over it."

"Don't worry about that, Elizabeth. I will be here for you."

"That's another thing—you will be leaving to go back home soon, and I will be left all alone. I sure do miss Karen something awful. I wish she was here to help me through this operation."

"I miss her too. Everything will be all right. When do you think you will have to have the operation?"

"I don't know. By the end of the week, I should know more about it. I am terrified about having it. I just don't know."

Charlie sees the frightened look in Elizabeth's eyes. He reaches over and kisses her on her cheek and says sweetly, "Elizabeth, you might think this is silly, but I find you very attractive. I don't think I have ever met a nicer woman in all my life, except maybe Karen." He notices her face brighten up somewhat. Her tender eyes show a yearning look of innocence. She looks as if she has the sweetness of a sixteen-year-old schoolgirl. She holds Charlie's hand nervously as if he were her first boyfriend. With his other hand, Charlie begins to rub her nape.

She gazes into his eyes. "I am very attracted to you too, Charlie."

"I find you very alluring."

"For a twenty-six-year-old man, I find you very alluring too."

Flattered by her compliment, he blushes. "Elizabeth, for a thirty-nine-year-old woman, you are very attractive and very sexy and very compelling to be near."

Elizabeth laughs a girlish laugh, and Charlie follows with a subtle laugh of his own.

Holding hands and looking at each other with glassy stares, they continue to talk, acting like a couple of high school kids. Elizabeth interrupts the conversation to go into the kitchen to fix them something to eat. When she leaves the room, Charlie reaches down and begins to read the newspaper once again. Ten minutes into reading the paper, Charlie turns the page and encounters the obituary section. He casually reads the people's names until a rush of horror floods him.

"Oh no! Dear God in heaven, please don't let it be!"

Elizabeth runs out from the kitchen and sees Charlie in a panic. "What's the matter, Charlie? Tell me—what's the matter?" She looks with worry at his ghost-white face.

Not saying a word, Charlie hurries to the phone and picks it up.

Elizabeth rushes over to him. "Please, tell me. What's the matter, Charlie? What has happened?"

Charlie's hand shakes as he tries to dial the phone. He decides to put the phone down as sweat runs down his brow and he begins to tremble. His voice cracks as he speaks. "A very dear and close friend of mine … the paper said she died Saturday night. Oh my God! I can't believe she would do such a thing." Charlie runs back over to the newspaper as Elizabeth stands there confused and dumbfounded.

Charlie tries to find the name of Dee's mother in the phone book. His nervous hands and disoriented thoughts compel him to call information instead.

After jotting down the number, Charlie looks over at Elizabeth and nervously says, "I want you to call this number and find out how Dee ... no ... find out how Deborah died. I gotta know how she died! I just gotta know!"

Elizabeth looks at Charlie with confusion but nods her agreement.

"Ask for Sonya O'Brien, Deborah's mother. Tell her you worked with Deborah at the Dodge City Saloon. She was a very close friend of yours. Then ask how Dee—I mean how Deborah died. This is very important. I will be listening in on the other phone. Will you do that?"

"Yes, Charlie, I will do that," Elizabeth says, still looking confused. Elizabeth dials the number, and a woman answers it.

"Hello."

"I just read about Deborah in the newspaper. Is this really true?"

"Yes, it is."

"Is this Sonya, Deborah's mother?"

"Yes, it is."

"I am deeply sorry to hear about Deborah. I worked with her at the Dodge City Saloon a while back. She was one of my best friends there."

The voice on the other end of the line is soft and fragile. "The funeral services are tomorrow night at Hayworth-Nelson Funeral Home on Third Street. She will be buried Wednesday at the Shiloh Cemetery. Do you know where that is?"

Elizabeth's heart aches when she hears the word Shiloh. That is where Karen is buried. "Yes, ma'am, I know exactly where it is. I don't mean to burden you, Mrs. O'Brien, but could you tell me how Deborah died? It sure would mean a lot to me if I knew how."

"Sure, I guess so," says Deborah's mother, her voice depressed. "My daughter committed suicide. She took an overdose of Valium and took it with half a bottle of liquor. I found her Sunday morning over at her mobile home."

Charlie's heart aches with a terrible pain of loss. Tears fill his eyes, and his breathing becomes unsteady as he continues to listen to the very difficult conversation.

"Oh my goodness, I am truly sorry about the loss of your daughter. Did she leave any message about why she would take her life?"

"Yes, there was a short note on her pillow. It said, 'I can no longer live in this world without the man I love beside me.' That's all it said. By the way, who am I talking with, anyway?"

Elizabeth, not knowing what to do next, says, "This is just someone who feels awful about her passing. Thank you so very much for your time." As she hangs up the phone, she hears Charlie crying from a distance. She too sheds a tear of sorrow for the girl whom she never met.

Elizabeth walks into the kitchen and finds Charlie sitting on the floor crying. She slowly walks over to him and sits down beside him. She wraps her arms around him, and they both sit there and cry together.

The next day, Charlie thinks about attending the funeral services. But he fears what might happen if he does. He is afraid of what Dee's mother might do when she sees him there. She probably knows he is the one Dee wrote about in her note. A strange force compels him to attend the services though. He puts on his gray suit, the one he asked Elizabeth to bring over from his house. Around seven o'clock Charlie decides to go ahead and get it over with.

Just as Charlie walks downstairs, Elizabeth says, "You sure look handsome in that suit. Are you sure you don't want me to go in with you, Charlie?"

"No. I just want you to drive me there. That's all. I won't stay long. This is something I feel I should do alone. Oh, by the way, I called Mr. Bowman today—you know, the PI. I will meet with him tomorrow morning at ten o'clock."

"Okay."

"He will find out where that Corporal Philip Spencer lives. He is good—really good."

"Are you ready to go now?"

"Yeah, I guess we should go now if we are going."

Charlie and Elizabeth walk out to her car. She drives them both to the funeral home.

Once there, Elizabeth helps Charlie out of the car. She kisses him on his cheek before he slowly walks away and enters the building.

Inside, Charlie doesn't waste any time. He begins to walk straight to the casket. He is filled with anxiety. He looks around and notices all the mourning people around him. Charlie begins to feel the loss of his first love with great heaviness. As he gets closer to the casket, the ache grows even more intense. He waits patiently in line for his turn to view the lifeless love for whom he had so much affection. The people keep moving on until Charlie is standing right in front of Dee's casket. He looks down and sees her beautiful face for the last time. He reaches over and holds her hand for the last time. A tear runs down Charlie's cheek as he gazes down at her still body.

"Oh, Dee. Dear God in heaven, why did you do such a thing? Oh my God, Dee, why? Why did you have to do such a thing?" As Charlie looks down and says his last good-byes to his beloved friend, he hears a loud female's voice.

"You! Not you!"

Charlie turns around and sees Dee's mother standing behind him. Her face is red with anger. Her livid expression frightens Charlie.

"You are the one responsible for this! My daughter took her own life because of you! You killed my baby! It was because of you! I hate you! I hate you!" Mrs. O'Brien rears back and slaps Charlie across the face as hard as she can. The sound echoes throughout the room like a gunshot. The smack makes Charlie's face burn like fire and turn a shade of magenta. Everyone in the funeral home directs their attention toward Charlie and Mrs. O'Brien.

After receiving the mighty blow, Charlie tries to explain himself. "Please, Mrs. O'Brien, please! I cared greatly for Deborah! I truly loved her. I truly did! I never wanted to see Deborah do anything like this!"

Mrs. O'Brien shakes her head in disbelief. Her face is full of fire and fury. With red, teary eyes and a vicious-looking expression, she looks like an uncontrollable and furious woman. Her words are loud and vicious. The people in the funeral home look disturbed at hearing such words spoken there. Mrs. O'Brien begins to pound on Charlie's chest as she yells at him. Charlie stands there and takes all she gives to him.

"You killed my little girl! You killed my little girl. It is all your fault!" Mrs. O'Brien screams as Charlie stands there in a terrified stupor, not knowing what to do next.

Suddenly, Dee's ex-husband, Danny Patterson, walks over and pulls

Mrs. O'Brien off Charlie and tries to calm her down. Seeing a way out, Charlie hurries down the aisle in a state of public humiliation. The faces of the mourners are filled with disbelief and wonder. Some of the faces are filled with hate. Charlie manages to walk out of the building and to the car.

"Let's go! Right now!" he shouts as he climbs in. "Let's get the hell out of here, right now!"

Elizabeth starts the car quickly and begins to drive off. A group of mad, angry faces is staring at them when they pull out of the parking lot.

Elizabeth drives them straight home without stopping for anything. Charlie tells her everything that happened inside the funeral home.

She feels strongly for Charlie. Her weak heart aches after hearing the terrible news. His whole body shakes as they drive. His face is full of pain. His worried look makes Elizabeth feel the same way. They soon arrive home. She helps Charlie out of the car, and the two go inside the house, where the humiliation begins to wear off.

The next day, Charlie tries to keep his mind off the prior day's bad incident. He looks forward to seeing Mr. Bowman again. But the hurt he felt yesterday has a prolonged effect. His love for Dee hasn't been scorched any by her mother's harsh words. He does feel a strange sense of guilt, feeling partially responsible for her death. He tells himself not to let it bother him, but it still does. The only regret he feels is that he will miss the burial services today. He missed Karen's burial services and so will also miss the burial services of his first true love.

Charlie climbs into the little red Mustang and starts it up. He remembers all the good times he has had in this little car. Charlie puts the car in drive, and for the first time since the wreck, he is driving again. He looks at his watch and then heads for the bank to withdraw some money. He knows the car is worth more than two thousand, so he adds another five hundred to the envelope of two thousand for Elizabeth. He stuffs the rest of the money from his withdrawal in his wallet. He doesn't know how much Mr. Bowman will want for helping him; as a result he carries plenty with him.

As Charlie pulls into the parking lot outside Mr. Bowman's office, he remembers looking over and seeing Karen's innocent smile as she gazed at him. He remembers the sweet-sounding laugh she had when he told her a joke. The loss of her presence makes the task of walking up to Mr. Bowman's office difficult. He struggles but manages to make himself get out of the car and walk in the door. It is hard to do.

"Hello. Aren't you Nancy Walker?"

"Yes, that's right. And aren't you Charlie Delaney?"

"That's right. That's me."

"It's good to see you again, Mr. Delaney. Mr. Bowman will be right with you. Why don't you have a seat? I will call you when he is ready to see you."

"Yes, ma'am. I will do that." Charlie sits down, holding the envelope containing the report. Charlie looks around the vacant room with an isolated feeling.

Just as Charlie picks up a magazine, he hears Ms. Walker's voice. "Mr. Delaney, Mr. Bowman will see you now."

Charlie gets up and walks toward her.

She smiles as she points and says, "Just go down the hall, third door on your left."

Charlie thanks her, walks to the office, and goes inside. Mr. Bowman is sitting behind his desk.

Mr. Bowman, with a big smile on his face, says, "Well, hello there, Charlie. How are you? Come on in. It sure is good to see you again."

Charlie tries to smile. "It is good to see you again also."

"Please sit down. Now, what can I do for you?"

Charlie sits down. He looks at Mr. Bowman seriously. "Let me first thank you for helping me the last time. The information you gathered for me was very helpful."

"Good. Good."

"Matter of fact, that is why I am here today. Do you remember the report you got for me about the downing of Colonel Alan Thomas's plane?"

"Oh yeah. How could I forget about that? A two-star general from the air force paid me a visit on that report."

"Well, there is a marine corporal who filled out part of that report."

"Yes, yes. Go on."

"Well, I want you to locate him for me."

Mr. Bowman gives Charlie a very stern look. After a few tense moments, Mr. Bowman breaks the silence. "Charlie … That report got one of my best friends into a lot of trouble. He lost a good connection in the process. If you pursue what I think you are trying to pursue, you are going to get yourself into some really deep shit."

"I had a feeling you were going to say something like that. You see, Mr. Bowman, I'm not trying to make a case against the air force or any other military organization. The man who died, Colonel Alan Thomas, well … his wife just wants to know exactly how he died."

Mr. Bowman gives Charlie a puzzled look. "I thought that report made it clear, Charlie. He was shot down by friendly forces in South Vietnam. What more does she need than that?"

Charlie opens the envelope, pulls out the report, and shows him the part about the radio. Charlie waits while Mr. Bowman reads it.

As Mr. Bowman looks up, Charlie says, "How could the colonel radio other planes that his aircraft wasn't working properly when the ground forces said that the radio wasn't working at all? There are several other things that contradict each other, things I don't think I need to go over. I just want to meet the corporal who wrote the part about the shooting down part."

"You want to meet whom?"

"Okay. Elizabeth and I … I mean Mrs. Thomas."

Mr. Bowman gives Charlie another stern look. "Now look, Charlie, if you are just telling me this just so you can file some kind of lawsuit against the air force …"

"No, sir! I would not do that. You see, Mr. Bowman, Mrs. Thomas has a bad heart. She just wants to know the truth about her husband's death before she dies. I promise you we are not thinking about any such lawsuits."

Mr. Bowman studies Charlie very thoroughly and says, "Okay, Charlie, I guess I could locate this corporal … What's his name again?"

"Corporal Philip Spencer of the United States Marine Corps."

Mr. Bowman writes down the name and then hands back the report. He jokingly adds, "You keep this, Charlie. I don't want to be caught dead with it." Mr. Bowman laughs as the atmosphere relaxes. "Oh, by the way, Charlie, I have had to go up on my fee since the business has been so slow here lately. The rent has got to be paid."

"So how much is it now?"

"Three hundred a day plus expenses. It shouldn't take but a day or two to find out about this fellow unless he is a fugitive or something."

"That's sound fine. I don't think you should have much of a problem."

"I probably will know something by Friday. You still live at the same address?"

"Oh yes, the same."

"I will call you sometime Friday. If I can't reach you, just give me a call sometime late Friday. Okay?"

"Okay. That sounds just fine."

"So you want to pay me for one day's work today?"

Charlie hastily pulls out his wallet. "Yeah, here you go." Charlie hands Mr. Bowman three one-hundred-dollar bills. Mr. Bowman smiles as he takes the money.

As Charlie puts the report back into the envelope, Mr. Bowman says, "Hey Charlie, I heard you got married. I read about it in the paper a week or so ago."

Charlie feels a little uneasy as he nods his head.

Mr. Bowman grins enthusiastically as he continues. "Yes, sir, married life. I have been married for over thirty-three years now. It's been one of the best decisions I have ever made. My wife has been real good to me all these years. So tell me, Charlie—where did you go on your honeymoon?"

Charlie looks at Mr. Bowman sadly. After a long pause, Charlie finally says, in a soft tone, "You see, Mr. Bowman, right after we got married, my bride and I were involved in a terrible automobile crash." Anxiety floods him as he tries to finish. "My wife Karen was killed in that wreck. I just got out of the hospital last Saturday."

Mr. Bowman's happy expression turns sour and bleak. He looks down at the floor and softly says, "I am very sorry to hear that. I really am. You say you got into an automobile accident right after you got married?"

"Yes, sir. We had not traveled a mile before a drunk driver ran into us."

Mr. Bowman contorts his face. The two men sit quietly in the office, neither knowing what to say. After a few moments of uneasy quiet, Mr. Bowman finally breaks the silence.

"Charlie, I feel devastated at hearing this. On your wedding day, gosh … This makes me sick. These goddamn drunk drivers! I had a cousin who was killed by one them sorry bastards."

"The police said he was driving down the road, and the light turned yellow, and instead of slowing down to stop, he thought he could make it by stepping on the gas. He didn't! He slammed right into us as we were under the light. He had the pedal all the way down. I was just lucky I didn't get killed."

Mr. Bowman shakes his head in disgust.

"I hope you find out where this Corporal Spencer lives. It is my wife's mother who wants to talk to him."

Mr. Bowman thinks for a moment and then gives Charlie a determined look. "You bet, Charlie! I will find him. Don't you worry a bit about anything. I'll find out where he lives. I will get in touch with you sometime Friday."

"I will be waiting to hear from you. Good-bye, Mr. Bowman."

"Good-bye, Charlie."

Charlie turns and leaves the office and the building. Charlie drives over to his house to pick up a few things. He doesn't retrieve too many belongings, for he will be moving back home in a couple of days. He sits down on his couch and thinks about all that has happened. He thinks about Karen being crushed by that car. He thinks about Dee and how she must have felt before she took those pills. He sees the tears run down her face as she places those pills in her mouth. He sees visions of her swallowing them with that bottle of liquor. He wonders what she must have gone through. He remembers what she said to him over the phone after he told her he was going to marry Karen. "If you do, I will kill myself. I will, Charlie. I will kill myself!" Those words haunt Charlie now.

He begins to think about Elizabeth. His love for her has grown tremendously over the last week. He has become addicted to her very presence. She has become very important to him. He lies back on his couch thinking until he falls asleep.

When Charlie awakes in the quiet house, he casually looks at his watch. "Oh my God! It's five thirty!" Charlie gets up slowly but hurries to his car. He drives quickly over to Elizabeth's house. As he drives, he thinks, *Oh my! She will be wondering where I am. I don't want her to worry about me. She has had enough on her mind lately.* He pulls into the driveway and gets out. He walks into the house.

Elizabeth is sitting on the couch as Charlie walks in. She jumps up and runs over to him. She throws her arms around his neck and hugs him warmly. "Oh Charlie, I am so glad you're home. I didn't know where you were. I was afraid something had happened to you. I have been waiting here since three o'clock."

Charlie puts his arms around her and rubs her back. Pulling back, he stares directly into her glassy eyes. "I went over to my house. I guess I fell asleep on the couch."

There is a long silent pause between them. Charlie stares deeply into her eyes, and Elizabeth stares deeply into his. They look at each other with a sense of ecstasy. They continue to stare at each other with their arms fixed tightly around each other. Charlie slowly turns his head slightly sideways and moves closer to Elizabeth's mouth. His lips touch hers for their first passionate kiss. Charlie's mouth presses harder and harder against hers. She responds by opening her mouth, and he does the same. As their passionate kiss becomes more and more titillating, their hands move more freely on each other's back and shoulders. Charlie pulls back slowly to break their first seductive and passionate kiss.

Charlie gazes down at Elizabeth, who with her soft, gentle voice says, "Charlie, I … I … I love you!"

Charlie smiles an intoxicated smile at his new love as she runs her fingers through his hair. "I love you too, Elizabeth." Charlie reaches down again and bonds his mouth to hers. He feels her body quiver as he kisses her moist, enticing lips. As Charlie presses his mouth harder against hers, Elizabeth pulls away and breaks the seductive bond.

"Oh my, Charlie. I haven't been kissed like that in a long time."

Charlie smiles as he looks deep into her eyes. "I truly love you, Elizabeth. Since you asked me to call you by your first name, I … I have looked at you differently. I need you so much now. I love you, Elizabeth."

Elizabeth takes Charlie by the hand and walks him over to the couch, where they sit close to each other. "I was hoping you would say something like that, Charlie. I feel the same way toward you. You are all I have in the whole world now. I feel a need to be close to you. When I didn't know where you were a while ago, I began to get scared. I don't know what I would do if I didn't have you near me."

Charlie reaches over and kisses Elizabeth passionately again. His eager lips cover hers completely. Elizabeth just sits there, completely motionless, like she is paralyzed by Charlie's aggressive, loving mouth.

Moments later, Elizabeth reaches up with her left hand and pulls Charlie's hair forcefully. She breaks the oral bond and lets out a loud, deep, feminine moan. She pulls Charlie's head toward her eager open mouth with passion and desire. She plunges her tongue into Charlie's waiting mouth. He responds in kind. As he feels her seductive tongue for the first time, his right hand automatically finds her large, full bosom and begins to caress it. Moments later, with a full, hard erection, Charlie begins to ejaculate. Realizing what is happening, Elizabeth watches with awe as Charlie experiences this most wonderful feeling. Elizabeth witnesses these fourteen seconds in complete silence. She understands and accepts the moment and realizes the passionate time has past.

After a few minutes, Elizabeth begins to run her fingers through his hair, and Charlie tries to explain what just took place. She places two fingers on his lips to stop the words. She softly says, "You don't have to explain. I know. I know. Shhhh." As he begins to kiss her again, the telephone rings.

Charlie whispers, "Should we let it ring?"

Elizabeth barely moves as she whispers back, "We better not. It might be important." She slowly gets up and walks over to the phone. She picks it up and says, "Hello."

As Charlie watches, her excited, loving expression turns dry and sour, and the mood in the room changes dramatically.

"Okay. I will be right over." Elizabeth puts the phone down and then walks over and sits next to Charlie, her face full of worry. "Charlie. That was my doctor. He wants me to come over to his office right now."

Charlie looks at his watch. "It must be important for a doctor to still be at his office. I will go with you."

"No! No, Charlie. I don't want you to go. This is something I must do by myself."

"I will! If it is important, I want to be beside you."

She gives Charlie a loving smile. "Charlie, I know you mean well, but—"

"But nothing! I want to hear it too."

"Charlie, my doctor said it wouldn't take long to tell me about the results of my tests. I will be back in about an hour. So please don't insist on going. Please, pretty please … pretty please, with sugar on top."

"Well … I don't know."

"Pretty please, with sugar on top, master."

Charlie remembers that's what he liked to make Karen say. "Well … if you don't want me to go, I'll stay here."

Elizabeth smiles lovingly and then kisses him on his forehead. "I love you, Charlie Delaney. I love you, I love you, I love you. I will let Little Charlie in. He will keep you company until I get back." After collecting her pocketbook, Elizabeth leaves to go see her doctor.

Charlie is left sitting on the couch, playing with his little friend. Charlie is amused as the basset hound puppy chews on his finger.

In a little more than an hour, Elizabeth comes back home. Charlie is watching TV when she enters, and Little Charlie runs toward her. She picks up the little basset hound as she sits down next to Charlie. Charlie doesn't waste any time. He looks at Elizabeth sternly. His voice is deep and serious. "Well … you better tell me what that doctor said, or I will put you across my lap and give you a spanking you won't forget!"

Elizabeth smiles playfully. "You know something, Charlie. I might even like that," she says, giggling.

"Well, let's hear it, young lady."

"Young lady? Charlie, I am thirteen years older than—"

"I am not kidding. You tell me what that doctor said, or I'll—"

"Okay, Charlie, I won't keep you in suspense … or you'll what?" Elizabeth playfully looks over at Charlie, whose expression is serious. "Okay, Charlie, okay. I just wanted to have a little fun with you. The doctor said I have three days to live."

Charlie's mouth falls open, and Elizabeth begins to laugh.

"Okay, you asked for it," Charlie says. He pokes Elizabeth in the side, and they begin to wrestle, rolling onto the floor. Elizabeth's face glows like a sixteen-year-old schoolgirl's as Charlie gets on top of her.

They wrestle a few more minutes before Charlie starts spanking Elizabeth's behind. Enjoying it, she yells out, "Harder! I want it harder!" Charlie strikes her harder and harder until Elizabeth eventually surrenders. "Okay, Charlie! Okay! You win, Charlie! I will tell you. Please let me up! Please let me up, master!"

When Charlie hears this, he feels more attracted to her than he has ever felt. His dominant role as her master amplifies his masculine ego. He lets her up off the floor. They sit down close to each other on the couch. Elizabeth's face is flushed.

She hugs Charlie's neck and says, "The doctor said I should refrain from any roughhousing, including being spanked by any young handsome men."

Charlie leans over and kisses her intensely. She responds by opening her mouth, and the two engage in a seductive and passionate kiss. After a couple of minutes, Elizabeth breaks the passionate bond.

"Charlie, the doctor said I will need to have a triple bypass operation sometime in the next month. I have known about it for quite some time now. But he said I can't keep putting it off any longer."

Charlie runs his fingers through her hair. "If the doctor said you have to have it, then go ahead and arrange it so that you can be done with it."

"That's what I did, Charlie. I scheduled it for one month from today." Elizabeth puts her head on Charlie's chest as she rubs his stomach. "Hey. How did you make out with the private investigator?"

"I should know something by Friday. It's still not too late to forget about going to see that corporal."

Looking angry, she snaps back bluntly, "Charlie, if you don't want to go with me, then that will be fine with me! This is something personal anyway. I will go alone if I must. So if you're trying to talk me out of it, then you can just—"

"Okay, okay. I'm sorry, Elizabeth. Hey … don't be angry at me, Elizabeth. I know how much it means to you. I was only thinking about your heart. The trip might be far away."

Elizabeth's angry expression disappears into a sincere, loving, affectionate gaze. "So you were thinking of my well-being and not just trying to discourage me."

"Yeah, that's right, young lady."

Hearing Charlie call her "young lady" makes Elizabeth feel more attracted to him. "Why do you keep calling me young lady, Charlie?"

Charlie smiles. "It's your eyes. You have the eyes of a sixteen-year-old schoolgirl."

Elizabeth's face glows with joy and happiness. Her radiant expression captures Charlie's heart.

Charlie gets distracted from her enticing face by Little Charlie, who is pulling on his pant leg. Charlie reaches down and picks up the little basset hound. "You know something, Elizabeth, I really have become attached to this little booger. Just look at those ears! And those eyes! Just look at those sad, innocent eyes. That face has personality all over it."

Elizabeth takes the dog and hugs him lovingly. "I have adored this puppy ever since the first time I saw him. He is part of the family now. I just love him to death." As Elizabeth hugs the little dog again, Charlie remembers something.

"I will be right back." Charlie gets up and walks out the front door. Elizabeth stares at Charlie's ass as he leaves. As Charlie walks to his car, he remembers how it felt to spank Elizabeth's soft buttocks. This brings forth thoughts of lust and sexual desire.

While Charlie is gone, Elizabeth begins to develop powerful thoughts of lust of her own. Her heart invites her lusty thoughts about Charlie to come down for a little visit.

Charlie reenters the house, and Little Charlie runs toward him as he approaches the couch. Elizabeth stares at the crotch of his blue jeans as he comes closer. When he sits down, Elizabeth's innocent girl-like expression has been replaced with a look of seduction. Her glassy eyes radiate her feminine intentions. Just as she casually puts one hand on Charlie's leg, he hands her an envelope. She removes her hand to take it and gives Charlie a curious look.

"Here's the money for the car. I want to thank you for selling it to me."

Elizabeth doesn't open it. She simply says, "You're welcome, Charlie. Thank you for being so prompt. Oh, by the way, how much is the private investigator going to charge me?" She opens the envelope and waits to see how much to pay Charlie.

Little Charlie begins to tug away on Charlie's pant leg again, so he reaches down and picks him up. "Don't worry about it, Elizabeth. I took care of it."

"Young man, I said how much is he going to charge me?"

Charlie, seeing how stern Elizabeth looks, decides to talk with compassion. "Hey … I know this operation is going to cost you a bunch. I would feel much better if you would just let me—"

"If you don't tell me how much it is, I am going to put you across my lap and give *you* a spanking."

Charlie looks at her with a grin. "You know, I might like that."

Elizabeth cracks a quick grin and then returns to her stern expression. "Okay. Just give me back the keys and the title to the car then."

Charlie, seeing how serious she is, gently says, "Hey, come on. I am just trying to help, but if you're so compelled to pay, it's three hundred dollars a day. Mr. Bowman said it might take only one day. So I paid him three hundred dollars this morning."

Elizabeth pulls out three one-hundred-dollar bills from the envelope. "Here you go, Charlie."

Charlie takes the money and says, "Okay. Now, when do I get my spanking? I am looking forward to it now."

Elizabeth gazes at him with surprise.     "Maybe that's just what you need—a good whipping."

"Oh, is that so?"

"Yes, that's so."

Charlie reaches over and holds her with a possessive grip. His mouth covers hers, and she welcomes his lips. She once again becomes paralyzed by Charlie's passionate mouth and seductive grip. He places his hand around her neck in order to press harder with his mouth. Just as Charlie's tongue enters her wet, warm mouth, she begins to quiver again. She turns her head to break the bond and lets out a quiet feminine moan. Hearing her, Charlie becomes extremely aroused.

She looks at him with seductive eyes. "Charlie, I haven't felt like this toward a man since I was twenty years old."

Just as Charlie moves in closer to her mouth, Little Charlie begins to fight for some attention. His sweet, frail bark captures the attention of both. Little Charlie bites gently at Charlie's fingers. Elizabeth laughs happily as the little innocent pup tears away at Charlie's hand.

Now that the mood has been broken, Elizabeth says, "Charlie, are you hungry?"

"Yeah."

"How would you like it if I cooked you a big thick steak?"

"I have a better idea. How would you like it if I took you out for dinner tonight?"

"That sounds wonderful. I was hoping you would say that." She giggles in the same "tee-hee" way that Charlie often does.

"Hey, that's my laugh."

"What? You got a patent on it?"

"Well, aren't you in a good mood, Miss Silly Putty?"

"Yes, I guess I am, Charlie. My doctor said I have nothing to worry about. I will be good as new after the operation. I feel much better about it now." There is a long pause as the two stare at each other. "Charlie, I love you. I love you so much." A single tear runs down her sweet, innocent face.

"Well, sweet sixteen, since you love me so much, I will let you take me out for dinner. By the way, I have decided to go back home Friday."

Elizabeth frowns, and her voice is melancholy when she speaks. "I had a feeling, now that you have started driving again, you would be going back home soon. I sure will miss having you around the house, Charlie." A devious grin appears on her face, and she reaches over and quickly pinches Charlie's nipple, hard.

"Ouch! You mean little rascal! Why did you do that?"

Elizabeth playfully replies, "You swindled me out of Karen's car, you let me take good care of you while you recovered from that terrible automobile accident, then you let me fall deeply in love with you, and now you want to just leave me as if I am all used up."

"You are going to feel pretty silly after I tell you this."

Elizabeth looks at him curiously.

"First of all, I put twenty-five hundred dollars in that envelope instead of the two thousand we agreed on."

Elizabeth gives Charlie a surprised look. "Well … I'll just give you five hundred of it back."

"Oh no! You can't do that."

"Why not?"

"Because you have already accepted the money, and besides, you have already spent some of the money. Remember the three hundred you gave me?"

"So? I will just give you five hundred more. That's no problem." Elizabeth tries to get up to retrieve the envelope, but Charlie holds her down.

"Oh no, young lady! You wait just one minute. A deal's a deal. You can't back out of a deal. You accepted twenty-five hundred for the car, and that's what you will have to keep. If you give me back five hundred dollars now, you will be breaking the law. You could even get arrested. You might even end up in prison. And all they give you in prison is bread and water, so make it light on yourself and just accept the deal as it was made."

Elizabeth laughs so hard that she can't stand it.

"Now don't you feel pretty silly?"

"Charlie, I have never met a man like you. You make me laugh, and you make me happy." Charlie and Elizabeth forget about the other things they were speaking about earlier. They stare into each other's eyes with a profound passion. A strange quite feels the room. The stare lets the other feel warm and open to touch each other's soul. A joyous, blissfulness consumes each other's heart compelling each to move closer. Their hearts beating harder! A strong force of affection pulling at each other's physical bodies compel each to explore those pleasurable territories. Charlie's hand begins to move towards Elizabeth's large full breasts until Elizabeth, seeing this, breaks the moment.

Elizabeth stands up and says, "Okay, Charlie, How would you like for me to take you out for dinner?"

Charlie, still in a state of seduction and allurement remains silent as he looks at Elizabeth with a blank look. His mind slowly returns to normal as his expression of playfulness also returns.

"I guess I could take you to McDonald's for a hamburger."

"Huh?"

"I'm just kidding, Charlie. Burger King is better," she says, giggling.

Charlie gives her a playful look as he says, "There you are, stealing my laugh again."

"Serves you right. You have stolen my heart, and now you are fixing to gallivant off."

The playful smirk on her face compels Charlie to grab her and take her into his arms. Just as Charlie starts to stand up, Elizabeth pushes him back down on the couch. Charlie marvels at her playful actions.

Elizabeth giggles. "What's the matter, big boy? Can't you stand on your own two feet anymore?"

"I don't know what that doctor gave you, young lady, but I'm going to give you another spanking, one you won't soon forget."

"Oh no, you won't either, at least not on an empty stomach. I'll tell you what, Charlie Brown …"

"Who are you calling Charlie Brown?"

"Is there anybody else in the room, silly boy?"

Charlie grabs her by the hand and pulls her onto his lap. He begins to kiss her. Just as soon as Charlie's lips cover hers, she is in his grip. She allows Charlie to kiss her any way he wants to. After a few moments, Elizabeth jumps up from Charlie's lap. Her eyes are flooded with seduction and want. Her glassy-eyed stare stirs Charlie's sexual desire immensely.

She turns around and says, "If we are going out for dinner, I need to take a shower first."

This thought activates the fire in Charlie's heart. The look in her eyes draws his attention.

Elizabeth walks halfway to the steps and then turns all the way around, catching Charlie staring at her ass. She giggles like a schoolgirl and smiles at Charlie from a distance. She walks about halfway up the staircase and says, "I will be down shortly, Charlie. It shouldn't take me long to shower." She turns her head, still smiling flirtatiously, as she disappears upstairs.

Charlie remains on the couch, his wonder and excitement growing. He hears the bathroom door shut. Little Charlie snuggles up to him and begs for his attention with his innocent-sounding bark. Charlie picks the puppy up and begins to play with him. After only a minute or so, Charlie hears the shower in the bathroom come on. The noise of the water opens a valve of lust from Charlie's mind to his heart. He suspects that she might be naked by now. He gazes up in the direction of the bathroom and continues to listen to the water.

As Charlie's desire and lust grow stronger, his mind becomes weaker. He begins to deceive himself. He thinks, *So what if I do make love to her. So what? I don't think there is anything wrong with it.* His lust takes over his thoughts and then begins the battle to take over his heart.

When Elizabeth walks into the bathroom, she closes the door but doesn't lock it. After turning on the shower, she walks over to the mirror and looks at herself. She unbuttons her blouse and removes it. She then takes off her slacks. She casually glances at the door. After a short pause she unsnaps her bra and lets it fall to the floor. She then slides down her panties and tosses them aside. She stares at her naked body in the mirror and then once again glances at the door. She puts her hands over her head and stretches. She cups her large, white breasts in her hands and begins to massage them, trying to get her nipples hard. After a few minutes, she quietly says to herself, "I guess these droopy boobs aren't going to respond." She turns around and stares at her buttocks in the mirror. She takes one hand and tries to lift each cheek. She says to herself, "I guess you are getting old, Elizabeth. Your ass has dropped four inches now, and your droopy boobs have gone into retirement." She casually looks at the door one more time before entering the shower.

Charlie listens to the shower like the children of Hamelin listened to the Pied Piper. Charlie gets up and walks up the stairs, approaches the bathroom door, and curiously turns the knob to see if it is locked. It isn't. As Charlie thinks about the subtle invitation, Little Charlie begins his sweet, innocent bark once again. Charlie shuts the door and walks back to the stairs. He looks down the staircase and sees Little Charlie's sweet, humble face looking up at him. His long floppy ears are on the first step, and his sad eyes and innocent face overcome the army of lust that has been battling for Charlie's heart. Charlie eagerly walks down the stairs and picks up the little basset hound. Charlie's compelling love for the little dog sobers up his mind.

Soon, the sound of the shower stops. Charlie takes the playful puppy back to the couch. His thoughts are only with his long-eared friend now. Charlie begins to talk to the little dog as if he understands what he is saying. He forgets what Elizabeth is doing.

After her shower, Elizabeth gets out disappointed. She second-guesses herself as she dries off her wet, naked body with a towel. The lust that started in her mind earlier has poured into her heart and conquered her. Her mind now begins to manufacture a reason to hate Charlie for not coming up. It tells her, Charlie has rejected you. He has repudiated and spurned your love. She begins to construct a resentful picture of Charlie. She finally pushes these thoughts to one side as she grabs the bathrobe. She looks at her naked body in the mirror one last time and then wraps the robe around her tightly. She opens the unlocked door and exits the bathroom slowly with an expression of anger and resentment. As she gets to the staircase, she disguises her anger with a wry smile. She walks halfway down the staircase and puts on a happy expression as if nothing is wrong.

"Hey, Charlie."

Not having realized she was so close, Charlie jumps a little. Charlie quickly looks toward the staircase and sees that Elizabeth is wearing a bathrobe.

"What would you like for me to wear tonight, Charlie?"

As he thinks about the question, she comes down the stairs and walks to him with seduction in her eyes. Charlie looks directly at her as she walks. His sensual thoughts about seeing her naked body beneath that robe activate his lust mechanism. He studies her with great admiration.

Too proud to say anything seductive or brash, she simply says, "Well … tell me, Charlie … what do you want me to wear tonight?"

Her voice is soft and alluring. Not knowing what to do, Charlie says, "Uh … duh … well … how about some clothes?"

Elizabeth laughs as her seductive eyes come alive. "I know that, silly boy. Do you want me to wear a dress or slacks?"

Charlie, who always likes to see a woman wearing a dress instead of slacks, answers quickly. "How about a dress?"

Elizabeth smiles at Charlie. "Any particular color, Charlie?"

He is still thinking about what she would look like without that robe hiding her naked flesh. He thinks about asking her to remove it before him but decides not to. "Blue is my favorite color."

"Fine then. I will wear a blue dress. It will go good with your eyes, Charlie." Elizabeth turns around and begins to walk away.

Charlie fixes his eyes on her buttocks as she walks. She takes only a half dozen steps before turning around quickly. She catches Charlie staring at her ass again. She smiles at him and then turns her head away.

Giggling, she says, "You think about where you want us to go for dinner. I'm going to my bedroom now to slip into that blue dress. It shouldn't take me more than ten minutes or so." She turns around, not waiting for Charlie to say anything, and walks until she is halfway up the staircase. She gives Charlie one last seductive smile as she disappears from his sight.

Charlie sits on the couch wondering why she didn't just get dressed in the first place instead of coming down like that. He interprets her actions as another subtle invitation to her feminine flesh. Charlie listens with great care for her door to close. He holds his breath and rubs Little Charlie's belly to keep him quiet. As Charlie listens, he doesn't hear the bedroom door shut. The silence in the house becomes more enticing than the sound of the shower pounding through the walls. The sound he didn't hear creates a curiosity too overpowering for Charlie to resist. He gets up and walks to the staircase. Little Charlie continues to lie on his back with his paws up in the air. Charlie walks halfway up the stairs and looks down the hall. He can see the entrance of Elizabeth's bedroom from this angle. The door is open. He remembers her words: "I am going to my bedroom now to slip into that blue dress."

Charlie thinks about her naked body so close to him now. He envisions her soft naked flesh as milky white and eager for his touch. As he stands there on the staircase, his thoughts bring on a hard erection. His lusty thoughts once again move toward his heart, and the shield that is protecting his heart from his mind's lust weakens. The idea of seeing her naked body in the bedroom lures him up the rest of the steps. He takes one step, then another, and then another, until he finally makes it all the way to the top. His length is fully enlarged now. He is fully consumed by the visions in his mind of her totally naked flesh. His heart continues to struggle to prevail against the lust of his saturated mind.

Charlie stands at the top of the stairs, and his heart weakens more and more with every passing second. It is close to capitulating.

Just then, Charlie hears Little Charlie's frail bark. Charlie turns and gazes down the stairs. The basset hound barks away like his heart is breaking. Charlie smiles down at the puppy with love and kindness. His thoughts of seduction evaporate as he gazes at the little dog's sweet face. His long floppy ears are once again on the first step. His sad brown eyes and humble expression fill Charlie's heart with love as he continues barking. Charlie knows the little dog won't stop barking until he picks him up and carries him back to the couch.

As soon as Elizabeth enters her bedroom, she quickly removes the bathrobe and tosses it on her bed. She walks over to a mirror near her bed. She turns and glances at the door and smiles. Naked, she faces the mirror so that she can look at herself and also watch the entrance of her room, and she thinks about Charlie. Her milky-white bare buttocks face the door in complete view of anyone who might walk in.

She reaches over, picks up a jar from her dresser, and begins to rub the cream on her body. She sets the jar down and then cups her breasts and begins to caress them. Her nipples become stiff and hard. She pretends she is being touched by Charlie's masculine hands. Her twenty-year-old dormant lust has awoken abruptly from its long restful sleep, like a grizzly bear waking up from its long hibernation. She fantasizes about seeing Charlie walk into her room while she is fully naked, hoping to catch her unsuspected and to thrust himself inside her. She looks down as she rubs the cream from the jar on her stomach. She is putting it on only as an excuse for Charlie to walk in and see her exposed bare buttocks. She wants to remain naked as long as she can, so she slowly rubs the substance over her white flesh without hurry. As she rubs the slick cream around her large breasts, she looks down at her thick, coal-black, bushy triangle. Her mind is polluted with desire and passion. The lust that was in her mind eagerly enters her heart. She wants to feel Charlie's young naked body on top of hers. She glances over at the mirror but quickly looks away. She doesn't want Charlie to catch her looking at him if he happens to walk in. She wants Charlie to find her accidently exposed.

As she glances at the mirror again, she fantasizes about seeing

Charlie's young naked body walking toward hers. She imagines seeing his long full length, erect and hard, slowly coming toward her. He then takes her into his arms and lays her down on her bed. She fantasizes about lying there on her bed motionless as Charlie loves her long-waiting body. She starts to breathe faster as she fantasizes about him kissing her madly as she remains helplessly still in the face of his youthful manipulations.

Her burning lust grows until it becomes dominant over everything else. It begins to burn a hot fever of sheer madness in her eager body. Her desire takes over as she grabs her hairbrush and thrusts the handle deep into her wet, juicy warmth. She closes her eyes as she pulls up on her primitive sensual device. She tries to hold back her feminine moan but to no avail as her moment arrives. She begins to tremble and shake as she climaxes instantaneously. Her nearly minute-long orgasm is strong and intense!

Suddenly, she hears something. She holds her breath and listens with great care. She hears Little Charlie's frail bark. She knows that Charlie is no longer sitting on the couch. The bark tells her that Charlie has gotten up and left the little puppy. She smiles with contentment as her extremely horny eyes glimmer with a look of intoxication! She feels the presence of Charlie's body nearby. She eagerly awaits his active mouth, the touch of his gentle hand, and the texture of his tongue!

As Charlie stands at the top of the stairs, he looks down and sees his little friend barking away continuously. He sounds as though his heart is breaking. Little Charlie tries to climb up the stairs, but his tiny legs are still too small. Little Charlie cries out for someone to pick him up and love him. Charlie smiles at the meek expression of his adorable little puppy. Charlie breaks up the mental image of Elizabeth standing nude and begins to think about simpler things. Charlie can't stand the temptation to pick up Little Charlie any longer. He walks down the stairs, picks up the frail-sounding little basset hound, and begins to talk to him. He carries his little friend back to the couch as his seductive mood passes away.

Elizabeth continues to wait eagerly. Her nipples are erect. Her naked body begins to quiver with excitement as she glances at the mirror. The sound of Little Charlie's barking makes her heart beat faster and faster. Then the barking stops. She holds her breath and realizes the barking is completely gone. She curiously walks over to the door and sticks her head out into the hallway. She hears Charlie's voice from a distance talking to Little Charlie. She furiously turns and walks back into her bedroom. Her disappointment evaporates her horny, seductive thoughts. When she sees her naked body staring back at her in the mirror, she quickly tries to cover her breasts with one hand and her coal-black triangle with the other. She feels totally humiliated! Lusty thoughts have made her act like somebody else. She feels shame as she quickly puts on a bra. She snaps it on with an expression of guilt on her frustrated face. She then hastens to the drawer where her panties are kept. She grabs the first pair she sees and then pulls the delicate silk panties up. Another powerful emotional force invades and takes over her mind and heart: hate! Her mind is eager to serve the new host. Elizabeth quickly finishes dressing. She begins to rebel mentally against Charlie. She begins to trick herself into thinking he is to blame for her feeling so humiliated. She once again starts to manufacture, in her mind, a completely ridiculous reason to dislike Charlie. She looks in the mirror one last time before going downstairs. The person she stares at in the mirror has aged tremendously in only ten minutes. The sixteen-year-old's girlish expression that she had earlier has been replaced by the face of a resentful, angry thirty-nine-year-old woman. The hate numbs all of the shameful thoughts she had just a few minutes ago. Elizabeth finishes dressing and then leaves the room with a disappointed, indignant, and wrathful expression showing boldly on her face.

Charlie, happily playing with Little Charlie, smiles gladly when he notices Elizabeth walking down the stairs. He smiles at her like he did earlier. As she walks closer to him, he notices her unusual expression.

"Wow! That sure is a beautiful dress you're wearing! You definitely look sexy in blue."

These words activate disgust in Elizabeth in her current state of mind. With her noticeably irritated expression she stares directly at Charlie. She speaks in a coarse manner. "If we are going, then let's go!"

Charlie, detecting that there is something wrong, speaks to her in a very soft manner. "Is there anything the matter, Elizabeth?"

"No! There is nothing the matter with me." She looks at Charlie angrily and then turns her head away.

Charlie pauses for a second, trying to figure out what is wrong. "You know something, Elizabeth—you might have your girdle on too tight. I heard that makes some women irritable." He giggles at his own joke.

His remark and his laugh make Elizabeth grin. But she quickly goes back to her cold expression. With her hands on her hips, she says, "For your information, I'm not wearing a girdle."

Charlie smiles and quickly says, "Then it might be your bra—one cup might be smaller than the other one." Charlie's high-pitched laugh puts a grin on her cold indignant face once again.

Little Charlie raises his head and begins to seemingly listen to the conversation. He looks on with sad eyes and long ears as Charlie and Elizabeth talk.

"I don't think that is very funny, young man."

"Young man? You sound like Karen now. She used to say that when she was … aha! That's it!"

"That's what?"

"I know what the matter is now—you're peeved!"

Elizabeth's face turns red. She shakes her head and quickly says, "I am not!"

"Yes, you are. You're peeved," he says, giggling.

"What are you talking about, Charlie? And quit laughing like that! Let's go eat. I'm starved."

Charlie doesn't move. He just sits there, looking at Elizabeth with a shit-eating grin on his face. He snickers as he looks at her angry face. "No. I'm having too much fun to leave now. You behave exactly as Karen did."

Elizabeth begins to look angrier as he puts his hand over his mouth, trying to muffle his snickering. Little Charlie begins to bark that innocent bark of his, crying out for attention. Charlie reaches over and begins to rub the little puppy, as Elizabeth stands there looking angry.

"Well … are you going to take me out to dinner or not?"

"I thought you were going to take me out for dinner."

"You thought wrong again."

Charlie begins to snicker once again. "You remind me of Karen. That's exactly how she acted when she was peeved."

"You quit saying that! I am not peeved!"

"You're peeved."

"I am not peeved."

"You're peeved."

"I am not peeved!"

"You're peeved, you're peeved, you're peeved."

"I am not peeved! I am not peeved! I am not peeved!"

"You're peeved."

"Oh! … I ain't peeved!

"There is no such word as 'ain't,' Karen … I mean Elizabeth."

"I ain't peeved! I ain't peeved! I ain't peeved! Don't you say I'm peeved anymore, young man!"

Charlie laughs as Elizabeth's face gets red as a pepper. "I see why I love you so much now: you're identical to Karen. Even your face and hair remind me of her," he says, giggling. "By the way, what happened to my sixteen-year-old schoolgirl smile?"

"I guess she grew up."

Charlie snickers more. "No. I think she just got peeved."

This makes Elizabeth furious. "I told you not to say that anymore!"

"You know something, Elizabeth, I think I know why you're peeved."

"Oh really? Then why don't you just tell me why I'm peeved?"

"You see! You admitted it. You just admitted it! You're peeved!"

Elizabeth gets upset almost to the point of crying. "If that is all you're going to say, I think I will just go to my room."

As she attempts to walk away, Charlie jumps up from the couch and grabs her. He pulls her to the couch and gently places Little Charlie on the floor. Charlie kisses Elizabeth a few times on her cheek as she puts up a halfhearted struggle to escape from his strong grip. Charlie and Elizabeth wrestle a little as they did before, until Charlie holds her down on the couch. She doesn't struggle anymore as Charlie begins to kiss her neck. She lies still as Charlie begins to gently blow in her ear.

"That's why you got peeved."

Elizabeth comes back to earth as her mind focuses on what Charlie just said. She doesn't say anything at first. She just stares at Charlie with curiosity and concern in her eyes. After a long pause she finally breaks the silence.

"That's why I got peeved? I don't think I know what you're talking about, Charlie." Charlie raises her up, and they both sit in an upright position on the couch. Little Charlie cries out for some attention with his frail appealing bark. Elizabeth picks up the small dog and places him on her left. She turns to Charlie on her right and says, "Please try to explain that, Charlie. I am eager to hear your explanation."

Charlie smiles as he holds her soft delicate hand. Charlie gets close to her and says, "When you were taking your shower, I was compelled to walk upstairs. I turned the doorknob to the bathroom and realized you accidently left the door unlocked."

Elizabeth turns her head and looks down. Her expression is one of guilt.

"Then as I was playing with Little Charlie, you came down in your bathrobe. I saw a very romantic look in your eyes. I felt an urge to see what was behind that robe. Then you left to go put your blue dress on. I became curious when I didn't hear your bedroom door close."

Elizabeth looks at Charlie, turns her head away, and looks down.

"Still thinking about you in that robe, I was curious to see why I didn't hear the door close, so I once again went upstairs to investigate. I noticed from an angle that your door wasn't closed. I then got the impression you wanted me to come on up."

Her face now begins to turn a shade of magenta. Charlie takes his other hand and puts it under her chin. He moves her head up until she is looking him square in the eyes.

"I wanted to go in your bedroom and see your naked, sexy body waiting for me."

Elizabeth's eyes begin to get teary. Her glassy-eyed expression captivates Charlie's heart. "Why didn't you?"

Charlie, releasing her chin, says, "Little Charlie came running over to the staircase, barking his little head off. You should have seen him standing there, barking away. He sounded as though his heart were breaking, so I went to him and took him back to the couch."

Elizabeth, now on the brink of crying, gently asks, "Is that the only reason, Charlie?"

Charlie looks into her tender, curious eyes. "No, it's not. No, Elizabeth. You see, sweetheart, ever since you asked me to call you by your first name, I have looked at you differently. I have come to realize that I love you as Elizabeth, not just as Karen's mother anymore."

Little Charlie begs for their attention again. His eagerness begins to agitate Elizabeth. The pup's innocent voice is interfering with Charlie's explanation.

She tells Charlie, "Wait one second, Charlie. Let me put Little Charlie out."

She picks up the little pup. "Come on, you little troublemaker. If it wasn't for you, I would be ... Well, come on, Mr. Ears. It's to the doghouse for you." She takes the little basset hound outside and chains him to his little doghouse so he won't run away. She eagerly hurries back inside the house and walks with anticipation over to the couch and sits down. The room is quiet once again. She snuggles up as close to Charlie as she can. Their loving hands bond together as he wraps his other arm around her, rubbing her nape with a gentle up-and-down motion.

"Now that the little troublemaker isn't barking, what were you saying?"

Charlie hugs her tighter. "I was just saying ... well ... I was going to wait until after we got back from dinner, but I think now is the better occasion."

"What occasion are you talking about, Charlie?"

"I went home today, right after I talked to the private investigator. I picked up a few things I thought I might need. I picked up something there I want you to have." Charlie reaches in his pants pocket and pulls out a tiny yellow envelope. "Go ahead and open it."

Elizabeth releases Charlie's hand and curiously opens the top of the envelope and slides a ring out into her hand.

As the object comes into view, Charlie announces, "It's Karen's diamond engagement ring. I want you to have it. Here, let's see if it fits your finger."

Elizabeth marvels with excitement and intrigue as Charlie puts the ring on her finger. She stares at the sparkling gem surrounded by gold. "Charlie … I … can't accept this."

"I don't want you to accept it like just another piece of jewelry. I want you to wear it because I want you to be my wife."

There is a long quiet pause as Charlie and Elizabeth stare at each other happily. Elizabeth is stupefied at hearing Charlie's words.

"You … you … you want me to be your what?"

"No, no, no. I don't want you to be my what. I want you to be my wife." Charlie's funny face turns sincere as he stares at his third true love. "I love you, Elizabeth. I have had two terrible tragedies happen to me here lately. I never got a chance to love my first bride as I wanted to. I am eager to love someone. I am eager to love someone whom I care about. I am eager to love you."

Tears of joy begin to rush out of Elizabeth's eyes. Her face becomes jubilant. She hugs Charlie in a tight embrace.

Charlie holds her face in front of his. "Elizabeth, will you marry me?" Just as she begins to answer, Charlie quickly says, "No, wait a minute."

"Huh? Do what?"

Charlie looks at her as he gets up. He then kneels down on one knee. "I have to get down on one knee first. I don't want you to think I don't know how to propose to a woman." He takes her left hand, and with a single tear on his cheek, he says, "Elizabeth, will you marry me?"

Elizabeth gazes down, trying to comprehend what is really taking place. She tries to hold back her tears as she speaks. "Yes, Charlie, I will marry you."

Charlie gets up. "I love you so much, Elizabeth. You make me so happy."

"Oh Charlie, I love you too. I love you. I love you. I love you so much!"

"I don't know if I'm marrying you out of sorrow, or despair, or even out of loneliness. It might even be because of the suffering I have endured these last couple of weeks. I don't know. I do know that I don't want to begin another relationship with anyone else. It takes a long time to build a relationship. I do know that I love you and care for you. I want to be close to you and be with you for the rest of my life. I just want you to know that I will be there for you no matter what hardship we may encounter. I want to share the bad times as well as the good times. I want to share the rest of my life with you."

"Okay, Charlie. Okay. I am the luckiest woman in the world right now. I love you so very much."

Charlie reaches over and covers her mouth with his. His mouth presses hard and passionately against her mouth. She sits there paralyzed, her lips bonded to Charlie's. He easily divides her lips and enters with his tongue. After a few minutes of passionate kissing, Charlie breaks the seductive kiss tenderly. He then goes for her neck and kisses it wildly. He runs his tongue up to and inside her ear until she begins to moan exotic sounds of sheer pleasure. The sound gets louder as Charlie's wet, warm tongue goes deeper into her ear. He breathes long hot breaths into the canal, which drives her to moan more erotic sounds. She holds Charlie's free hand with both of hers firmly while they embrace each other lovingly. She releases it as she cries out softly in a state of passion.

"Oh, Charlie! Make love to me! Make love to me right now, Charlie! Make love to me!"

Charlie stops kissing her ear as he says, "I have a better idea. Let's get married, right now! We could fly off to Las Vegas and get married tonight. Tomorrow morning we could wake up as husband and wife. The first time I make love to you, Elizabeth, is when you will be my wife! So what do you say?" Charlie looks at her eagerly for a response.

"Charlie? Are you okay? We can't act like that. We have other things we are planning on doing. Remember the private investigator?"

"We could put all of that aside for now. We could start out with a brand-new slate. We could just forget about the past and plan for the future."

When Elizabeth hears this, it strikes a very sensitive nerve. Her passionate desire for Charlie erodes. She turns and looks straight ahead in disgust. Charlie, seeing this, tries to hold her hand.

She repels his attempt and says indignantly, "You don't care one bit about finding out how Alan died. You don't give a damn about it, do you, Charlie Delaney?" She turns her head and stares at Charlie's surprised-looking face.

"How can you say that? I went to see a private investigator today and paid him three hundred dollars to find this Corporal Spencer. I paid him because I knew you wanted to find out what really happened. I did it because I love you. I am very disappointed in you!"

Elizabeth begins to cry tears of sorrow and regret for what she just said. "I am sorry, Charlie. I am so sorry I said that." She reaches over and wraps her arms around him. Charlie in turn accepts her loving affection.

Charlie kisses her lightly and says, "I care deeply about you. I just want you to be my wife before we start engaging in sex. Let the rest of the world do what they want to. I don't want to start treating you like my mistress or like a … well … you know."

Elizabeth finishes Charlie's statement. "You don't want to start treating me like a whore. Isn't that what you were going to say?"

There is a short pause from Charlie before he replies, "Well … yeah. I'm too much of a gentleman to use words like that while a lady is present, but you did answer the question correctly. If we engaged in one act of fornication, you would become my mistress. I don't want you to become my mistress, Elizabeth. I want you to become my wife."

Elizabeth looks deeply into Charlie's sincere eyes with love. "Charlie, I want to become your wife too." Charlie kisses Elizabeth sweetly, kindly, and gently for a few tender moments.

Charlie looks deeply into Elizabeth's eyes and says tenderly, "Elizabeth, let's make an agreement right here and now. Just as soon as we finish talking to this Corporal Spencer and find out what happened to your former husband, after we do that, promise me we will go to Las Vegas and get married. I am eager to love you. I am eager to be a part of you, but I want to keep you a respectable woman no matter what worldly desires I have. I want to make you a permanent part of my life. Will you promise me that?"

After a few brief moments to think about it, Elizabeth agrees. "Okay, Charlie. If you still want to get married, then so will I." Charlie hugs her warmly, and she responds affectionately.

"Get used to the idea of being called Mrs. Charlie Delaney because that's going to be your new name."

"Okay, Charlie. Whatever you say. Whatever you say, Charlie."

# *Chapter 2*
# A JOURNEY BACK INTO THE PAST

C harlie packs his belongings the next day and moves out of Elizabeth's house. Back in his own house, Charlie tries to cope with the sudden loss of Karen and Dee as best as he can. He tries to understand why God permitted this to happen. He feels alone now that he is away from Elizabeth. If it weren't for the lithium Charlie is taking for his depression, he wouldn't be handling this painful situation as well as he is. This tragic blow is a dull, rusty dagger cutting deeply into his soul. Charlie experienced this kind of loneliness early in his life—the time when his mother and father died—but he thanks God for Elizabeth. She is there to comfort him through this most difficult time. Having her prevents him from blaming all his troubles on God.

Charlie looks forward to the day when he and Elizabeth are married. He lives for the day when he can hold Elizabeth in his arms as his wife. While Karen was alive, Charlie didn't realize that he was developing two relationships at the same time—one with Karen and one with Elizabeth. His early relationship with Elizabeth was filled with anger and resentment, but now they love each other more than they ever thought possible. They need each other so very much now.

Now that Charlie has exposed the cover-up of Elizabeth's former husband's death, Elizabeth is compelled to find out what really happened the day her husband died. She lives for the day when she can finally put to rest the uncertainty of all those years of doubt. She has something to live for now—the chance to learn what really happened.

Elizabeth's heart condition has gotten worse since Karen's death. Her doctor reassures her that the operation is necessary and safe. She feels confident about having the surgery now. She has put it off for quite some time, but now she is eager to finish it. She is glad to have Charlie by her side now more than ever. She loves Charlie immensely! She looks forward to the day that he will make love to her. For years, Elizabeth has yearned for a man to be intimate with her. Her long wait to feel a man's seductive touch, to feel his hard, masculine body, is finally coming to an end. Although she is facing surgery and coping with the sudden death of her only daughter, Elizabeth Thomas handles herself in a brave, courageous manner.

But now to remove the doubt that has plagued her for so many years, she must take a journey back into the past.

It is Friday, the day after Charlie proposed to Elizabeth. Charlie is trying to organize his house, moving things from one place to another. As he finishes, the phone rings. He picks up the kitchen extension and hears a familiar voice.

"Hello, good-looking. How's my favorite fiancé?"

"I'm doing about the same since I last saw you five hours ago. What's on your mind?"

"My doctor has confirmed it. My operation will be one month from yesterday."

"Did you tell him that you were getting married soon?"

"Yes. I told him." Elizabeth is reluctant to tell Charlie that the doctor said it would be a serious mistake to excite herself before the operation. She quickly changes the subject. "Have you heard anything from the private investigator?"

"Uh … well, no, I haven't. I should hear something today, though."

"Good. Call or come over just as soon as you hear something. I'm eager to find out where this Corporal Philip Spencer lives."

Charlie replies, "I am too, Elizabeth. Oh, by the way, what did your doctor say about getting married before the operation?"

Panic floods Elizabeth's body. She doesn't want to ruin Charlie's plans, but she doesn't want to lie to him either. Realizing that he will sense something is wrong if she hesitates to answer, she quickly says, "He told me congratulations and that I would make a beautiful bride."

Charlie isn't convinced that Elizabeth is telling him the whole story. "What else did he say? And tell me the truth."

Elizabeth finds she can't lie to Charlie. "Okay, Charlie, if you must know, he doesn't want me to exert myself much before the operation," Elizabeth confesses. "He didn't like the idea of us getting married."

Charlie pauses for a moment and says, "Did he tell you not to get married?"

"No, Charlie. He didn't say, 'Don't get married.' He just didn't recommend it right now."

"So what do you want to do?" Charlie asks.

"I want to carry on just as we planned. You will just have to be gentle with me, that's all," she says with a laugh.

Charlie smiles. "I guess that means you won't be getting on top much."

"Charlie Delaney! You shouldn't be talking like that over the phone."

Charlie hesitates. "You do still want to marry me, don't you?"

"Yes, Charlie. That's what I want more than anything in the whole world, darling. That's what I want."

"Good. I'll go ahead with the arrangements."

"I love you, Charlie."

"I love you too, Elizabeth," Charlie says softly.

After Charlie hangs up, he grabs a bite to eat and takes off to run errands. As he does his errands, he thinks about making love to Elizabeth. The anticipation of feeling her warm, loving body next to his puts him in a positive state of mind.

Charlie returns from his errands around five thirty in the afternoon. He notices a car sitting in his driveway. In the car is Mr. Bowman, puffing a cigarette.

"Have you got good news for me?" Charlie asks.

"Charlie, I have some good news, and I have some bad news," Mr. Bowman replies with a mysterious look. "Maybe we should speak in the house. I can lay out the reports better in there."

Charlie unlocks the door, and the two men walk inside. Mr. Bowman looks around the modern, quite large house before saying, "You sure have a nice house, Charlie. I hope you don't mind me stopping by. Your house is on my way home."

Charlie, still curious, says, "No, I don't mind at all. I'm glad you did. It will save me a trip to your office."

"Good. A lot of my clients don't like private investigators sitting in their driveways when they drive up. It makes them jumpy."

Charlie, eager to hear the investigator's news, says, "So tell me the good news first, Mr. Bowman. I sure do need to hear some." They both sit down at the kitchen table.

Mr. Bowman crushes out his cigarette and lights another. "Okay, Charlie. I found our Corporal Philip Spencer. He lives on a farm near Bowling Green, Kentucky." Mr. Bowman hands Charlie a big orange envelope containing his report. As Charlie peruses the report, Mr. Bowman continues. "Spencer has been married one time and is presently divorced. He has one son who lives with his mother. Where? I don't know."

Mr. Bowman rises, walks across the kitchen, and flips his ashes in the sink. Charlie glances up and notices Mr. Bowman looking at him strangely. Charlie quickly looks away.

The blunt Mr. Bowman says, "Charlie, I hope you aren't lying to me because if you are …"

"Lying to you? What are you talking about?"

"Let me explain, Charlie." Mr. Bowman takes a big draw on his cigarette and looks Charlie in the eye. "If you're going to talk with this Corporal Spencer in hopes of getting enough information so you can bring a lawsuit against the United States Air Force, you will be making the biggest mistake of your life."

Finally understanding Mr. Bowman's concern, Charlie reassures him, "Neither Mrs. Thomas nor I have any intention of filing a lawsuit. Mrs. Thomas just wants to know what happened to her husband."

"That's plain to see, Charlie. He was shot down by friendly fire in South Vietnam. Why does she want to pursue this matter? There were a lot of men who died by friendly fire in that war."

"This is something she won't accept until she talks to someone who was there. She has been lied to by the air force. She doesn't know what to believe. She just wants to know the truth."

"Okay, Charlie, I believe you. I just want you to know, if you do change your mind about pursuing a lawsuit, you will be getting me and a lot of other people in trouble. I talked to my buddy up in Washington,

DC, today. He told me he lost a good resource because of that report about Colonel Alan Thomas."

Charlie listens attentively as the room gets smoky, with Mr. Bowman puffing away on his cigarette as he speaks.

"You see, Charlie, my Washington buddy had a buddy who worked at the Pentagon. That man is the one who tapped into the computer and located the report about the downing of Colonel Alan Thomas. It just so happened that file was top secret. When the Pentagon brass discovered that a copy of that report had been printed up, they went ape shit. That's when the shit hit the fan."

"You aren't scared of those high-level men messing with you, are you, Mr. Bowman?"

"Is that what you think, Charlie? No, Charlie, but let me finish. When my buddy's source was found out, he was moved out of the Pentagon. My buddy lost an important source. That's why he was so upset. Over the years, he will lose thousands of dollars' worth of information because of that one single report."

Charlie scratches his head. "Did your source break the law when he took that report?"

"No, Charlie. If he had, he would be on trial now. He had access to that computer file, so there was no law broken. They threw him out of the Pentagon because the paper he printed the report on was government property. Those Pentagon people get mighty unhappy when one of their secret files is leaked out. They didn't want to go through the crap they had covered up years ago. They just needed some excuse to get him out of the Pentagon. Stealing government paper is what they decided on."

"I see. So nobody really broke any laws."

"Correct. Matter of fact, that report was not really top secret; it had been declassified. It was top secret when it first came out, but it was declassified several years ago."

Charlie begins to feel better about the report.

"So," Mr. Bowman says, "I hope your lady friend isn't using you to find out information so she can start some legal crap. I don't care to be subpoenaed into some faraway courtroom over this."

"You can rest assured that won't happen, Mr. Bowman. She happens to have a heart condition. She will have an operation next month."

Mr. Bowman gives Charlie a smile and then a frown. He says, "I'm glad that you aren't planning any lawsuits, Charlie. But I'm sorry to hear about Mrs. Thomas's heart operation. If she did decide to pursue this in the courts after talking to this Corporal Spencer, it would surely kill her before she saw the final outcome of it."

"Whiskey on the rocks?" Mr. Bowman asks.

Charlie gives Mr. Bowman a reluctant smile. "I'm sorry, Mr. Bowman. I don't keep any liquor in the house. I seldom drink."

"That's all right, Charlie. Just whatever you have will be fine."

"How about some iced tea?"

"That will be fine."

Charlie fixes them both a glass of tea as Mr. Bowman smiles contentedly now that he knows Charlie's intentions.

"Here you go, Mr. Bowman." Charlie hands Mr. Bowman a glass of iced tea.

"I feel much better about this now, Charlie. I just didn't want to see you get involved with something that can get as sticky as this can."

"I am involved, Mr. Bowman, but only with what Mrs. Thomas wants. And all she wants is to lay to rest how her husband died in Vietnam."

Charlie doesn't want to start calling his future bride by her first name in front of Mr. Bowman. He doesn't want to give Mr. Bowman the impression that he is having a romantic relationship with her. He wants to keep this matter to himself for now.

Mr. Bowman appears to think about something for a moment before he speaks. "Charlie, while I was investigating this Corporal Spencer, I did a check on several other things."

"What other things?" Charlie asks.

"My buddy in Texas, the one I call to get the whereabouts of military personnel, is the one who found out where this Corporal Spencer is living. I also had him do a check on Colonel Alan Thomas's commanding officer."

"How come?"

"Just curious, Charlie. The colonel's commanding officer was

General Curtis Anderson. Just thought I would mention it, Charlie. This general died a couple years ago about the same time the report was declassified."

Charlie is confused. He doesn't know why Mr. Bowman is telling him this.

"I hope you pass this information on to Mrs. Thomas. I think she will want to know this."

"Sure," Charlie says, scratching his head. "I'll be sure to tell her."

"Good," Mr. Bowman replies with an intriguing grin.

Mr. Bowman believes Charlie when he says he doesn't intend to take legal action against the air force, but Mr. Bowman doesn't exactly trust Mrs. Thomas. He figures if she still has any hate and wants revenge, the one she might want to seek revenge against will be this General Anderson. Mr. Bowman has been a private investigator too long to trust the uncertainties of a woman seeking revenge. He hopes to diffuse her hate as much as possible since it was General Anderson who lied to her about the tragic incident in which her husband was killed in Southeast Asia.

Charlie sips his iced tea and stares at Mr. Bowman. He sets the glass on the table. "So … tell me the bad news now."

Mr. Bowman reaches down and picks up a large black envelope lying beside his chair. He seems anxious as he refuses to meet Charlie's cold stare. "Charlie, you wanted to know where Corporal Spencer lives so you and Mrs. Thomas could talk with him. But before you talk with this man, let me tell you a little bit about his character. And what I'm about to tell you is the bad news."

Charlie's eyes fill with apprehension. Mr. Bowman takes a swallow of his tea and then lights another cigarette.

"Charlie, Philip Spencer was dishonorably discharged from the Marine Corps. That's right—he received a dishonorable discharge. After looking deeply into his military file, I have come to the conclusion that he isn't a very nice boy. He struck an officer, a Major Lester Cain. Spencer beat him up so seriously that the major was hospitalized. So you see, Charlie, you may be going to meet a very dangerous man."

Charlie considers Mr. Bowman's information.

Mr. Bowman takes a long drag from his cigarette before saying, "I just want you to know this before you make any little trip to see him. Being a marine myself, I know that anybody in the Marine Corps who would strike an officer is a complete idiot! That has to be one of the most stupid things a soldier could possibly do."

"Does the report state why he did such a thing?"

"No, Charlie, it doesn't. It doesn't make any difference. He struck a major of the United States Marine Corps. There is no excuse for that. The report does say the corporal threw the first punch, so be careful when you meet this man."

"Oh, I will. I'll be extremely careful."

As Mr. Bowman drinks his tea, Charlie reads over the high points of the report to himself. Finally, he asks, "Mr. Bowman, since you were in the marines, tell me something. Why would someone strike an officer?"

"Well, Charlie, I guess the fellow didn't like him very much. He couldn't control his behavior and probably acted out of impulse—you know, without thinking." Mr. Bowman points to a special part in the report. "He was a complete idiot in the true sense of the word. Spencer had only three weeks left before his term was up."

Charlie considers this and says, "You mean to tell me Corporal Spencer would have served his entire tour in only three more weeks if he hadn't had that fight with the major?"

"That's right, Charlie. He would have been going home, but instead he got a dishonorable discharge. He spent those last three weeks in the stockade. After his court-martial, he came back to the States, according to the report in his file."

Charlie examines the papers before him.

Mr. Bowman shakes his head, puzzled. "Charlie, there is something about that fight that bothers me. The corporal and the major were both stationed at the Chu Lai Air Base. That was where Colonel Alan Thomas was stationed the day he was shot down."

A curious fright comes over Charlie. Before he has time to say anything, Mr. Bowman continues.

"It might not mean anything, but then again, it seems that those two probably had a feud brewing while they were stationed at Chu Lai. I don't know. There are no other reports of quarrels between the two."

Charlie gets up and pours himself another glass of tea. He gazes at the reports lying on the table. Intrigued with everything, he is compelled to ask, "Where on God's green earth did you get all this? There must be thirty pages here!"

Mr. Bowman smiles. "I told you, Charlie. I have a buddy in Texas who has connections. He can get anything about any veteran's background. I just want you to know the expenses alone for gathering all this was nearly three hundred bucks."

Charlie gives Mr. Bowman a very nervous look.

Mr. Bowman continues, "You do remember my fee is three hundred bucks a day plus expenses? My buddies and their resources are expensive."

Charlie hesitates for a moment with a tense feeling of curiosity and says, "Well, I guess they are. These reports are loaded with important information. I must admit, they do contain more information than I ever thought I would see. How much extra do you want?"

Mr. Bowman's smile evolves into a laugh. He gives Charlie a firm look as he says, "I paid my buddies two hundred and eighty-nine dollars for their help. That amount is just for the outside expenses. My fax machine has been working overtime these last two days. Additionally, my secretary has been working her fingers to the bone compiling and sorting all those reports. When I have a lot of clients, I try to divide those expenses among everyone. But business has been slow this month."

Charlie braces himself.

"Then after all those faxed reports come in, they have to be entered into our computers. That's not a big expense. We feed the entire report into the slot, and it records all the data without our having to type it in. When we print the reports up on our printers, they come out looking like professional reports. Don't you agree?"

Charlie tries to put on a halfhearted grin. "Yes, they do. They look very professional. So tell me, how much?"

Mr. Bowman finishes his tea and smiles. He looks around the kitchen and sees a picture of Karen hanging on the refrigerator door. He asks, "Is that a picture of your wife, Charlie?"

Charlie turns his head and sees the picture of Karen. In a quiet voice, he says, "Yes, sir, it is."

Mr. Bowman gazes at the photograph. He is delighted by the

sweetness of Karen's smile and admires her luscious red hair and radiant blues eyes. "She sure is beautiful, Charlie! I mean, she is an absolute knockout!"

Charlie says sadly, "Yes, she was. She was nineteen years old when that picture was taken."

Mr. Bowman looks at Charlie's distressed face and then glances back to Karen's picture. He looks down toward the floor as he tries to imagine the grief Charlie must be feeling. He tries to put himself in Charlie's shoes—to think about what it must feel like to marry a beautiful girl like Karen and have her taken away on their wedding day.

As Mr. Bowman is thinking, Charlie softly says, "It's her mother. It's her mother who wants all this information. You see, Mr. Bowman …" Charlie looks at Mr. Bowman with sincerity. "The main reason Elizabeth—Mrs. Thomas—wants to talk to this corporal is …" Charlie pauses for a moment as he tries to finish his statement. "You see, Mrs. Thomas has been lied to about the death of her husband, Karen's daddy. She thinks … well, you know how women are. She thinks her husband is a POW. She has never seen his body, so she thinks the air force lied to her because he was shot down and captured. All these years, Mr. Bowman, she has believed in the back of her mind that he was living in a prison camp somewhere in Southeast Asia.

"If those liars had just told her the truth, it would have relieved her of all doubt. No matter how bad the truth was, if they would have been honest with her, she wouldn't have had to live in doubt all these seventeen years. That's why she wants to talk to Corporal Spencer. Then she can lay to rest this matter once and for good and not have to worry anymore."

Mr. Bowman feels like a very selfish man right now. He has been planning to charge Charlie an enormous amount for all the expenses he has incurred this month because of the lack of business—everything from the rent to his employees' salaries to the utilities. But now what Charlie has told him has touched him. He remembers when he fought in Korea and all those soldiers who were also POWs who didn't come home. He recalls the families who had to live never knowing the whereabouts of their loved ones. He is disturbed by Karen's picture now. He thinks about what that happy-faced person in the picture must have gone through while growing up without a daddy to be there for her all those years. Mr. Bowman's rough, hard character is smoothed and softened by her enchanting smile.

Charlie speaks again in a soft tone. "I guess that's why she is having the heart surgery next month—because of all the worry and stress she has been through these last seventeen years."

Mr. Bowman breaks his silence. "I see, Charlie. I see why now … Tell you what, Charlie." Mr. Bowman gets exuberant as he continues. "You can just forget about any of those other expenses. You paid me three hundred bucks. I'll use that to pay the expenses. How does that sound?"

Charlie is bewildered. He can't believe Mr. Bowman is doing this. He looks at him excitedly and says, "Mr. Bowman, thank you, but please let me give you something. I know your time is worth a lot. Let me at least pay you the three hundred dollars for the expenses."

"No! Charlie, this might sound stupid, but I don't want to make anything on this case." Mr. Bowman looks at his watch. "Just look at the time. I must be going now, Charlie. Let me know if you need any more investigating." Mr. Bowman quickly gets up and proceeds to the door.

Charlie follows him. Just as Mr. Bowman reaches the door, Charlie says, "I sure do appreciate this, Mr. Bowman. I really do, and Mrs. Thomas will appreciate it too."

"Think nothing of it, Charlie. I feel better about this case now. Tell Mrs. Thomas that I hope this information helps some."

"I will, Mr. Bowman. I will."

Mr. Bowman smiles contentedly as he leaves.

After seeing Mr. Bowman off, Charlie looks through the reports for only a few minutes before he picks up the phone to call Elizabeth. When she answers, Charlie happily says, "Hello there, sweet sixteen. I just received the reports on our Corporal Spencer. Just hold still, and I'll be right over."

"No!" exclaims Elizabeth before he can hang up. "Don't come over here now, Charlie!"

Her voice is filled with anxiety.

Charlie quickly responds, "What's the matter? What's going on?"

Elizabeth speaks with a determined tone. "Charlie, I have a guest here, and I don't want you to come over right now."

"Who? Who is there?"

"Charlie, I can't talk now. I'll come to your house, let's say, around seven o'clock."

"I don't like the tone of your voice. Tell me what's the matter."

"Charlie, please don't be so persistent. I will tell you when I see you later. Just promise me you won't come over here."

Charlie pauses for a moment, not liking the mood of this conversation. "You promise you will be over here by seven o'clock?"

"Yes, Charlie, I promise."

"Okay, Elizabeth. I won't come now, but if you aren't here by seven, wild horses won't prevent me from coming over there."

"Okay, Charlie. I've got to go now. I really do, Charlie. I'll see you at seven o'clock. I love you." Elizabeth hangs up the phone without waiting to hear any more from Charlie.

Charlie sits in a chair, impatiently waiting for Elizabeth. He doesn't look over the reports while he waits. He feels something is wrong, but he does what she asked him to do; he stays home until she arrives exactly at seven o'clock.

When Charlie hears Elizabeth knocking on the door, he eagerly jumps to answer it. Opening the door, he immediately sees that the area around her eyes is red. She has been crying. She smiles, though, as if nothing is wrong.

"So tell me, do the reports say where Corporal Spencer lives?"

"Forget about that right now. First of all, come in and tell me what's going on."

Elizabeth kisses Charlie on the cheek as she enters the house. He shuts the door. Charlie is disturbed to see Elizabeth acting this way.

Elizabeth walks into the living room and sits down on the couch. Charlie follows and sits down beside her. He reaches for her hand, and this makes Elizabeth smile. Charlie speaks first. "What's this kissing-me-on-the-cheek stuff? You are my future wife, not my future mother-in-law."

Elizabeth kisses Charlie sweetly on his lips. She says quietly, "Charlie, I had a visitor."

Charlie listens in silence, giving her his complete attention.

"This visitor was in a bad state of mind."

"Who was it?"

Elizabeth hesitates. "Charlie, the man who came to see me was … well, Charlie, he was the man who slammed into you and Karen on your wedding day."

Charlie's curious expression is replaced with one of fury. He says, "I see. That's why you didn't want me to come by."

"Yes, Charlie. I didn't think it would have been appropriate."

"So tell me, what did the scum want?"

"I know you have a lot of hate for this man, but Charlie, after hearing what he told me, I feel like he is also a victim."

"What are you talking about? A victim?"

"Charlie, I saw a grown man cry like a baby two hours ago. He cried and then fell on his knees in shame. He just wanted to ask for my forgiveness for what he did. If you could have seen him, you would probably understand the grief this man is going through."

Charlie sits in silence, a feeling of anger and resentment beginning to fill him. Finally, he gets up and walks into the kitchen.

Elizabeth watches Charlie disappear from the room with wonder but says nothing. Charlie comes back into the living room with two cans of soda. He hands one of them to Elizabeth and then sits down.

Charlie stares at Elizabeth. "So go on. Tell me this man's sad story."

"Charlie, you're not taking this like you should."

"Like I should?" Charlie yells. "That man killed Karen. He took her away from me and from you. Now you are telling me that I am not taking this like I should."

Elizabeth pauses before saying, "This man didn't purposely kill Karen. It was an accident."

"I guess it was just an accident that all that alcohol got poured into him too."

"No, Charlie. That was no accident. But by drinking and then driving, this man has done something that will torture his conscience for the rest of his life. When I told him that you and Karen were just married before the accident, he broke down and fell on the floor and bawled. Have you ever heard a grown man cry like that, Charlie? It was one of the most heartbreaking sounds I have ever heard. It was awful, Charlie. It was just awful!"

Charlie takes a long swig from his soda. He thinks for a moment about what Elizabeth has told him. The visions of that tragic day come back to him. He remembers Karen's bloodstained wedding gown, the loud noise of metal twisting and bending, the glass crashing in, and those last words Karen spoke to him: "I love you, Charlie." Charlie feels the loss of his bride with a great sense of helplessness and despair. His heart aches to be near her again. He wraps his arms around Elizabeth and with tears in his eyes says, "Ma, I sure do miss Karen. I miss her more now than I have ever missed anyone in my life. Oh my God, do I miss her so! I love her more than I love myself."

Elizabeth and Charlie hold each other with deep emotions as Charlie says gently, "Although the man who ran into us didn't mean to, he still killed Karen."

Elizabeth holds Charlie close to her. "I know, Charlie. I miss Karen a great deal too. But hating someone else because of his mistakes will only ruin your life. It will ruin it! If this man intentionally killed Karen, then I would feel differently, but hating this man will not bring Karen back. It will only bring you bitterness and negative feelings."

Charlie listens to Elizabeth with compassion as his lonely heart aches with sadness and grief.

"You see, Charlie, when people are deceived into doing something wrong, they don't have much control over the outcome. The damage has already been done. But if they feel bad about it later and repent to the person they did the wrong thing against, then you should try to understand and forgive them. You should forgive them not just for their sake, but for your sake as well."

"For my sake? What do you mean for my sake?"

"So the hate won't get into your heart and destroy your soul."

Charlie thinks for a moment and says, "I guess so, Elizabeth. I guess you're right."

Elizabeth runs her fingers through Charlie's hair and says, "Jesus would want you to forgive him. Right?"

"You sound like my mother now. I guess he would, though. I guess he would."

Elizabeth comforts Charlie, and he comforts her in return with a loving hug. They remain quiet, both thinking about Karen, about the man who killed her, and about themselves.

Finally, Elizabeth says in a teasing voice, "So are you going to tell me what that private investigator found out, or am I going to have to beat it out of you?"

Charlie grins and kisses her gently on her enticing lips. He gets up and says, "Come on. I can't stand another beating right now."

Elizabeth gets up from the couch and follows Charlie into the kitchen, where she sits down in a chair and begins to look through the reports that are lying on the table.

As she reads, Charlie says, "Mr. Bowman did a very good job. Spencer lives in Kentucky." Charlie points to various papers as he tells Elizabeth about Spencer and his dishonorable discharge.

As she reads the file, Elizabeth grows excited. "Wow! This stuff tells everything about him: where he went to school, his parents' names, and the color of his eyes. It tells everything I need to know about Corporal Philip Spencer. How much did all of this cost? And don't tell me it only cost three hundred dollars."

Charlie pauses as he sees Elizabeth's excited face. "It only cost three hundred dollars."

"Charlie, don't lie to me. I have had enough people lie to me in my lifetime. Even a white lie is a lie. If you want to marry me, we must have an understanding right now. I don't want any lies told to me, even if you are thinking of my well-being. Tell me the truth on all matters or—"

Charlie interrupts her. "Hey, slow down, little girl. Slow down. I am telling you the truth. Mr. Bowman only charged me three hundred dollars."

Elizabeth looks puzzled. "But these reports look too professional. Just look at all this! There is a complete life history of this man here."

Charlie bites his lower lip and then grins at Elizabeth's stern-looking face. Finally, he points to Karen's picture on the refrigerator. He looks back at Elizabeth and says, "Mr. Bowman was leading up to tell me all the expenses he acquired by gathering all this information. I told him about you and about why you wanted this information."

"Why did you have to tell him anything, Charlie Delaney?"

"He thought you wanted the information so you could bring a lawsuit against the air force. He wouldn't give me the information until I made it clear to him that no lawsuits were being planned. He then saw Karen's picture hanging on the refrigerator. I told Mr. Bowman that it was her mother who wanted to know about Spencer. When he saw Karen's face, he changed his mind. Maybe it was because she died on our wedding day, I don't know, but he told me to forget about the expenses. Said he would take it out of the three hundred I gave him earlier. His exact words were 'I don't want to make anything on this case.' That's what he told me."

Elizabeth smiles as her eyes become teary. "Charlie, I'm glad you explained this to me. I probably wouldn't have believed you if you hadn't explained it. Whenever there is any doubt about something, please explain it to me. I will try to explain anything you have any doubts about. This way, I won't have to wonder if you are telling me the truth. I have lived with doubt about Alan's death all of my life. It is more painful because doubt lives with you twenty-four hours a day. Let's not have any doubts between us, Charlie. Okay?"

"Okay, Elizabeth. I will try to explain anything you want me to. So feel free to ask me anything at any time, so I can remove any doubt that you might have—because I love you, Elizabeth."

"I love you too, Charlie."

Charlie reaches over, and they share a pleasant, grateful kiss. Their eyes gleam with a look of devotion, faithfulness, and love.

Charlie says, "So now that we know where Spencer lives, when do you want to leave?"

Elizabeth responds quickly. "Tomorrow. I want to leave tomorrow."

"Come on, that's too soon. We have to plan where we are going to stay, how to get there, and then, of course, there's the honeymoon. What do you say about … next Thursday?"

"Next Thursday? I'm not waiting that long. I have waited seventeen years to find out if Alan was really killed or not. I'm not waiting any longer. I'm leaving tomorrow!"

"You will not! We are going to go together. There are a few things I need to discuss with my boss."

"What kind of things?"

Charlie replies, "I need to tell him about the wreck. I don't think the vacation time I originally scheduled for my and Karen's honeymoon covers the time I was in the hospital. I need to call and tell him this, so I will know when I am supposed to come back to work."

Elizabeth doesn't like this delay. She is eager to leave now. She says bluntly, "You can call him."

Growing impatient, Charlie says, "I have to talk to the doctor at the health care center and fill out all those papers my boss will need."

"Can't you fill them out after we get back? I want to leave tomorrow."

Charlie looks at her with a twinge of anger and says, "You know who you are acting like?"

"Who?"

"You are behaving just like Karen would behave. Exactly like Karen! If she wanted something, she had to have it right now, or she would get hysterical. I see where she got her lack of patience. The only difference between you and her is that she had red hair."

Elizabeth stares at Charlie. Her stern look evolves into an affectionate smile. She wraps her arms around him and begins to kiss his neck, ears, and face.

They walk into the living room and sit on the couch. Elizabeth whispers sweet things into his ear. She kisses him until he breaks. "Okay, Karen—I mean Elizabeth. You win. We will leave tomorrow. I'll call my boss Monday and see if the paperwork can wait. I just hope we can get rooms without making any reservations."

Elizabeth lets out a joyous cheer. "Oh boy! We leave tomorrow! Don't worry about anything, Charlie. I will make all the arrangements. I'll call the airline and book us a flight to Kentucky. All you have to do is be here tomorrow morning by ten o'clock, ready to go. Everything will be fine."

Charlie shakes his head in amusement at her happy face. They stay up late reading the information about Spencer. Around eleven o'clock, Elizabeth kisses Charlie good night and goes home.

The next day, Charlie gets up around nine o'clock. He gets dressed and eagerly drives over to Elizabeth's house. When he gets there, she has her suitcase packed. As Charlie walks in, he says, "Hello, sweet sixteen. I see you are ready to go."

Elizabeth gives Charlie an exuberant kiss. "Good morning, darling. I hope you slept well."

"I would have slept better if you were lying next to me."

Elizabeth gives Charlie a seductive kiss and says enticingly, "Who knows, big boy? Someday you just might get your wish."

Charlie holds her tightly as he says, "Oh God, I love you so. I can't wait until we are married. The anticipation is wonderful, but the event will be more wonderful."

Elizabeth kisses Charlie as though she has wanted to kiss a man for a long time. Her body is filled with the excitement of a schoolgirl.

Elizabeth outlines for Charlie her plans for their trip. Her kind, sweet voice controls Charlie's very existence. Whatever she says, Charlie is eager and ready to oblige her. He will do anything to make her happy. Elizabeth drives them to the airport. She leaves her car in long-term parking, and they catch their flight to the town of Bowling Green, in the unspoiled state of Kentucky.

On the airplane, Charlie says to Elizabeth, "Please don't be upset if Philip Spencer doesn't want to talk to us. He might tell us to leave when we get there. I hope he doesn't, Elizabeth, but I want you to be prepared if he does."

Elizabeth looks at Charlie with a little apprehension as she says, "I understand that he may tell us to leave. I will be polite and delicate when I talk to him. I'm nervous about how he might react to us. I hope he will accept us, but if he doesn't, I will be prepared to leave without making a scene."

Relieved, Charlie sighs. "I'm so glad to hear you talk this way. It makes me feel better about the whole situation. Still, Elizabeth, just as soon as we talk to Philip Spencer, we're getting married. I don't want to waste any time. I will spend the rest of my life making you forget about all those years of misery."

Elizabeth looks at Charlie with love. "I love you, Charlie. I am so glad you are with me. Just having you near me makes me happy. I just want to thank you for doing this for me. I don't know if I could have taken this trip without you. I thanked God last night for you coming into my life."

Charlie smiles at Elizabeth with compassion and reaches over and kisses her gently. They hold hands until the plane lands.

As soon as Elizabeth and Charlie claim their luggage, they hurry to the rental car location, where their car is waiting for them. Elizabeth drives as Charlie takes out a map he finds in the glove compartment. They drive for over an hour, asking people for directions along the way, until they finally reach the home of Corporal Philip Spencer.

Spencer lives in a farmhouse down a dirt road, and his name is painted on the mailbox. As Elizabeth parks the car, she and Charlie look at each other nervously. They hold hands as they walk up to the front door. The anticipation of meeting this man is intense. Charlie knocks on the door several times, but no one answers.

Elizabeth asks, "Charlie, what time do you have?"

"It is five minutes after five o'clock."

Elizabeth looks around the old farmhouse with fascination. She decides to walk around back to see if she can find anybody. Charlie remains at the front. He feels even tenser now that no one is home.

The day is hot and humid. The June temperature in Kentucky is like that in North Carolina. It is sticky, miserable, and wretched. The humidity makes it hard to breathe and think clearly. The beaming sun glares down on them like a merciless villain with a sweltering vengeance.

The fields around them are full of corn, long and tall. Everywhere Charlie turns, he sees the long green stalks sticking out of the brown dirt. Cows graze on green pastures in the distance. The farm looks clean and orderly. Chickens are walking around and cackling.

Elizabeth returns to the front and sits down on the front porch step. Charlie sits down beside her and says, "Cows, cornfields, and coal trucks. That seems to be what Kentucky is made up of. I haven't seen one McDonald's, Burger King, or any other type of eating franchise for the last twenty miles."

Elizabeth wipes her forehead with a handkerchief. "I wish I was in the house. I hear the central air-conditioning going. I don't know if I can stand it out here much longer."

Just then, they hear something. Charlie gets up and spots a tractor coming toward them. He says, "Hey, Elizabeth. I think our wait is over."

Elizabeth gets up and looks. "Yeah. It sure looks like a man is coming." Elizabeth walks under the shade of a tree; she nervously watches as the tractor approaches and pulls up before them.

On the tractor is a stocky man with a neat, close-shaven beard. He is wearing blue jeans and a white T-shirt. His cap says "Thank God I'm a Country Boy" in all capital letters. The man is well built for his medium size. His arms are big and strong. He looks at Charlie and Elizabeth with curiosity. The man cuts the tractor motor and, with a clear voice, says, "Hello there. Can I help you with something?"

Elizabeth walks up to the man and says, "Hello. Are you Philip Spencer?"

The man nods his head as he says, "Yes, I am. Who may you be?" The man gets off the farm tractor as Charlie walks over to join Elizabeth.

Elizabeth smiles at the man and says, "My name is Elizabeth Thomas. You probably don't know me, but you might remember who my husband was: Alan Thomas, Colonel Alan Thomas of the United States Air Force."

The man gives Elizabeth a peculiar look. Charlie, seeing this, kindly says, "Hello, Mr. Spencer. Glad to meet you. My name is Charlie Delaney." Charlie holds out his hand, and the man shakes it with a firm grip.

The man looks back at Elizabeth and says, "Did you say your husband was Colonel Alan Thomas?"

Elizabeth replies, "Yes, sir, I did. Do you remember him?"

The man studies Elizabeth carefully and smiles. "Red Man. You're Red Man's wife!"

"Yes, that's right!"

"Well, what do you know? What makes you come all the way out here?"

Elizabeth softly replies, "I was wondering if you would tell me about how my husband died. I sure hope you can remember what happened those seventeen years ago."

Charlie begins to relax now that Spencer is smiling and talking to Elizabeth in a friendly manner.

"Mrs. Thomas, I have—"

Elizabeth interrupts to say, "Please, call me Elizabeth."

"Oh no, ma'am. I can't do that. It would be disrespectful to Red Man if I called you by your first name. I would feel better if I could call you Mrs. Thomas."

"Okay. You can call me Mrs. Thomas, if you like. What would you prefer me to call you, Mr. Spencer or Corporal Spencer?"

"Why don't you call me Philip? That's what everybody calls me." He looks over at Charlie and says, "You too. Please call me Philip."

Charlie replies, "Okay, Philip."

Elizabeth eagerly asks, "Do you remember the day Alan was shot down?"

Philip looks at Elizabeth with a serious look. "Mrs. Thomas, there hasn't been a day of my life that I haven't thought about what happened that day. I remember it like it was yesterday. You two come on inside the house, out of this miserable heat, and I will be glad to tell you about that day."

Philip walks up to the house, opens the front door, and enters. Elizabeth and Charlie follow him into the cool farmhouse. Philip says, "It sure feels better in here than out there."

Elizabeth smiles kindly and says, "It sure does."

"I keep the air conditioner on all the time during the summer. I don't know how people lived without one. Can I fix you both something to drink?"

Elizabeth answers first. "Yes. That would be nice. Whatever you are having." Charlie answers likewise.

Charlie and Elizabeth look around at the cluttered house. There are magazines, newspapers, and books lying everywhere. It is apparent that there hasn't been a woman in the house for quite some time. They continue following Philip until they reach the kitchen. The sink is full of dirty dishes, and the floor beneath their feet is sticky. The appliances look like they haven't been cleaned in years. The only clean spot in the house is the kitchen table.

Philip takes down a full bottle of bourbon whiskey, Kentucky Gentleman, and sets it on the kitchen table.

Elizabeth asks, "Do you have any iced tea?"

"Sure do."

Charlie stares at the whiskey briefly and then gives Elizabeth a concerned look. Charlie announces, "I'll have tea also."

Philip opens the door of the refrigerator and takes out a pitcher of tea. He puts ice in three glasses. He pours tea in his guests' glasses and bourbon in his. After he returns the pitcher of tea to the refrigerator, they sit down at the kitchen table.

Spencer takes a long swig of his whiskey before he speaks. "Yeah, that was a long time ago. Red Man was one of the best fellows I ever knew. If my memory serves me right, he had a little girl."

Elizabeth looks at Philip with a sad expression and says, "Her name was Karen. She died a couple of weeks ago in an automobile accident. This is her husband." She points to Charlie, who turns sad and distraught.

"I see," Philip says, shaking his head with sorrow. "Red Man told me he never saw his daughter. He was always talking about going home and picking her up for that first time. Oh well … I guess they both are with each other now."

Elizabeth says, "Please tell me what happened the day my husband was killed."

Philip looks at Elizabeth and seems to notice the worried look on her face. "I hope what I am about to tell you doesn't upset you. You look like this matter has bothered you for quite some time. It has bothered me for the last seventeen years of my life. Just like I told you earlier, there hasn't been a day of my life that I haven't thought about the day your husband was killed, Mrs. Thomas.

"It was July 1970. We were stationed at Chu Lai Air Base, about fifty-seven miles from North Vietnam. I was just a twenty-year-old kid then. I had been in the marines for about two years when that tragic day occurred."

Charlie and Elizabeth listen intently to the corporal's words.

"Yeah. I remember that day like it was yesterday. I wish I could forget it, though. It was a day I wish never came."

Spencer finishes his whiskey and refills the ice. The atmosphere becomes more relaxed and tranquil. But Charlie still remembers what Mr. Bowman told him about this man. Charlie tries to envision how this gentle-looking, soft-spoken man could turn violent enough to strike an officer of the United States Marine Corps.

Spencer glances at Charlie and says, "Would either of you care for a sip of bourbon?"

Charlie and Elizabeth kindly say no. The corporal fills his glass nearly full. "I believe I am going to need this whole bottle to get through this story. It's going to be hard to open these old wounds again. Before I tell you this story, let me explain something. Right out of high school, a few of my buddies and I decided to join the marines together. We knew we would have to serve sooner or later, so we decided to enlist. We all piled in one car and joined up. I graduated in the class of 1968. Six months later, I was in South Vietnam, a private in the Marine Corps."

The room is filled with anticipation. Elizabeth listens with wonder and intrigue. Charlie listens warily, feeling uneasy about the bottle of whiskey on the table. The only sound in the room is Corporal Spencer's gentle, deep voice.

"The first week I was in Nam, I saw what the war was all about. I happened to be out on patrol in the jungle around the base. Well, anyway, our corporal got shot and killed. I got along with all the guys in my platoon fairly well, so the sergeant promoted me to corporal—just like that. They needed someone to be a corporal, so I was elected to fill the position."

Spencer picks up his glass and says, "I hope you don't think I drink like this all the time, because I don't. This story has more victims in it than just Colonel Thomas. The bourbon will make it easier for me to tell you the entire story."

Elizabeth takes a drink of her tea and says, "Please go on. I am very interested in your story."

"Yes, please go on," says Charlie.

"Okay. Well, after I became a corporal, nothing really much changed. We were still in a war zone twenty-four hours a day. I was moved around quite a bit until I ended up at Chu Lai. Yes, that's where all the trouble began, at Chu Lai." Spencer stretches out in his chair and looks up at the ceiling as he thinks about that time. After a few moments, he says, "Yeah. That was a bad week."

Elizabeth and Charlie, not knowing what he means, sit quietly and listen patiently.

"About a week before Red Man was shot down, we were—"

Elizabeth anxiously interrupts. "You saw him get shot down! Is that what you are saying? That you saw him get shot down?"

Philip calmly says, "Yes, ma'am. That's right. I saw Red Man get shot down. But if you would please listen to the whole story, maybe you will understand why." The room grows quiet as Spencer continues. "You see, Mrs. Thomas, about a week before that fateful day, we suffered a great deal of casualties."

Elizabeth holds her breath.

"We went on patrol around the base on a Sunday. It was hot, humid, and sticky. As we were walking down this little trail, we heard gunfire, single-action gunfire. We knew that was the enemy. Two of us got killed; another three were wounded. One of the fellows who died was a close friend of mine. Billy Atkins was his name. We grew up together. We played on the same baseball team. We went to the same school. I knew him all my life. We even joined up the same day. He was the best friend I ever had." Spencer pauses for a minute, and the room is quiet and still. Finally, the corporal breaks the silence as he says with a frown, "Now he was gone. They just hit us quickly, then ran away. I guess that was the worst part of that war. That vicious hit-and-run tactic that the Vietcong used. It was horrendous!"

Charlie's eyes focus on the corporal with sympathy. Elizabeth drinks her tea until it's gone. Seeing this says, Philip says, "Would you like some more tea, Mrs. Thomas?"

"No, thank you. Please go on," Elizabeth anxiously replies. Charlie drinks his tea as the corporal continues with his story.

"The next day, Monday, the same thing happened. We were on patrol, and we walked into another ambush. They were waiting for us. Just as soon as we were all visible, here came the gunfire. This time three of us got killed, and four got wounded. You had to be there to feel the misery we were going through. It was extremely hot, it was so humid you could hardly breathe, and our buddies were getting killed like flies. But that's not the worst of it. It's seeing your buddies suffer before they die. That's gotta be the hardest thing to bear."

Elizabeth's face is filled with grief and despair as she looks at the corporal. Charlie too is touched by the corporal's words.

"Tuesday was the next day. It was the worst day of the week. Our lieutenant ordered a whole company out on patrol. He was anxious to stop the hit-and-runs for good. There were thirty men in my company; after Tuesday, there were twenty. We killed several of the enemy, but we suffered more casualties. They had everything ready for us. This time they were lobbing grenades and firing mortars at us. I remember seeing one grenade drop four of my buddies at one time. We found the rest of them. We killed every one. Would you believe there were only five of them? Two were firing the mortars, one was lobbing grenades, and the other two were shooting rifles, I guess. There were three men and two women, or should I say, there were three boys and two girls. They were all real young. None of them could have been much older than nineteen."

Now the atmosphere in the room is full of sorrow and grief.

The corporal looks at Charlie with sympathy and says, "After I saw who we killed, I felt a little differently about who the enemy was. Don't get me wrong, though. I hated the enemy, and I always did my best to kill them. But after you see their young, dead corpses, you wonder: why the hell would young kids like that be trying to kill us? I guess someone put them up to it. I guess anybody can be deceived, especially young kids who don't know any better."

Elizabeth slowly shakes her head with sympathy. "I believe I will have another glass of tea."

"Sure thing," Spencer answers softly. He gets up and brings the pitcher of tea from the refrigerator and pours Elizabeth and then Charlie another glass. He sets the pitcher down on the table and pours himself another whiskey. Spencer looks at his full glass and says, "You know something, Mrs. Thomas?"

"What?" she replies gently.

"I didn't start drinking liquor at all until about seven years ago. I don't really know why I drink so much. I lied earlier about not drinking like this. I usually drink a fifth of bourbon almost every night. Maybe after I tell you this story, I will learn why I drink so much."

Elizabeth pauses before saying, "You could just stop drinking, you know."

Spencer laughs and says, "That's easier said than done. That's like saying you could have stopped worrying about Red Man seventeen years ago."

Elizabeth stares at the corporal.

"I can see the worry in your eyes. I know the air force lied to you, and since they did, they put doubt in your mind. Am I not correct, Mrs. Thomas?"

Elizabeth nods before saying, "Yes, I guess you are right. Please finish your story, if you may."

The corporal smiles a halfhearted smile before taking another drink. "Well, after Tuesday, the lieutenant's commanding officer got into the picture. He is a man who will be troubling to you, Mrs. Thomas, as much as he was troubling to me. That man's name is Major Lester Cain."

A mysterious sensitive nerve erupts in Charlie's consciousness. Both Charlie and Elizabeth have read about this man, but they don't let on that they know anything about him. They continue to listen with their complete and undivided attention.

"You see," Philip continues, "Major Cain was a crude and somewhat difficult man at times. When everything was going his way, he was all right to be around. But when anything wasn't going his way, he was like the devil in a green uniform."

Charlie asks, "Did Major Cain dislike you?"

Philip answers immediately in the same gentle tone. "No. Not when I first met him. As a matter of fact, he kinda took a strange liking to me. You see, all Marine Corps majors do is go around and give sergeants and lieutenants a hard time. They chew them out over the smallest things, anything and everything. The majors get their orders from the generals through the colonels. Then they pass them along down the line through the lieutenants. In the meantime, they just ride around looking for someone to chew out. You see, I used to drive Major Cain around for his daily ass-chewing-out sessions. Oops … I'm sorry, Mrs. Thomas. I don't usually cuss like that in front of ladies."

Elizabeth politely says, "That's quite all right, Philip. Please go on."

"Like I said earlier, Major Cain took a special liking to me—I guess because nobody else liked him very much, and he just wanted someone to like him. Major Cain and I got along exceptionally well in those early days at Chu Lai, but that didn't last long." The corporal pours himself another drink. The sound of the liquor filling the glass is the only sound in the house besides the air conditioner humming its gentle noise. He stares at the glass with a look of depression.

Spencer takes a stiff drink from his glass and says, "Well, anyway, Wednesday came along, and once again we went out on patrol. This time our sergeant got shot. I came over to where he was lying. He spoke to me through excruciating pain. 'Corporal,' he said, 'I am putting you in charge now. You go after them, and when you find them, you send them all straight to hell!' That's what he told me. So I ordered a few men to carry the sergeant back to base. Then we went after them. It didn't take us long to find them. We killed four and wounded two. We dragged them all back to the base. None of them could have been older than nineteen this time either."

He takes another stiff drink from his glass. "I sure was shook up about being put in charge for the first time. Later we found out that the sergeant died. I never did like him very much, but when I heard he died, I felt as though my own father had died. It sure was a funny feeling—hating someone for such a long time; then they die, and you feel a sense of love for them. Anyway, when Major Cain found out that Sergeant Adams was dead, he hit the roof. He literally went berserk. I've never seen a major act the way he did. The deaths of our men were finally taking a toll on his nerves.

"Thursday rolled around, and this time I didn't have to go on patrol. I drove Major Cain around the base. Planes were flying in and out like bees around a hive. I drove the major anywhere and everywhere he wanted to go. He was fit to be tied."

Elizabeth listens more eagerly now because she knows Alan was supposedly shot down on Friday.

Philip continues, "He blamed everything on the closest man around him. He used his rank to intimidate and humiliate every lieutenant and every sergeant he saw. He was a class A asshole—excuse my language, but that was just what he was. I don't think he cared about anybody except himself."

The corporal gets up to put more ice in his glass. When he returns, he doesn't waste any time pouring more whiskey in his little glass. The smell of bourbon fills the kitchen. The ice makes a crackling noise as the amber liquid hits it. The atmosphere is filled with great anticipation.

The corporal thinks for a few seconds, trying to recollect the images of that day. Finally, he speaks. "Yeah. It was Thursday when I saw Red Man for the last time. I didn't talk with him long, but I did shake his hand and speak with him for a couple minutes."

Elizabeth leans forward. "What did you talk about?"

The corporal slowly sips the bourbon. "I don't remember exactly what we talked about, but it was something about the mission he was going on the next day. I only talked with him a few minutes." Spencer smiles up toward the ceiling as he remembers. "He was some kind of man. He would pull out a pouch of Red Man chewing tobacco and put a wad in his mouth the size of a baseball. And with that bright red hair of his, it was an automatic thing for him to get a nickname like Red Man. He was one of the friendliest men I ever knew. He was a hell of a nice guy."

Elizabeth smiles with pride. Seeing Elizabeth's happiness makes Charlie smile even more robustly.

"You should have heard him talk about his missions," Spencer continues. "He used to tell us how he would sweep in behind an enemy aircraft and shoot it down. I used to love to hear him tell those stories. Everybody liked Red Man. I don't think he had an enemy in the world, except those MiGs trying to shoot down our bombers. He was really one hell of a nice guy."

Suddenly, the corporal slams his glass down on the table. The sounds of ice banging together and the glass hitting the table echo throughout the room in a disturbing way. The corporal quickly says, "Yeah, Thursday was a bad day too. Sometime around three o'clock, casualties started coming in. I can't remember how many, but there were a bunch."

Elizabeth and Charlie exchange glances.

"Major Cain had me drive him over to see them. There were a least a dozen, possibly more. None of them died, but they were in excruciating pain. The VC's hit-and-run tactic was working." Spencer looks directly at Charlie with sincerity. "Here we were, United States Marines equipped with multimillion-dollar armament, and we couldn't stop getting hit like that. Every single day that week, we had casualties. We were all so mad. We wanted to kill the enemy so bad, but they were nowhere to be found. All that energy built up inside us to kill someone, and we couldn't find them. Not even one enemy was found that day. Every marine at the entire base was mad as hell! We were all eager to kill the enemy with a passion."

Elizabeth becomes nervous as she listens to this but remains silent.

"The next day, Friday, is the day that haunts me like a living nightmare. The day started out like any other day. I had breakfast like everybody else. I did my normal duties as usual. I was in Major Cain's quarters typing a few papers for him. As I was typing a report, the major looked at me through the open door of his office. There was nobody else in the room."

Elizabeth holds her breath, so as not to miss a single word. Charlie listens with eagerness and with his eyes focused directly on the corporal.

"The major pulled out a bottle of whiskey from one of his drawers. He opened the full bottle and began to start drinking. I saw him take the cap off the full bottle, but I didn't say a thing. I just kept on typing. I guess this was around noon."

The corporal keeps talking as he pours more whiskey in his glass. "As I was typing, I happened to look up. I saw the major turning the bottle up. He didn't use a glass. He drank right out of the bottle. I guess he drank for about thirty minutes or so before he spotted me looking at him. Our eyes met. I tried to turn away, but he said, 'Hey, Corporal, would you like a drink?' I replied politely, 'No, thank you, sir.' He said, 'Suit yourself, Corporal. Just thought you might like a drink.' I again politely refused."

Charlie asks, "Did he get mad at you for not wanting to drink with him?"

The corporal laughs as he says, "No, Charlie, just the opposite. Like I said earlier, he kinda liked me for some reason. As he turned up the bottle and drank, he spoke to me like a decent person for a change. For several minutes he asked me about where I was from, about my folks—you know, those kinds of things. I guess the alcohol was making him feel a little friendlier toward me. Then he gave me a peculiar stare and said, 'Hey, Corporal, how would you like to be a sergeant? I can arrange for you to get a promotion. I like you, Corporal. I like you, boy.' I told him no thanks. I told him as soon as my hitch was up, I was going home to get married to my high school sweetheart and settle down. He didn't say much after that. A little while later, the major wanted me to drive him to the airport. I remember him putting the cap on that bottle of whiskey. The bottle of Jack Daniel's was half-full when he put it away."

Charlie, Elizabeth, and the corporal simultaneously look at the bottle of bourbon sitting on the table. It is half-full by now. "Yeah," Spencer says, now with a slur in his speech, "just like this bottle here, about half-gone."

Elizabeth and Charlie look at each other, thinking the same thing. Major Lester Cain would then have been in the same condition as the corporal is now.

"After he put the bottle away, we left for the airport. The major really liked to see our bombers take off. Red Man was there. Red Man, being in the air force, was flying a fighter, a Phantom, and that was some fighter! The best in the world at that time."

Elizabeth's eyes shine with pride. Charlie's attention grows stronger with every word.

The corporal continues, still slightly slurring his words. "Well, the air force fighters and our bombers took off to go on their mission. The major's face was filled with self-pride and revenge when they took off. He told me, 'Corporal, those planes are going to make up for what we couldn't do out there in the jungle.'

"I saw a sinister grin on his face. It was a look that would make your stomach turn sour. I never did like to see a self-proud look on a man's face. And that's what he looked like, a man full of self-pride." Spencer looks over at Charlie and then over to Elizabeth. "You remember seeing those old World War II films of the dictator of Italy? Mussolini? The major looked just like Mussolini after he made one of his speeches."

Charlie nods his head in understanding.

"The dictator in those old war films would put his arms across his chest and gaze out into the crowd with that vile, repugnant, proud, loathsome, atrocious look. Well, that's about what Major Cain looked liked, except he had hair. Maybe not so extreme, but you get the picture."

Knowing the story is nearing the part where her husband was shot down, Elizabeth listens nervously and curiously. She is finally going to hear what happened to Alan seventeen years ago.

The corporal turns his head and stares at Elizabeth. She looks at him with tender, anxious eyes. The corporal gently says, "After your husband took off, along with the other planes, the major wanted me to drive him around to some of the antiaircraft batteries. He just wanted to make sure the troops were alert. This is where it gets difficult to talk about it."

Charlie and Elizabeth both are becoming more anxious, but they listen in complete silence as the corporal continues.

"Somewhere around ten minutes after the planes took off, I saw an aircraft flying just over the horizon. I was sitting in the jeep while the major was talking to some lieutenant at one of our batteries. I turned on the radio, and I heard Red Man's voice. He was in trouble. His plane was experiencing some type of mechanical problem. He was asking for permission to land. I heard his voice over the radio—'This is Red Man. Need to land immediately! Need to make an emergency landing!'"

Elizabeth frowns on hearing this. She realizes now that the report about Alan's radio not working was indeed just another lie. She listens intently.

"That's all I heard before Major Cain looked up and started screaming, 'Enemy aircraft! Enemy aircraft! Shoot down that plane! Shoot down that plane!' He went berserk! I never saw any marine major act in that manner. He was hysterical."

Charlie's and Elizabeth's faces are full of concern as the corporal gets more exuberant.

"The lieutenant got on the radio and ordered everyone to fire on the aircraft. The major was still running around, screaming at the top of his lungs to shoot down that plane. Then our fifty calibers began to unload on the aircraft. I jumped out of the jeep and ran over to the major. I yelled, 'It's Red Man! It's Red Man! Stop! Stop! It's Red Man up there!' The machine guns were still blazing. The noise was loud and fierce. The lieutenant and I looked over at the major. His face turned red with dismay. He was dumbfounded! He looked like a schoolkid who'd just gotten caught stealing an apple from a sidewalk stand—you know, a real stupid look. The lieutenant took over at our batteries and ordered everyone to stop firing. Everybody at those batteries was upset. It was a really bad scene."

The corporal gets up from the table, visibly angry and disoriented. His voice grows louder as he acts out what happened on that tragic day. The room is filled with uneasiness as the corporal stares at Charlie and Elizabeth, with energy radiating out of his intoxicating eyes. The corporal gestures wildly as he speaks. His motions begin to bring more meaning to his words. Elizabeth is absorbed in his story. Charlie too is on the edge of his seat. He listens attentively as the corporal continues.

"While the lieutenant was trying to stop the firing, Red Man managed to outmaneuver most of the ground fire. I saw him fly away from the airstrip. The machine guns finally stopped firing. Just as the fifty calibers stopped firing, a surface-to-air missile was launched. Red Man was nearly out of sight as we watched it go up. I followed the trajectory of the missile until I saw it hit Red Man. From the angle where we were standing, only the major and I actually saw the explosion. His fuel tanks were still pretty full, so when that missile hit him in the rear, it gave off a burst of yellow flames like nothing you have ever seen."

The corporal looks at Elizabeth with sympathy and compassion. He moderates his voice, speaking gently now. "I am sorry, Mrs. Thomas. I'm sorry I had to be the one to tell you this."

Elizabeth tries to smile at the corporal as a tear runs down her ivory-white cheek. She rubs it away and says, "Please go on. I want to hear the rest." Charlie reaches over and holds her hand as they both focus again on Spencer.

Philip Spencer sits down and pours himself another drink. He takes a sip and a few quiet moments before continuing. "We found the aircraft in the jungle. There was nothing we could do. The plane kept burning for hours. We had hoped Red Man would have parachuted out, but there was no time. He probably didn't know what hit him. The partial remains found in the aircraft left no doubt that he died there.

"Major Cain ordered me to drive him back to his quarters because he was in a state of panic. When we got there, he went straight to his top right drawer where the half-full bottle of Jack Daniel's was. He quickly poured it out and threw the empty bottle deep into the jungle. He looked at me with a wicked look and said, 'Corporal, if you ever tell anybody you saw me take a drink today, I will personally destroy you! Do you understand me, boy?' His voice was cruel and sinister. His face was like that of the devil!"

Now Charlie understands why there was a cover-up. However, he still has some doubts. This might just be a story the corporal cooked up because he resented being dishonorably discharged from the marines. Charlie wonders how he can get the corporal to prove his story without offending him.

Elizabeth's thoughts are centered mostly on finally knowing how her beloved husband died. She believes the corporal's story completely. The tumor of doubt has been removed from her mind. Her grief and sorrow are complete now, and she finally can let Alan go. She tries to smile so as not to upset Charlie and the corporal, but she can't keep from showing tears of sadness and grief for the loss of her husband. She now knows he wasn't a POW. She is happy and sad at the same time. Her mixed emotions show in her face.

After the corporal takes a long drink from his glass, he says, "When the investigation took place, I at first didn't tell anybody about the major drinking on duty. If I had, it would have cost me my life. I took his threat seriously. The next day, Red Man's commanding officer, General Anderson, came into my quarters. He asked me if I knew anything about the mishap on Friday."

Elizabeth listens eagerly. She remembers General Anderson. He was the one who came to her house in 1970 and told her how Alan had died.

"I remember him looking at me with that stern look of his. I couldn't lie to a general, even if he was a general in the air force, so I told him I saw Major Cain drink half a fifth of whiskey prior to the downing of Colonel Thomas's plane. He already knew that Major Cain had given the order to open fire on the aircraft. He shook his head in disbelief until I told him the brand of whiskey, Jack Daniel's Black Label. I told him where the major had thrown the bottle. He ordered someone to retrieve it. I remember him saying, 'Corporal, you did the right thing telling me about this. I'll make damn sure Major Cain doesn't retaliate against you.'"

Elizabeth thinks angrily, *The general knew. He knew all along what happened to Alan. He looked me in the eye and flat-out lied to me.*

Spencer continues, "They confronted the major about drinking the whiskey. When they produced the bottle, he admitted that he did drink that day. If he had been a lieutenant or a sergeant, he would have faced a court-martial, but since he was a major, and virtually no one else saw the missile hit Red Man's aircraft, they covered it up. The major simply got away with it. Or at least somewhat."

"Why?" Elizabeth cries out.

"Why didn't they do something to Major Cain?" Charlie asks.

"You see, Charlie, Mrs. Thomas, the people in Washington were taking a lot of heat about the war. The top brass didn't want to escalate it by telling the American people that a colonel of the United States Air Force had been shot down because of a drunken marine major. And since the major and I were the only ones admitting to seeing the plane get hit, it was easier for them to simply cover it up. Not even the lieutenant saw Red Man get hit. He was yelling at the top of his lungs for everybody to stop firing. If anybody else saw the impact, they kept it to themselves."

Charlie looks at Elizabeth with a glum expression. He pours them both another glass of tea as the corporal takes another stiff drink.

"When the other planes returned from their mission, we learned that three others didn't make it back either. We lost two bombers, a fighter, and of course, Red Man. They told everybody at the base that Red Man was wounded by machine-gun fire from a MiG. He tried to make it back home but crashed in the jungle. They said none of the artillery that mistakenly was fired at him ever hit his plane. And since nobody saw the brief explosion far away in the distance, everybody believed it. The top brass lied about why we fired on Red Man. They said his radio didn't work."

Elizabeth nods her head. This was the reason she read on the report.

"This gave the marines a defense in case anything came out later. They simply would have said they thought Red Man was an enemy aircraft because he didn't radio for permission to land. They covered up the incident so well that even if the truth did break that Red Man was shot down by friendly fire, they would have an alibi for firing."

"A cover-up on top of a cover-up," says Charlie.

The corporal nods. "Exactly. The war was so unpopular then that they had to stoop to these types of tactics." There is a long silence in the room as everybody thinks about what they have just said and heard.

The corporal studies Elizabeth and Charlie, waiting for the right moment to speak again. Finally, he says, "The day after I told the air force about Major Cain, I knew I was going to catch hell for doing it. The lieutenant wanted me to drive him to the airport. He was mad as hell at me for talking to the air force. He made that perfectly clear."

The strong smell of bourbon fills the room as Charlie and Elizabeth look on with blank expressions.

"The lieutenant wanted me to see Major Cain for the last time. The top brass was transferring him out of Chu Lai. I'll never forget the way he looked at me when he was escorted to his plane. He didn't get a chance to say anything to me, but he nodded his head as if to say, 'One day I am going get you for this, Corporal!' I was glad to see the bastard leave. He got away with what he did because of the pride of the Marine Corps. But I knew what he'd done, and so did the top brass. He got away with drinking on duty, killing Red Man, and causing a stir between us and the air force. But I promise you this, Mrs. Thomas: he will have to answer for it someday."

Elizabeth says in a depressed tone, "My husband died because of liquor, and my daughter also died because of liquor." There is a short pause. Elizabeth is on the verge of crying. "What makes people drink liquor?"

Her question stuns the corporal for a moment. He stares at her misery-filled face and then at his glass. The smell of bourbon seems even stronger as the corporal continues. "Mrs. Thomas, maybe after I tell you the rest of the story, I will find out the answer to your question—because what happened after Major Cain left Chu Lai changed my life in a very dramatic and horrendous way. And I mean for the very worse!" The corporal gets up and gets himself another glass and fills it with ice.

Charlie is still wondering how to find proof that the corporal's story is true. Charlie waits until the corporal sits down before asking, "After you told that air force general what happened, didn't you write up a report on the incident?"

The corporal begins to pour the bourbon in his glass. He thinks about it and announces, "As a matter of fact, I did. Yeah, I sure did. Right before the lieutenant came in the next day to have me drive him to the airport, I remember handing him that report."

Charlie smiles subtly.

"Yeah, but the lieutenant tore it up. That's when he began to chew me out about telling on Major Cain. The lieutenant tore that report to shreds. That's when he told me I was a disgrace to wear the uniform … and a few other very unpleasant things."

Charlie's smile disappears at the disappointment.

The corporal says, "But I made two copies. I knew every report had to be made in duplicate."

"What did you do with the other one?" Elizabeth asks quickly.

The corporal takes his time before answering. "I simply kept it. I couldn't make myself throw it away, so I just kept it."

Charlie asks, "Where is it now?"

The corporal gets up from his seat. He gently says, "Wait a minute. I think I know where it is."

The corporal leaves the room for a few minutes and then comes back carrying a small, dusty brown box. He quickly opens it as the anticipation grows stronger and stronger. The corporal thumbs through the small box until he finds what he is looking for. "Here it is." He takes one more look at the report before handing it to Charlie.

Charlie reads through the three-page report quickly. He nods his head in agreement. He looks up toward Elizabeth and says, "It's correct. This document tells about Major Lester Cain drinking while on duty, which resulted in the downing of Colonel Alan Thomas of the United States Air Force." He hands the document to Elizabeth as the corporal finishes the bourbon in his glass. Elizabeth reads it carefully all the way through.

The corporal resumes speaking with a slur. "Now let me tell you what the major did to me after he left Chu Lai."

Charlie and Elizabeth both take a drink of their tea as the corporal fills his glass once more. The pair look at each other, each knowing what the other is thinking.

"After the major left the Air Base, they transferred me out the following week. The top brass in the Marine Corps didn't like the idea of me ratting on the major to the air force, so they sent me all the way to Saigon. I stayed there and worked mostly as a clerk until June of 1971. At that time we were in the process of preparing everybody to evacuate Vietnam. I had only three weeks left before I could go home. I counted the days with excitement. I was really looking forward to going back home. My mama was in the hospital, so that made me that much more eager to get out of this rotten war and go home. I'd had enough of it."

Charlie, like Elizabeth, knows what happened in Saigon. They both read about it in Mr. Bowman's report. But they don't say anything to the corporal about what they know. They just sit and listen quietly.

The corporal gazes over at Charlie as he speaks. "Like I said, I had only three weeks left to go. But I just happened to be in the wrong place at the wrong time. I didn't know then, but the major had everything arranged to get me, just as he said he would." The corporal looks over at Elizabeth. "I was at this little nightclub. I can't remember the name of it, but it was a hangout for military personnel. That's when I saw the major. When I spotted him, he was grinning at me with a fiendish, devious little grin. I got up to leave, but he met me at the door. Although I did manage to leave the club without any incident, his cronies were waiting for me outside."

The corporal gazes back and forth between Charlie and Elizabeth as he talks. "The major was wearing civilian clothes. This is a direct violation of military dress codes. I then heard his voice. 'Hey, Corporal. What seems to be your hurry? Don't you want to talk to an old marine buddy?' That's what he said. I told him I didn't have anything to say to him. Then he said, 'Now that's no way to be. I just want you to know that I had to leave the Marines Corps because of you. They made me retire a couple of weeks ago. You see, I'm not wearing my uniform anymore.' Being an idiot, I believed him. Why else would a marine major be wearing civilian clothes? Well, that's when the trouble began."

Charlie and Elizabeth are on the edge of their seats. The corporal takes a stiff drink as his voice gets louder. "He started calling me all kinds of names. I could tell he was looking for trouble. I tried to ignore the insults about me. But when he started calling my daddy a stupid dirt farmer and a host of other nasty things, I began to get angry, very angry. But when he started talking about my mama is when I blew up. He started calling her a whore and … well … other things I don't feel comfortable saying right now. Those things got under my skin. The major even did some research and found out my mama was sick in the hospital."

Charlie begins to get upset now. He thinks, what would he have done if somebody had said those things about his mother? Elizabeth holds her hands tightly and breathes slowly, not wanting to miss anything being said.

The corporal shakes his head. "But when he said men were lining up outside her room to get laid, well, that did it! I tore into him like a tornado in a Kansas cornfield. I beat the living hell out of him. It was what he wanted me to do. That's when his cronies came running up from behind some cars, one lieutenant and a couple of MPs. They threw me in the brig. As I was being taken away, the lieutenant said, 'Corporal, you will stand to be court-martialed for this.' I said to him, 'A court-martial? What are you talking about?' The lieutenant's voice was deep, loud, and clear. 'You will stand before a court-martial for striking an officer. You just struck a major of the United States Marine Corps.' I said, 'Do what?' I couldn't believe it! He was still in the corps!"

Charlie and Elizabeth gaze at the corporal in amazement.

"I yelled, 'Look at him! He isn't wearing a uniform!' I think later he got a citation for being out of uniform, but it didn't make any difference to him because he was getting out the next month anyway. He tricked me! That low-life bastard tricked me! I spent the rest of my tour in the brig. I sat back in my jail cell with an awful, terrible feeling in the pit of my stomach. I couldn't believe it! I just couldn't. The conspiracy the major had planned to ruin me was working."

Elizabeth pulls her chair closer to Charlie's. Charlie holds her hand firmly as they wait for the corporal to finish the story.

The room is still as the corporal continues in a gentler tone. "The next thing I remember, I was standing before a court-martial. The stooge witnesses were eager to tell what they saw. When the court asked who threw the first punch, I knew it was over. It didn't take them long to slap me with a dishonorable discharge."

Elizabeth is puzzled. "If the major didn't get into trouble because of the incident at Chu Lai, why did he still want revenge?"

The corporal considers the question for a moment. "I guess it was mainly because of pride. He may not have gotten into much trouble over the incident at Chu Lai, but the top brass did make him retire early."

Elizabeth nods her head, trying to understand.

"I found out later that his term was up, and they didn't let him stay in for another term. He only had eighteen years in the corps, not twenty, so he didn't get a full retirement. But having to leave the marines, I guess, is what did it. He was a hard-line military man. No matter, he did what he said he was going to do—he destroyed me."

Charlie and Elizabeth look at the corporal with sadness. Charlie pours Elizabeth another glass of tea as the corporal stares down at the floor. Charlie and Elizabeth begin to feel for the corporal, whose face is plagued with misery.

After a few moments of uninterrupted quiet, the corporal says, "After I got home, things began to get worse. My mama was still in the hospital when I got off the plane, so she wasn't there to welcome me home. My girlfriend and my father were the only ones there. My girlfriend threw her arms around me with great jubilation, but …" The corporal's voice trails off.

Charlie and Elizabeth both sense that something bad is about to be said. They listen quietly as the soft-spoken corporal resumes his story.

"My father greeted me like I had the plague or something. He was disappointed because I got a dishonorable discharge. He never was one to hold back anything when he talked to me. He told me flat out on the way to the hospital, in front of my girlfriend, that I'd brought shame to the family name and that I was a total disgrace." Spencer looks at Charlie. "Let me tell you something that hurts more than anything. When your own father has no respect for you, then you don't have much respect for yourself." The corporal tilts the bottle of bourbon once again, and the amber liquid dances into his glass.

"My mother, on the other hand, didn't care one way or another. She loved me more than anybody in my life. I believe if I had told her that I robbed a bank, she still would have loved me. I guess mothers are supposed to be like that."

Charlie asks, "Didn't you tell your father why you got a dishonorable discharge?"

The corporal quickly replies, "No, Charlie. I didn't tell him or anybody else. I didn't want to sound like a crybaby. My father wouldn't have accepted anything I said anyway. I knew him too well. He was too angry with me to understand or accept anything I said. I guess he'd seen too many John Wayne movies. He thought I was supposed to capture the enemy, win the war, and come back home like a real Sergeant York. He just didn't understand that this war wasn't fought like the ones fought on TV. And because he didn't understand, he inflicted some awful psychological wounds on me."

The corporal takes another stiff drink before saying, "Yeah, after I got home, things weren't the same by a long shot. Because of the discharge, I couldn't get a job. I guess I filled out twenty applications, but just as soon they found out I had a dishonorable discharge, the reply was always the same: Don't call us. We'll call you. And they never did."

Although Elizabeth is relieved to know how her husband died, she feels compassion and sympathy for the man who suffered so much because he witnessed that death.

"But not getting a job didn't stop me from marrying my childhood sweetheart. We were married less than a month after I got back from Nam. I talked Daddy into giving me two acres of land. We bought a small mobile home. She had a job with an insurance company, while I helped Daddy on the farm. It wasn't easy listening to him yell at me. When he ordered me around, I felt like I was still in the marines. But it was the insults I despised. Those were some bad times, and it got worse.

"My mama died a year later. That was a terrible blow to me. She was the one person I needed more than ever."

Elizabeth shakes her head in sorrow.

"Daddy managed to take control of the entire farm. Mama made out a will before she died. She willed me half of what she owned, but it wasn't notarized properly, so Daddy managed to get it all. Daddy and I got into an awful fight over her estate. But he won. I wasn't about to sue him or anything like that. He had lawyers put everything in his name after she died. He did give me things over the years, though, things that should have been mine all along. He thought he was giving me this or giving me that, but he didn't realize most of those things should have been mine from the start. I guess it made him feel generous to give me those things, but I developed a dislike for him for being that way."

Charlie suspects that the alcohol is making the corporal open up more than he would normally do. He gazes over at Elizabeth and sees the compelling look in her eyes as she listens.

"Daddy and I got along pretty good before I went to Nam, but after I got back, he treated me exceptionally bad until he died. I think he used me as a scapegoat for all the things he failed at in life. You see, my father always wanted to be rich. He tried to make people think he had money. He would carry large sums of money around to show people how rich he was, but when it came to me and Mama, he never had any. He made several outrageous investments that resulted in disaster for the farm."

Elizabeth asks, "What type of investments?"

"Tell us if you don't mind," Charlie adds.

The corporal takes another sip of his bourbon and says, "I was just a boy when my daddy thought up this get-rich-quick scheme. To make a long story short, he went to the bank and borrowed thirty thousand dollars. That was a fortune back then. He used the farm as collateral for the loan. My mother was totally against it, but she eventually gave in to Daddy's persistence. He bought a half-interest in a peanut company. For every dollar he invested, he thought he would get ten back. Boy, was he mistaken! Six months later, the company filed for bankruptcy."

Elizabeth and Charlie shake their heads empathetically.

"My father was devastated! The bank nearly foreclosed on the farm. He managed to get another loan to cover it. We all worked real hard, and seven years later it was paid off. My daddy made the last payment right before I left for Vietnam. After I came home from Nam, would you believe he blamed me for everything? Every failure that he'd had in his life, he blamed on me. He would tell me straight out, 'It was all your fault.' I was his scapegoat for every failure he experienced in his life. That damn dishonorable discharge cut deep into his soul."

The mood in the room grows oddly tranquil. "It's strange," Spencer ponders, "that a man would work hard all of his life hoping to be a big shot someday—make a million dollars, live in a big house, drive a nice car, and wear fancy clothes. But when it doesn't ever happen, I guess you need somebody to blame. So I let my father blame me. I guess it made him feel better. That's why I don't care to ever be a millionaire—because if it never comes to pass, and I'm sure it won't, I won't be looking for someone to blame. And if I didn't find anyone to blame, I would go through life resentful and angry for not achieving what I wanted life to be—you know, feeling like a failure."

Charlie's eyes begin to get glassy, and Elizabeth's expression is melancholy. They both hurt for the corporal.

Spencer turns up his glass and peacefully says, "My daddy died four years after I got back from Nam. I remember the day he died. He was in the hospital. He never apologized one time for the things he said to me. I never once heard him say he loved me. The last words he said to me were 'Why did you have to disgrace me by hitting that officer?' Let me tell you, that hurt. That's when I began to think about finding Major Lester Cain and killing him. The hate I had for that man was tremendous."

Charlie also is beginning to develop a hatred for this man. He knows the grief Karen suffered while growing up without a daddy, plus the grief Elizabeth has endured all these years because of one man's stupidity. The seed of hate for Major Cain has been planted in Charlie's mind.

As the sun begins to go down over the western horizon, Elizabeth is consumed by the corporal's sorrow. Just as the saying says, misery loves company. Elizabeth, like the corporal, has been dealt a lot of hardship because of this one man. Charlie comforts her tenderly, patting her hand. They continue to listen to the corporal.

"My wife and I were married only five years. Like I told you earlier, she had a job with an insurance company. So she was making most of the money—which I didn't mind, but she put most of it in her savings account. She made it perfectly clear to me that it was *her* money. That money was the main reason that we broke up."

Elizabeth and Charlie look curiously at Spencer.

"There were things we needed around the house, but she was reluctant to use her money. She had changed dramatically. She had become a very materialistic girl. Her selfishness grew at a tremendous rate, and of course, her parents didn't help matters."

Elizabeth asks, "Didn't you get along with your in-laws?"

The corporal takes another sip of bourbon and notices Elizabeth staring at his glass. He says, "When I was growing up, they liked me a whole lot. But after the discharge, my in-laws practically excommunicated me. They seldom spoke to me. They never came over to our mobile home to visit. You see, my wife's father was in the army. So he thought I was a real loser when I got a dishonorable discharge." The corporal catches a look on Charlie's face and says, "I know what you think—they didn't like me because I drank."

Charlie and Elizabeth simultaneously reply, "Oh no."

The corporal smiles. "You see, I never drank liquor then. That's the God's truth. Even after my wife left me, I still didn't drink."

This satisfies Charlie and Elizabeth's curiosity for now. Strangely, they both believe him. They continue to listen intently, eagerly waiting for the part when the corporal has another encounter with Major Lester Cain.

"After my daddy died, my wife wanted me to sell the farm so we could move away. She hated Kentucky. She wanted to move to New York City. Can you believe that? Me, living in New York City!" The corporal laughs as the room grows darker. "She was offered a higher-paying job with the insurance company she worked for. Her boss was moving to New York, and he wanted her to go along to be his private secretary. She really didn't want me to move up there. She just wanted to manufacture an argument with me, so she and her boss could run off together, and she did."

Charlie and Elizabeth don't know what to say. They both feel a close bond to this stranger because their lives also have been plagued with disappointment and tragedy. They continue to listen with great interest.

Spencer fetches another glass, his third, and fills it. "My wife and I were happy together for the first three years of our marriage. But I guess we just grew apart. She had a steady job and money. The more money she made, the more money she wanted. She wanted the nicer things in life, things I never could have given her. Her attitude changed tremendously.

"The last two years of our marriage were filled with 'I want this' and 'I want that.' The nagging over the same things was like a knife cutting a rope, and the rope was about to be severed. She never threw the discharge up in my face until the very end."

Elizabeth holds her breath as she anticipates the outcome.

"You see, Mrs. Thomas, I wouldn't give her a divorce. I loved her too much. So she reduced herself to being mean to me. She threw everything up in my face, even the dishonorable discharge, saying, 'My mama and daddy were right about you. You are a loser! A sorry, good-for-nothing loser. Your own daddy didn't even like you.' You don't want to hear everything she said, but I can tell you it was awful. Her sharp, vicious tongue cut through me like a hot knife, so I finally submitted and gave her a divorce. She lives in New York City now with her boss."

Charlie asks, "You said you have a little boy?"

"That's right."

"Do you ever go up there to see him?"

"Oh yeah. I go at least three times a year. She doesn't like the idea, but I made it perfectly clear that if I didn't see my son, or if she left town without telling me where Scott was, I eventually would find her and kill her. That might sound harsh, but that boy is mine too. And I will kill her if she tries anything to stop me from seeing him. And she knows I would!" The corporal turns up his glass, and the only noise in the room is the bourbon making its way down the corporal's throat and then the ice in the glass rattling as Spencer returns the glass to the oak table.

Charlie, like Elizabeth, is somewhat shocked at hearing this threat but doesn't show any negative emotions. They both smell the scent of the liquor strongly now. The room grows quiet and still as the corporal reaches for the amber-colored bottle one last time. He pours the last drop into his glass. Charlie wonders why Philip has changed glasses so often but doesn't ask.

The corporal takes a small sip from his half-full glass with great care. The anger in his eyes is noticeable to both Charlie and Elizabeth. The corporal finally breaks the silence. "Now, let me tell you about what I was going to do to Major … or should I say Mr. Lester Cain!"

The way he is speaking gives Elizabeth chills. Charlie, on the other hand, feels content to hear about some type of revenge for this man.

Charlie has grown to hate Major Cain. He knows Karen and Elizabeth have both suffered greatly because of this man. He listens with a gleam in his eye.

"Four years after my wife left me, back in 1980, I got to thinking about things. When you are all alone, you can think pretty good. I thought about how I'd lost my daddy's respect, how I couldn't find a job to make something of my life, and how I'd lost my wife and son."

The room grows even darker as the sun makes its descent for the day. The corporal's voice gets softer with a stronger slur.

"After thinking it all over, I came to the unhappy conclusion that because of that dishonorable discharge, I'd lost everything. I'd been tricked into performing the act that resulted in my ruined life. Because I was deceived, I had to suffer the outcome of the deceiver." The corporal begins to sip his whiskey with great care. "At first I blamed God for my troubles, but I didn't do that for long. I might not know much about this world, but I do know this: you can't blame God for everything that goes wrong in your life. It's not His fault. If you get mad at anyone, you get mad at the one who is directly responsible, and you deal with that person alone."

Elizabeth's expression is blank as she finishes drinking her iced tea. Charlie's eyes gleam as he listens with great interest. The room grows darker, and the corporal pauses to turn on the lights. He first turns on the kitchen lights and then makes the trip to the other rooms in the house. Charlie looks at his watch and notices it is 8:45 p.m. Elizabeth glances at the wall clock and sees the time for herself. She whispers to Charlie, "We must be leaving shortly."

Charlie answers, "Not yet, not until we find out what happened to Major Cain."

The corporal walks back into the kitchen and sits downs at the table. "Now, where was I?"

Charlie says, "You were saying you don't blame God for everything bad that has gone wrong in your life."

Spencer replies, "Oh yeah. Right after President Reagan got shot, I got an idea to do some shooting of my own. I decided I was going to kill Lester Cain."

Elizabeth is shocked by this admission. She doesn't know if she wants to hear the rest, but she remains silent in her chair.

"Back in 1980, I hired a private investigator to see if he could locate Cain, and this is 1987, so it was seven years ago when I finally decided to even the score. It didn't take the investigator long to find out where he lived."

Charlie asks, "Where did he live?"

"He lived in Tennessee, just a few miles away from Lynchburg."

The corporal takes a sip from his glass and says, "So I got some of my things together and drove my truck there. The things I brought with me consisted of a half-empty bottle of Jack Daniel's Black Label whiskey—I had to pour the first half of it out because at that time I still didn't drink whiskey—a handful of bullets, and of course, my .357 Magnum handgun. I had decided I was going to kill this man."

Charlie and Elizabeth both listen nervously. Charlie, like Elizabeth, is uncertain about whether he wants to hear anymore, but he is reluctant to say anything.

The corporal continues, "So I drove to Lynchburg. I asked around for directions until I found his house. I pulled my truck next to the curb and read his name on the mailbox. I knew it was time to pay the major a little visit. It was time to pay him back in full!"

Charlie thinks, *This man's life was ruined by Major Lester Cain. Karen and my future wife also have been devastated by the acts of this man.* The anticipation is great as he waits for the corporal to continue.

Elizabeth, on the other hand, thinks differently. After hearing the story of the man who killed her daughter in the automobile accident, she has more forgiveness and more understanding. She remembers how the man who killed her daughter repented. Yet she hasn't heard anything from Major Cain, and she probably never will. Since Elizabeth hasn't heard any regret from this man, she too has developed a serious dislike for him. She now listens quietly for the corporal to finish his story.

"As I was walking up to the front door, I realized that the major had done well since Vietnam. The house was a large. It was a nice place. But as I got closer to the door, I realized he wouldn't be enjoying it much longer. I held the half-full bottle of liquor in one hand while my other hand was snugly in my pants pocket, keeping my .357 Magnum warm."

Charlie wonders, *Did he really do it?* He and Elizabeth both listen with intense emotion.

"I rang the doorbell. As I waited, I began to get a bad feeling about this. But the hate inside me had complete control of me, and it was too late to back out now. I told myself, *Just as soon as I see his face, I'm going to hand him the bottle, say a short farewell, and then blow his ass straight to hell.* I was eager to get it over with. My moment was finally here. I was nervous and scared, but I didn't care. This man had to be punished. I stood away from the glass in the door. I didn't want him to see me before he opened it. Just then the door opened."

Charlie and Elizabeth hold their breath.

"A young girl answered the door. She couldn't have been more than twelve years old. I asked if Lester Cain was home.

She answered, 'No, he's not.' She then called out to her mother. A woman came to the door. I asked if this was Lester Cain's residence. She told me, 'Yes, but he is not home from work yet.' There was a little boy holding on to her leg. He looked like he could have been about eight years old, about the same age my boy is. I looked at his tender eyes, and suddenly, I realized what I was doing. I couldn't believe it! I was there to kill those children's' father."

The corporal's hand begins to shake as he tries to take a sip from his glass. Charlie and Elizabeth are on the edge of their seats. They watch him with a great deal of anxiety. They wait patiently until the corporal gets control of himself.

"Here I was, a big man." The corporal stares right in Charlie's eyes. "My intentions were to kill a man who had done me wrong. By doing so, I was going to take away that little boy's father, not to mention the little girl's, plus this lady's husband." The corporal slowly turns his head until his eyes are focused on Elizabeth. "I was going to do to his wife like he'd done to you, Mrs. Thomas. I was going to kill her husband just like he killed your husband seventeen years ago."

The corporal turns away, visibly trying not to cry. He pauses for a moment before continuing. "The woman said, 'My husband should be home soon. Would you like to come in and wait for him?' Right then, I felt like a heathen. I couldn't believe myself! I was fixing to do something that I would be sorry for the rest of my life. I glanced down and saw the little boy smile at me. His sweet, innocent smile melted away the reason I'd come there. I told the woman, 'No, I must be going now.' That's it. I just turned and walked away. I got into my truck and drove away. I drove and drove and drove. I drove for hours before stopping at some little diner. That's when I took my first real drink of liquor."

Elizabeth frowns when she hears how he started drinking whiskey. The corporal picks up his glass and holds it right in front of his eyes. He says, "That's when I started drinking. I opened the half-empty bottle of whiskey and began to drink it—just like the major, right out of the bottle. I must admit, I hated the stuff at first. I don't know why I drank it. I ended up having to force it down, but before I started my truck to drive myself home the next morning, I'd drunk the entire contents of the bottle. Maybe it was because I almost murdered someone. Or maybe it was because I didn't have the nerve to finish what I had set out to do. Or maybe it was a combination of both. I don't know. All I do know is that I have been drinking whiskey ever since." The corporal turns up his glass and finishes the last drop.

Elizabeth waits a moment before saying, "Maybe you drink because you deceived yourself into believing that you did do something wrong. Then after thinking these false thoughts for so long, you needed to take out your frustrations on someone. Your going to the major's house to kill him should be a perfect example of that. Then because you didn't carry out your vicious plan, you felt like a failure. Maybe you drink because you won't accept the fact that you never did anything wrong in the first place. And by not accepting that, you let your father and your wife and even your own self convince you that you were at fault for what happened in Vietnam. Maybe you needed someone to blame for the untrue thoughts that were planted in your mind."

The corporal looks at Elizabeth with compassion, his eyes glassy. Without saying a word, he listens carefully as she continues.

Elizabeth says, "That's what's wrong with the world today. We all need someone to blame things on. That's how evil is perpetuated throughout this world. Someone does something to somebody, and they in turn do something wrong back. This starts a chain reaction until everybody is doing something wrong to each other. I guess that's why Jesus said, 'When someone smites you in the face, turn the other cheek.

And pray for your enemies.' As long as you are praying for them, you won't be hating them. I agree with you that this man did you wrong. But in wanting to do him wrong, you almost became just like him."

Spencer stares into his empty glass before saying, "But Mrs. Thomas, this man gave the order to shoot down and kill your husband. He never got punished for this act."

"He may not have been punished for shooting Alan down, but he has had to live with himself all these years for that act," Elizabeth says. "He will have to answer for his action one day! If you or I or even Charlie killed this man, then we also would have to answer for that sin. We are the ones who must answer for our own actions. Killing that major wouldn't have brought back Alan, or your father's respect or your wife. Just because somebody does something wrong to you doesn't give you the right to do something wrong back. Two wrongs don't make a right. As long as you hate this man, you will continue to drink liquor. You must learn to forget about what Lester Cain did to you, Philip, so you won't end up like him."

Charlie looks at his watch. It is 9:30 p.m. He listens to Elizabeth but still feels a strong dislike toward Major Lester Cain, not for what the major has done to him personally, which is nothing, but for what he has done to Karen and Elizabeth. The seed of hate and revenge has been planted in Charlie's mind. As soon as Elizabeth has finished, he says, "It also says in the Bible, a man must ask for forgiveness before he can be forgiven. Major Cain hasn't tried to rectify his murderous act—or his plot to destroy the reputation of Philip, either."

The room grows quiet as everyone thinks about what Charlie has just said. Elizabeth gives Charlie a stern look before the corporal breaks the silence.

"No, Charlie, Mrs. Thomas is right. If you let hate take control of your life, then you are destined to destroy yourself. I knew when I went to the major's house to kill him, I was doing something wrong. But I didn't care at the time because of what the hate was doing to me. It had affected me to the point where right or wrong didn't matter. I was, in fact, going there to kill myself."

Elizabeth smiles at Spencer, but Charlie just sits there in silence.

A tear runs down the corporal's face as he says, "Thank you, Mrs. Thomas. Thank you for coming by. I am glad I told you this story."

Elizabeth replies, "I'm glad I came by too. I want to thank you for telling me this story. You have relieved a great deal of doubt that has plagued my heart for many years. Thank you, Philip."

The corporal smiles gladly. "I have been drinking all these seven years just to numb myself to the truth. I will try to accept that what happened in Vietnam was not my fault. And I will try to stop blaming others for the way my life turned out. I was just another victim of deception. I have to try to live my life without feeling guilty anymore about how others have judged me. And I will try to stop hating Major Cain, so I won't keep torturing myself anymore. Maybe now I can stop drinking."

Elizabeth stands up and reaches out to him with her arms. The corporal does likewise, and the two embrace in a loving hug. Tears run down the corporal's cheeks as he gratefully says, "Thank you, Mrs. Thomas. Thank you so very much."

Charlie is touched by the love the two strangers show to one another. But he still feels a strong dislike for Major Cain. As the hate dissolves from the corporal's mind, Charlie captures it in his.

As Elizabeth and Philip embrace, Charlie turns his head and looks away. He sees visions of Karen growing up without a father. He recalls the tears Karen had in her eyes when she first told him of her father dying in Vietnam. He envisions Elizabeth trying to bring up Karen without a husband to comfort her in those difficult times. He thinks about all the years of suffering these two special women had to go through because of one man and his liquor.

The only way Charlie can forgive this man is if he repents. Then and only then can Charlie learn to forgive this man for his murderous act. He hates Lester Cain for what he has done to the two special women he loves so much.

Elizabeth and Philip release each other, and she kisses the corporal on the cheek. "Well, Philip, we must be going now."

The corporal replies, "You are welcome to stay the night. I would be honored to have you and Charlie."

Elizabeth smiles as she kindly says, "No, we must be going now. The next time I see you, I want to know you have stopped drinking."

"Yes, ma'am. I will try. I can only promise you that I will try."

Charlie shakes the corporal's hand and thanks him also. Elizabeth and Charlie get into the car. Then they slowly drive away, fulfilled and content, into the dark, warm Kentucky night.

# Chapter 3
## A TEST OF FAITH

After leaving Philip's house, Charlie and Elizabeth drive to a motel. Charlie parks the car, kisses her, and says, "I'll be right back."

Elizabeth smiles as she replies, "Okay."

Charlie walks into the lobby and gets two rooms. He eagerly walks back to the car and drives around to where the rooms are located.

Charlie's thoughts now are of Elizabeth. Although he paid for two rooms, he wishes he could have gotten only one. He wishes he could spend the night with her, but that will have to wait until tomorrow night.

Charlie carries Elizabeth's suitcase to her room, and Elizabeth stops him at the door. Charlie was hoping to spend a few moments with her before going to bed. But he doesn't even get a chance to see the inside of her room. Looking tired, she says, "Charlie, I can take my suitcase in."

Charlie feels momentarily stunned. Before he can speak, a tear runs down Elizabeth's cheek, and she says, "Charlie, I hope you understand. I have just fully realized that I have lost my husband. I just want to be left alone right now; please understand."

"Do you still want to marry me?" Charlie asks kindly.

Elizabeth smiles before saying, "Yes, Charlie, more than anything in the whole world. But before I take on another husband, I have to let go of the first one. I'll see you tomorrow."

Disappointed, Charlie says, "Okay, sweet sixteen. I'll be knocking on your door about nine o'clock."

Elizabeth nods, picks up her suitcase, and disappears into the room. She leaves Charlie standing alone in the warm night air. He turns and walks back to the car. He takes out his overnight bag and walks sadly back to his room, right next door to Elizabeth's.

After Elizabeth locks the door, she prepares for bed. As soon as she crawls under the covers, she begins to cry uncontrollably. She realizes her beloved husband is dead and gone. It's like he just died today. She mourns his passing with overwhelming emotion. Eventually, she cries herself to sleep.

Charlie undresses and gets into bed with an incredibly lonely feeling. His heart aches as he stares at the ceiling. Oh, how much he wants to touch Elizabeth's soft flesh right now! His desire for her grows stronger and stronger with each passing second. To be near her and not able to touch her is an agonizing pain. The heart and the flesh engage in battle.

Charlie stares up at the ceiling, feeling miserable. He whispers, "Oh, God, I know I haven't been praying to you like I should, but I do want you to know that I am thinking of you all the time. I have kept my promise to my mother; I finished my education. I fornicated only three times in my life, for which I am truly sorry. I know now why my mother wanted me to promise her this so I wouldn't hurt myself with this act. I deny myself tonight because I want you to join Elizabeth and me as husband and wife first. Until I have your blessing, I will refrain from practicing fornication with her. I want your blessing before I engage in any act of lust I have in my heart. And one last thing, Lord: be with me and watch over me, so I will never rebel against you. This I pray in Jesus's name. Amen."

After Charlie makes this prayer, the horrible ache that was in his heart vanishes. He falls into a deep, peaceful sleep.

The next day, Charlie hears Elizabeth knocking on his door. He gets up and walks to the door wearing only his underwear. When he opens the door, Elizabeth takes one look at the white undergarment and says, "Is that any way to answer the door?"

Charlie smiles and says, "I just thought I would give you a preview of what to expect. Come on in."

"I will do no such thing," she replies. She puts her hand over her mouth to hide her laugh. "I'll be back in fifteen minutes, and you'd better have some more clothes on then."

Charlie grabs her and pulls her into his room. He begins to kiss her neck, closing the door with his free hand. Elizabeth doesn't put up any resistance. She enjoys being controlled by his masculine strength.

As Charlie kisses her wildly, they fall on the bed. Elizabeth lies paralyzed as Charlie's mouth runs all around her neck, ears, and face. After only a few moments of his seductive kissing, Elizabeth whispers, "Oh, Charlie. Make love to me. Oh God, Charlie. Make love to me, right now! I need to feel you inside—"

"Nope," Charlie says, interrupting her and giggling.

"What do you mean, nope?" she responds, hitting him with a pillow. She mocks his high-pitched laugh. "Hell," she says.

Charlie playfully throws a pillow back at her and says, "Nope. Not until you marry me. Then … maybe."

"What do you mean, maybe?" she playfully asks.

Charlie doesn't answer her. He gets up from the bed and retrieves his pants and shirt. Elizabeth gazes at Charlie's half-naked body with horny eyes. She says, "Here I am, fixing to get married, and all I see is a man putting on his clothes. I thought it was supposed to be the other way around."

Charlie dresses quickly and looks at his watch; it is 8:29 a.m. "You sure are an early bird this morning," he says.

"You know what they say," Elizabeth says. "The early bird gets the worm." Before Charlie can respond, his alarm clock goes off. Elizabeth reaches over and cuts it off. Getting an idea, she looks at Charlie playfully and says, "If we aren't married by eight thirty tonight, I'm not going to marry you. I'm going looking for another fellow, one who takes his clothes off, not puts them on."

Seeing her playful smile and hearing her giggle like a schoolgirl, he smiles too. "Well, I guess I better hurry then." He walks over to the phone and dials the airline to make reservations for Las Vegas.

Elizabeth lies back on the bed for a few moments before saying, "Who are you calling, big boy?"

Charlie remembers how Karen used to talk like that. He glances over at her and says, "I'm calling the airline to—"

Elizabeth giggles, interrupting him. "I have already made the reservation. Our plane leaves in 3 hours."

Charlie gives Elizabeth a wry grin. "Why didn't you tell me?"

"You didn't ask."

"Well, what are we waiting for? Let's go." Charlie pulls Elizabeth off the bed and carries her out to the car.

She tries to put up a struggle, but not too much of one. She enjoys the attention he is showing her tremendously. She laughs with happiness and excitement all the way to the car. She has her things loaded in the car already. Charlie goes back for his overnight case; then they leave for the airport. They are both full of anticipation for the trip and expectations for the night.

When they arrive in Las Vegas, neither one can get over how beautiful the town is. All the lights are flashing and beaming out beautiful arrays of colors. The streets are clean and futuristic. The place looks like something from the twenty-first century. Charlie marvels at how everything looks. Elizabeth is bewildered by everything.

Before getting a room, Charlie flags down a cab to take them to the justice of the peace. As they drive, Charlie glances at his watch and makes the time adjustment. With all the stopovers the airplane had to make it is now 8:45 p.m. Las Vegas time. He just hopes Elizabeth has forgotten what she said earlier. As the cab drives along the glorious light-filled streets of Las Vegas, Elizabeth impulsively reaches over and grabs Charlie's arm. She turns his wrist until she sees the time on his watch. As she releases his wrist, she gazes up at his tender blue eyes and smiles playfully. She doesn't say anything until the cab drops them off at the justice of the peace.

Charlie waits for her to say something, and finally, she does. "Hey, Charlie, you remember this morning when I said if you hadn't married me by eight thirty, I was going to find me another fellow?"

Charlie turns his head sideways and with a blank expression says, "Well … I guess … yes, I remember."

"Since you didn't marry me before eight thirty, I guess I'll have to …"

Charlie gives her a sad, lonely look.

"Okay, I'll give you one more chance."

Charlie eagerly asks, "What's that?"

"You will have to promise me that nothing will ever come between us."

"I agree. Let's go."

"Wait just one minute, young man. I'm not through yet."

Charlie listens patiently as Elizabeth continues.

"I want you to promise me there will be no other women as long as we are married."

Charlie wraps his arms around her waist and says, "I promise there will be no other women in my life besides you." Charlie reaches over and kisses her lightly on her forehead.

Elizabeth says, "Promise me you will make me happy and be there for me whenever I need you."

With a tear on his cheek, Charlie softly says, "I promise. I promise." He kisses her again on the forehead.

With tears in her eyes, Elizabeth says, "And you gotta promise to love me forever."

Charlie smiles before saying, "I promise to love you forever and ever and ever. I will always love you, Elizabeth. Even after this life, I will love you forever." Charlie reaches down and lightly kisses Elizabeth on her tender red lips.

After Charlie breaks the kiss, Elizabeth buries her face in his chest. She hugs him as she has never hugged him before. She looks up with tears of joy running down her face. She says, "Charlie, I promise to be faithful to you all the years we are married. I will always be there for you."

As Charlie listens, a tear runs down his cheek too.

She continues, "I promise to always love you, and I will never let anything come between us. You come first in my life, and I will always put you first."

Charlie kisses her passionately. People passing by stare, but the attention of the passersby doesn't stop Charlie from running his hands through Elizabeth's hair as the kiss gets more intense. Charlie pulls her loving face tenderly away from his.

Charlie, wiping a tear from his cheek, says, "Well, Elizabeth. What do you say we get married?"

"Charlie, as far as I am concerned, we just did. But since we flew all the way out here, let's make it legal."

So Charlie and Elizabeth go inside the small building and say the traditional vows. They pray and ask for God's holy blessing.

After the ceremony, the happy couple flag down a cab. Charlie tells the cabby to just drive around for a while. "My wife and I haven't decided what hotel to stay at." Charlie throws the man a hundred-dollar bill, and this gets his attention. He drives them around for almost an hour. They both enjoy watching all the lights flash before their eyes. They finally pick a hotel and tell the cabby to drop them there.

Charlie asks, "Do I owe you any more, young man?"

The cabdriver, who must be at least fifty years old, laughs. "No, you don't owe me anything, but if you've got any more of what you're on, let me have some."

Charlie and Elizabeth laugh happily. "What I'm on," Charlie says, "is love. I wish you could feel this feeling. It is the most wonderful feeling in the world."

Elizabeth says, "Here you go, mister." She reaches over and kisses the driver on the cheek.

This makes the man smile. He says, "I see what you mean. You two have fun." The man drives off as Charlie and Elizabeth enter the hotel.

After Charlie gets a room, they both excitedly get on the elevator. They walk hand in hand as the bellhop carries their luggage. A nervous energy floods their souls as the elevator stops at their floor. At the door to their room, Charlie slaps a ten-spot in the man's hand, and he departs. Charlie opens the door and throws the luggage inside. He picks up Elizabeth, carries her over to the bed, and gently lays her down.

Elizabeth's eyes get glassy and seductive. She is filled with great expectation as Charlie walks back over to shut the door.

Charlie nervously says, "Well ... what do you want to do now?"

Elizabeth gives him a curious look. She says, "Well, what do you want to do?"

With a playful expression, Charlie says, "You want to play some backgammon?"

She replies, "Nooo."

"Do you want to play some checkers?"

She replies again, "Nooo," with a horny look on her face.

Charlie asks, "You want to watch some TV?"

Elizabeth pats the bed as she says, "Nooo."

"Do you want to make love?"

Elizabeth's eyes become full and intense. "Yesss," she replies.

Charlie sits down on the bed as she reaches up to kiss him. They kiss passionately for only a few seconds before Elizabeth says in a tender, soft voice, "Let me go into the bathroom and get myself ready for you."

Charlie nervously says, "Okay." She slides off the bed and proceeds to the bathroom.

The anticipation reaches its peak. The minutes Charlie spends waiting are the most exciting time of his life. He has waited for this moment all of his life. Most people in the world never get to experience this most wonderful time, a time filled with wonder and excitement without any guilt or worry about doing something wrong. The moment has taken on a special magical effect for Charlie.

Looking forward to this experience is one of the most wonderful moments in a person's life. The feeling of nervousness, the heart beating at a faster pace, the excitement of being close to that special one for the very first time—it is pure ecstasy. The atmosphere in the room makes it feel like a utopia!

Charlie takes off his clothes with a yearning that is strong and powerful. He lies down on the bed, wearing only his underwear. And then Charlie holds his breath as he hears the bathroom's metal doorknob begin to turn. The door creaks as it slowly opens. Charlie's heart beats faster and faster until Elizabeth comes out of the bathroom.

She stands right in front of him and makes a subtle girlish laugh as she allows Charlie to gaze at her beautiful naked body. Charlie briefly gazes upon her milky-white breasts before his eyes make their way down to her thick, coal-black triangle. His eyes grow large, and Elizabeth laughs girlishly again. "Well, Charlie, this is what you get."

Charlie says, "Oh boy!"

Elizabeth walks over to one side of the bed, staring at Charlie's underwear. She seductively says, "Umm, I think this is going to have to go." She rubs then tugs on the soft white cotton garment gently before pulling them down. As she slides Charlie's underwear off, she gazes at his exposed length with glassy horny eyes. "Oh my!" she says quietly. She begins touching then squeezing his full hard length while looking deep into his eyes. She whispers, "Relax, Charlie. Relax. Lie on back, darling."

Charlie lies back, paralyzed, as she positions her naked body on the bed. Their eyes never break away from each other.

Looking up at him, Elizabeth softly says, "I love you, Charlie," before touching her lips to his swollen body.

"I love you too, Elizabeth," he says. Reaching down to rub her long black hair, Charlie continues to look into her tender, loving eyes. He feels like he is in heaven now. Continuing to keep eye contact, Charlie says, "Oh, how I love you so. Oh God, you make me feel wonderful. I am so glad I married you." Her pace increases, and Charlie continues to fill her emotional needs by talking to her. His voice gets a little louder, "Oh! Oh my! Oh, Elizabeth. You are the most beautiful woman in the whole world. I love you."

Charlie, not able to keep eye contact, looks up to the ceiling. After the eye contact has been broken, Elizabeth's motion grows faster. Charlie begins saying her name over and over. "Elizabeth! Elizabeth! Oh, Elizabeth! Oh, Elizabeth!"

The more she hears her name, the more she loves what she is doing. Her mind is consumed by Charlie's wild, erotic voice and loving words. Elizabeth rolls over to get situated in a better position.

Charlie looks down and rubs her hair gently with his fingers. Once again, the motion gets fast. Charlie, loving every second, doesn't stop talking to Elizabeth. His intense sexual tone drives Elizabeth to go faster. Charlie doesn't let five seconds go by without saying or moaning something.

Thirty minutes have gone by when Charlie says, "Oh my God, Elizabeth! It's going to happen! Oh, sweetheart, it's going to happen." His voice is full of emotion. Charlie lies back as Elizabeth's motion doesn't let up. Feeling her pace get faster, he simply lies back and enjoys the moment. Charlie is experiencing this magnificent act for the first time in his life. He lets out a moan of sheer pleasure.

Elizabeth gets up and softly says, "I'll be right back." Charlie smiles contentedly as he watches her white buttocks disappear into the bathroom. He lies back motionless on the bed, paralyzed by the climax he just experienced.

Charlie doesn't say anything as Elizabeth returns and laughs girlishly. She lies down beside him, waiting for the touch of his mouth.

He pulls her head toward his, and their mouths are attracted to each other like magnets. Elizabeth moves on top of Charlie as their passionate kiss lingers on. Charlie rubs her back and then moves his hands down to her soft buttocks, caressing them. Elizabeth's passion grows wild and hungry. Her mouth presses harder against his, and her tongue freely invades Charlie's mouth. His does likewise as their passionate kiss becomes wilder.

Charlie rolls Elizabeth over and begins to rub her large white breasts. Elizabeth's eyes are extremely glassy and horny now. The gleam in her seductive eyes compels Charlie to say, "You were wonderful. I love you so much." He rubs his fingers through her hair, mesmerized by the gleam in her eyes. Elizabeth lets out an alluring feminine sigh. Her hand roams down to reach his soft sensitive length, but Charlie moves her hand away. A look of disappointment comes over her face. Charlie interlocks her fingers with his as he whispers, "It is too sensitive now, my love. Rub your fingers through my hair like you do so well. In a few minutes it will be yours again."

Elizabeth does exactly what Charlie asks, without saying a word. She belongs to him totally now. She yearns for him to enter her.

Charlie stares into her eyes as his hand moves down to her bushy triangle. His hand disappears as he moves in further. When his hand enters her warmth, Charlie sees from the look in Elizabeth's eyes that he is giving her a long-needed pleasure. Her moans are like music to his ears. Charlie's tongue invades her ear canal. He blows gently as Elizabeth's moans and heavy breathing fill the room with a tantalizing expression of pleasure. Charlie's hand gets very wet and warm as he moves his head down to her breasts. Her red nipples are stiff and hard. He gently sucks on the stiff red nipples, and Elizabeth's feminine moans grow louder.

Charlie moves down toward her navel. He kisses her stomach only a few times before looking up and saying, "Elizabeth."

She looks down at him and says, "Yes, Charlie."

"Talk to me. Talk to me the way I talked to you a while ago." His voice is soft and delicate.

She replies, "What do you want me to say?"

Her innocent question brings a smile to Charlie's lips. He kisses her navel once more before saying, "Tell me how it feels."

Elizabeth now definitely knows what is about to happen. She continues to listen to Charlie's requests.

"Say my name. I like to hear you call out my name the way I said your name. I want to hear you moan and groan out loud, passionately. I want you to talk to me. I don't care what you say, but please, let me hear your lovely voice."

Elizabeth answers, "Okay, Charlie. Anything you say. I will do it for you."

Charlie makes a subtle move down past her navel. As his hand touches her thigh, her legs begin to quiver. Charlie takes great delight in seeing this happen. He continues to watch her leg quiver until her coal-black triangle consumes his attention. He raises up and positions her legs with ease.

Elizabeth lies back, paralyzed. As Charlie begins, Elizabeth calls out, "Oh, Charlie! I love you, Charlie! Oh God! That feels so wonderful!" Her moans, along with her words, feed Charlie's appetite. The more he hears her voice, the more aggressively he performs. He loves to hear his name being called out this way. Charlie's mind is consumed by her words. He is in a different world now. It is a world of giving pleasure to Elizabeth and absorbing all the joy of giving it.

After only a few minutes, Charlie looks up and sees Elizabeth staring up at the ceiling with an expression of indescribable pleasure. Her head moves back and forth as she moans sighs of pleasure and enjoyment. She clenches the bedsheets with a tight grip, only to release them. She continues to call out, "Oh, Charlie! I love you so much, Charlie!" As he touches the sensitive spot, Elizabeth's voice gets extremely loud. Her legs begin to move wildly.

After thirty minutes, Elizabeth begins to get wilder. Her whole body begins to move as if she is having a seizure. Sweat beads on her forehead, and her seductive words send Charlie's movements into a wild sexual frenzy.

After forty-five minutes, Elizabeth's voice gets louder and firmer. Her sexual enjoyment now becomes agonizing. Her legs move wildly as her voice leads Charlie to perform even more exuberantly. Her face is full of erotic agony as she cries out, "Come here, Charlie! Come here!"

Charlie doesn't obey. He continues without letting up. He locates the spot that drives Elizabeth crazy and, without mercy, attacks this spot with a vigorous motion. Her agony gets louder. She continues to beg Charlie to come up to her, but Charlie doesn't budge from his position. Her hands grip Charlie's hair wildly. She pulls out shafts of hair from his head, but he still doesn't come to her. He continues to attack her sensitive spot without letting up for one second.

A full hour has gone by, and Elizabeth's voice becomes more demanding. She begs for him to come up to her. Over and over, she pleads for him to come up but her voice drives Charlie onward. The more she speaks, the more aggressively he performs. He shows no sign of stopping.

Finally, after an hour and ten minutes, Elizabeth lets out a long sensual moan. She grunts loud and long, as if she is holding something heavy. The sound drives Charlie nearly insane. The sound he has been waiting to hear all along finally comes. As her groaning stops and her body lies still, she presses her legs tightly together and demands, "Hold still! Damn it! Hold still! Don't move! Damn it! Just hold still." Charlie welcomes her demand and obeys her totally. He lies still until she releases the pressure from her legs.

Charlie raises himself up and begins to get off the bed. As he does, he says, "I'll be right back. Let me go get a towel."

Just as Charlie tries to leave the bed, Elizabeth grabs him and pulls him close to her. She says with determination, "You don't need a towel."

She kisses him wildly and without restraint. Charlie takes one of her hands and brings it down to his full length. She speaks softly as she holds him lovingly and firmly. "Oh, Charlie, I have never been that far before. I can't believe you went that long without stopping."

Charlie smiles as he says, "I love you so much." He kisses her softly. "I've never enjoyed doing anything for myself more than doing something like that for you. If that was wonderful and pleasurable for you, then I got more enjoyment out of it than you will ever know. I enjoyed doing that for you, Elizabeth. I enjoyed it because I love you so much."

Elizabeth responds softly, "I love you too, Charlie. I love you too."

Until now, Charlie and Elizabeth have loved each other without being intimate. Their first sexual experience together has been one of thoughtfulness and unselfishness, one of seeking to make each other feel pleasure. They have loved the other in a more loving and caring fashion by denying their own physical pleasures to fulfill the other's needs.

Charlie's mouth covers Elizabeth's with intense force. Their tongues rub against one another wildly. Elizabeth squeezes Charlie's swollen length as he rolls over on top. She directs Charlie to enter her. Charlie plunges deep into her wet warmth, and Elizabeth makes an intoxicating moan. Her horny eyes focus directly on Charlie as her hands reach up to caress his face. She runs her fingers through his hair as he moves gently but deeply into her wet warmth. Charlie says softly, "Oh, Elizabeth. You are so warm."

"You are too, Charlie." Elizabeth lies back and allows Charlie to make all the movements. She simply looks up at him and smiles in sheer pleasure. Tenderly, she says, "Come here, Charlie." Charlie brings his head down close to hers as he speeds up. She kisses him wildly and openly. Their heavy breathing and the sound of trapped air being released causes both of them to feel they are getting closer and closer to their moment. Elizabeth moans loudly.

Ten minutes into the unifying act, Elizabeth cries out in a crazed state of emotion, "Faster, Charlie! Faster!" Charlie does what she asks. His pace grows fast and rough. She screams out once again, "Faster, Charlie! Faster!"

Charlie moves with sheer determination as Elizabeth lets out a loud moan followed by a long, deep grunt. This sound causes Charlie to erupt at the same moment. The two bond together to become one for the first time, climaxing at the same time. Charlie lies still on top of her as she holds him in place, her fingernails digging into his back and buttocks.

Charlie tries to move, but Elizabeth continues to hold him tight. "Stay still. Don't move, Charlie. Just stay still right where you are!" Charlie does what she asks. He remains still until her fingernails release him, and her arms wrap possessively around him in a powerful hug.

Charlie raises his head to kiss Elizabeth's tender, soft, loving lips.

He softly says, "I guess this is what it means when two people become one flesh."

Elizabeth, exhausted by their lovemaking, manages to whisper, "That's right, Charlie. You are a part of me now."

Charlie kisses her tenderly. "I love you so much, Elizabeth. I love you more than I ever knew I could love someone." He kisses her one last time before they both fall asleep, still bonded together by their love.

During the night, Charlie and Elizabeth make love time after time, each time thinking more about the other than about themselves. Charlie never knew he could be so happy, and neither did Elizabeth. Happiness fills their hearts like a never-ending stream of joy flowing through their souls. They talk about the things they want to do together and how they plan to share their lives together. They agree to sell their separate houses and build a house together. They think about pleasing each other more and more as their bond of love and togetherness grows stronger.

They go shopping together while in Las Vegas. Charlie buys some clothes, and Elizabeth enjoys removing them once the couple is back in the room. Charlie even buys a suitcase to put his new clothes in. Charlie buys Elizabeth small things, but nothing too elaborate; he doesn't want material things of great value to interfere with what they have. Elizabeth enjoys everything about Charlie. The small things he buys for her make her feel just as happy as if they were expensive. She doesn't want Charlie to buy her anything expensive anyway. That would just make her feel guilty. She is happier with the thought of Charlie giving gifts to her than with the items themselves. They take long walks down the bright streets of Las Vegas, bubbling with joy like a couple of schoolkids.

On the seventh night they spend together, Charlie wakes Elizabeth up in the middle of the night to make love to her once again. Although she is fast asleep, she welcomes his touch. She allows him to maneuver himself until he is once again deep into her warmth. As he moves, Elizabeth cries out seductive, erotic words. These words bring Charlie to climax early. Every time Charlie and Elizabeth make love to each other, their communication makes the lovemaking process more real, caring, and meaningful.

After every session of loving Elizabeth, Charlie enjoys lying beside her and talking to her even more. They talk about anything and everything. These tranquil, peaceful conversations create an openness in their new marriage.

On this night, after Charlie has bonded once again to Elizabeth's warmth, he tenderly says, "Oh, how I adore you so. I never knew I could be so happy."

Elizabeth pulls Charlie's face to hers and opens her mouth, inviting Charlie's tongue to invade her mouth.

Charlie rolls over, pulling apart the bond of their flesh. He gazes into her eyes and says, "Let's go to Hawaii."

Elizabeth, aroused by this, says, "Are you crazy? We can't just go to Hawaii on the spur of the moment. You have to make reservations and—"

"Fine. We will leave tomorrow."

Elizabeth laughs. She lovingly says, "Okay, husband. But if we get over there and can't find a room, what will you do then?"

Charlie, caressing her large breasts, replies, "We could sleep on the sand."

Elizabeth laughs again.

Charlie runs his fingers through her hair and says, "As long as I am with you, I don't care about anything else." Elizabeth smiles happily at Charlie before they both fall asleep.

Charlie and Elizabeth do fly to Hawaii. They find rooms and everything they need; their impulsiveness makes their honeymoon even more exciting. They fall in love with the splendor and beauty for which Hawaii is famous. They spend two glorious weeks there and travel to each of the seven islands. They feel like they are in paradise. Everything is perfect.

After the two weeks, Charlie goes to the front desk to pay the bill with his credit card. He seldom uses any cash. He doesn't care what anything costs. This time with Elizabeth makes him feel as if life is a wonderful thing again. The horrible things he has experienced are in the past now. He loves life! He thanks God for allowing him to experience this glorious time with Elizabeth.

Elizabeth gathers all the luggage from the suite. Their bags are heavier than when they originally left home. She places them in the rental car for the journey back home, but Charlie has one last surprise for his lovely bride to experience first.

Charlie drives the rental car to the airport with a mischievous smirk on his face. He smiles gladly when Elizabeth senses he is up to something. After they get to the airport and return the car, Charlie tells her what he has planned. "We aren't going home yet."

"Oh, we're not? Then where are we going?" Elizabeth asks with a curious grin. Charlie turns his head and excitedly says, "We are going to Niagara Falls."

Excitement fills Elizabeth's face. "But Charlie, can we afford to go there?"

Charlie picks her up and swings her around with great jubilation. He excitedly says, "Don't worry about anything, sweetheart. I have enough money in the bank to cover everything. I have never been so happy in all my life, and I don't want it to end yet."

Elizabeth kisses Charlie impulsively. Her mouth presses hard against his as the excitement overtakes her. Her happy face brings great joy to Charlie's heart. He smiles a glorious smile at her and watches tears of joy run down her face. This spontaneous excitement of experiencing each other's happiness is what marriage is all about, he decides—being partners, not just lovers, and loving, sharing, and experiencing new adventures together. That is the force that surrounds the nucleus that holds the elements of marriage together.

Charlie and Elizabeth enjoy Niagara Falls more than their first two rendezvous combined—the romantic views, the falling waters, the effervescence of a new beginning. This location gives Charlie and Elizabeth a more sensual sensation toward one another. This time together provides the foundation to build trust and caring for their new life together.

Charlie and Elizabeth stay at this romantic location for only three days before they decide to finally go home. They leave with memories that will last for eternity. Their new life together has had a wonderful and spectacular beginning.

Now that they are back home, it is time for Elizabeth to have her operation. Her specialist, Dr. Parker, explains that he has done this procedure numerous times without any complications. Charlie is impressed by Dr. Parker's expertise in triple bypass surgery. The doctor gladly tells Charlie of the high rate of success he has had with this operation. Charlie feels confident but still worries. He will be glad when it's over.

Charlie takes Elizabeth to the hospital one week after they get back from their honeymoon and stays with her there until she is settled in for the night; her surgery will start the next morning at nine. They hold each other lovingly as Charlie gives her some encouragement about the operation. Elizabeth looks at Charlie with a radiant glow and an enchanting smile. She is so glad to have Charlie here with her now.

When it is time for him to go, Charlie reaches over and kisses Elizabeth softly and whispers, "I love you so much, Elizabeth. I love you so very much. Everything will be all right, sweetheart. I promise you."

Elizabeth reaches her hand to Charlie's neck and pulls him to her. She tenderly kisses him before saying, "I love you, Charlie Delaney. You are the most wonderful man in the entire world."

Charlie kisses her once more and says, "I love you too, Elizabeth. You are the most wonderful woman in the entire world. I am lucky to have such a wife as you."

Elizabeth's eyes sparkle in response to Charlie's beautiful words.

Charlie continues, "I have to make some phone calls, so I must be leaving now. I will be back early tomorrow morning. You behave yourself." Charlie tenderly kisses her once more before he gets up. Elizabeth watches lovingly as her handsome Prince Charming gracefully leaves the room.

At his house, Charlie makes his calls. One of them is to his realtor, who confirms that Charlie's and Elizabeth's houses will be going on the market the next day.

Charlie goes to bed early. He wants to be at the hospital first thing in the morning so that he can spend as much time as possible with Elizabeth before the operation. While Charlie lies in bed, he gazes up at the ceiling and prays out loud. "God, I just want to thank you once again for the happiness I have experienced lately. I never knew life could have so much purpose and joy. You may know my wife Elizabeth is going to be operated on tomorrow. Please let her come through this operation okay. I don't pray for anything for myself. I only pray that my wife will be looked after and taken care of tomorrow." After making this simple prayer, Charlie rolls over and falls into a tranquil, peaceful sleep.

The next day, Charlie gets up early and hurries to get ready. He goes to a twenty-four-hour grocery store near his house and buys a dozen red roses. He also buys a cup of coffee and a doughnut. He happily drives to the hospital and hurries up to Elizabeth's room.

Charlie taps on the door as he sticks his head inside. Elizabeth is lying on her bed, reading the newspaper. Charlie tries to hide the roses behind him, but Elizabeth sees them anyway. As he approaches her bed, he says, "Hello, sweet sixteen. I hope you slept well."

Elizabeth smiles a warm smile. Her face glows with joy at the sight of Charlie's happy face. She reaches for a hug, and Charlie wraps his arms around her and kisses her sweetly. He presents the brilliant red roses to her and watches her expression light up with more excitement and joy.

Just as Charlie sits on the bed, a nurse comes into the room. She reminds Elizabeth that they will be coming for her at nine o'clock. As the nurse tends to Elizabeth, Charlie finds a vase for the flowers. After the nurse leaves, Charlie lies down on the bed beside Elizabeth and kisses her passionately. He tenderly whispers, "I missed having you next to me last night, sweetheart."

She smiles and says, "I missed having you next to me too, Charlie. Just your being here right now makes me feel like I am the luckiest woman in the world."

Charlie kisses her softly. "I will be so glad when this is all over. I am looking forward to taking care of you when you get home."

Every word Charlie speaks brings a sweet smile to Elizabeth's delicate, soft lips.

Charlie glances at his watch and sees it is 8:05 a.m. He runs his fingers through her soft black hair as he looks deeply into her eyes. He whispers, "I still have about one hour with you. Do you think the doctors will mind if we make love first?"

"Charlie!" Elizabeth gives him a surprised but intrigued look. "Now you behave yourself, young man. You are just going to have to wait."

Her smile gives new life to Charlie's admiration for her. The more he looks at her, the more he loves her. They talk, laugh, and kiss each other happily for the hour.

Charlie tells her, "Don't worry about a thing, sweetheart. I'll have everything ready when you come home. I called the realtor, and they are putting our houses on the market today."

Elizabeth smiles as she sees how happy Charlie is.

Charlie continues, "I will be looking for some land out in the country, a place we can build our dream house on, a place we can call ours."

Elizabeth doesn't say anything. She just marvels at Charlie's robust energy.

He continues, "Maybe I can find enough land so we can build a ranch. We could start raising basset hounds. How would you like that?"

Elizabeth's eyes glisten with happiness. She quietly says, "That would be fine, Charlie."

Charlie holds her hand lovingly with one hand and runs his fingers through her hair gently with the other. He says, "Little Charlie will love that! When I fed him this morning, I could tell that he misses you by his sad face."

Elizabeth laughs as she says, "He looks like that anyway."

"Well, he was a little sadder this morning." Charlie stops talking long enough to kiss her glowing face, and the look in her eyes becomes a mesmerizing stare.

As Charlie's lips delicately kiss Elizabeth's, two doctors and a nurse walk into the room. They get Charlie's attention with a "Good morning." Charlie stands up and greets the two familiar faces with a firm handshake and a welcome.

One of the doctors is Dr. Parker, the specialist who will perform the operation. The older doctor is Elizabeth's family doctor, Dr. Steward. He has known Elizabeth for more than twenty years. After Charlie has greeted the two doctors, they both walk over to Elizabeth. Dr. Parker says with a smile, "I have never seen any of my patients in such high spirits before an operation."

She shakes his hand and says, "I'm just your typical happy newlywed eager to get back home to my wonderful husband."

The two doctors congratulate both Charlie and Elizabeth with smiles and handshakes.

Elizabeth asks the doctors a few questions as Charlie stands nearby listening. The doctors are in high spirits themselves. They tell Elizabeth that the operation should take between six and eight hours and that she should recover from the operation in about seven days. Charlie gives Elizabeth a wink of encouragement. As the doctors leave, Charlie shakes their hands.

Charlie walks over and holds Elizabeth's hand and kisses her forehead. He kindly says, "See, I told you there is nothing to worry about. Just as soon as you're home, I am going to love you as you have never been loved before."

Elizabeth again smiles at Charlie with love and admiration. She softly says, "Charlie, just your being here today shows me you love me more than anybody has ever loved me before. I love you so much, Charlie Delaney."

Just as Charlie reaches over to kiss Elizabeth, Dr. Steward comes back into the room. "Mr. Delaney," he says.

Charlie says, "Please call me Charlie."

Dr. Steward nods his head and says, "Okay, Charlie. It's time for you to leave so the nurses can prepare Elizabeth for the operation."

Charlie gets off the bed. As their hands separate, Charlie reaches over and kisses Elizabeth tenderly. "I'll see ya later, sweet sixteen."

Elizabeth waves to him and says once more, "I love you, Charlie Delaney. I love you."

Charlie just smiles as he disappears from the room.

Outside the room, Dr. Steward walks with Charlie down the hall and shows him where Elizabeth will be recovering. Together they walk toward the elevator that will take Charlie to the intensive care waiting room. "Charlie," the doctor says, "you sure have made one of my favorite patients happy. I have never seen Elizabeth so happy. Her face was glowing when Dr. Parker and I walked into the room."

Charlie grins before saying, "She has made me happy too. I don't think I have ever been so happy with anyone in all my life."

The doctor smiles, looking impressed by Charlie's words.

As Charlie and the doctor get on the elevator, Dr. Steward says,

"Elizabeth is a really fine lady. If it wasn't for this operation, she would be the healthiest woman I know. She has never had an operation in her life."

This makes Charlie feel much better. The elevator stops on the floor where the waiting room is located. Charlie and the doctor walk out of the elevator and proceed down the hall. After showing Charlie where to wait, the doctor doesn't stay long. He shakes Charlie's hand enthusiastically one more time before departing. He tells Charlie before he leaves, "This operation will take a few hours, so make yourself comfortable."

Charlie says, "Thank you, Dr. Steward. I will be here." He finds a seat and a magazine and begins the long wait.

Thirty minutes after Charlie left Elizabeth, he is trying to read but is too nervous. His mind is occupied with thoughts of Elizabeth. As he sits in the quiet room, trying to keep his mind on the article he is reading, the door opens. A loud, deep voice says, "Mr. Delaney."

Hearing his name makes Charlie's heart skip a beat. He quickly drops the magazine and looks up to see Dr. Steward standing near the doorway. His expression gives Charlie a fright.

Charlie jumps up. He stares at the older doctor with concern. The doctor walks over to Charlie slowly. "Mr. Delaney, something has happened."

Horror fills Charlie's heart. He says harshly, "I told you to call me Charlie. What … why are you looking at me like that?"

The doctor turns his head away from Charlie and looks down at the floor. The older man sits down, but Charlie remains standing in front of him.

Charlie loudly says, "What the hell is going on? Tell me! What the hell is the matter?"

Dr. Steward looks Charlie in the eye. He says quietly, "Charlie, while Elizabeth was being put under anesthesia, something happened. The third drug they administered …" The doctor pauses.

Charlie waits impatiently for the doctor to finish. His eyes focus on Dr. Steward with intense emotion.

Dr. Steward continues, "Elizabeth had a negative reaction to this substance. As the drug entered her bloodstream, she died instantaneously. We tried to resuscitate her, but her body wouldn't respond."

Confused, Charlie says harshly, "I thought you told me this operation was safe! You lied to me!"

The doctor quickly responds, "No, Charlie, I didn't lie to you. The operation is safe, but Elizabeth never made it to the operation. Elizabeth died before Dr. Parker even entered the operating room. I am truly sorry, Charlie. I really am."

Charlie falls back in the chair, dumbfounded. He is in a state of shock. He sits there bewildered; he doesn't act wild or out of control. Slowly, tears trickle down his face. He looks at the doctor with an expression of grief. He softly says, "But she can't die now. We were just married. We just started sharing our lives together. We are going to build a house together and …"

Charlie's words become jumbled as he cries. Dr. Steward listens to Charlie, though he surely can't comprehend all of what he is saying. Eventually, the doctor apologizes again and leaves the room. Charlie is left staring at the walls in a sad, quiet, heartbroken state of mind. He doesn't understand.

Three days after Elizabeth's unexpected death, Charlie buries her next to Karen at the Shiloh Cemetery. Charlie handles the hurt of losing Elizabeth worse than he handled the loss of Karen. He was bonded to this woman as one soul. Part of Charlie died with Elizabeth. He sits on a bench at the cemetery trying to understand why his life has been filled with so much tragedy and hardship.

He puts flowers on both graves and remains there for a couple of hours. He stands there like a man in the wilderness, alone and confused. There is no female presence to influence him now. There is no one now to prevent him from rebelling against God. He must handle this calamity all by himself. He feels like a wounded soldier on a battlefield of an unseen war.

His thoughts are not guided by anyone except himself. His faith is the only weapon he has to combat what he feels. He struggles from within himself to fight this strange, uncertain feeling. He remembers the prayer he made the day before Elizabeth's operation: "God, I don't pray for anything for myself. I only pray that my wife will be looked after and taken care of tomorrow." Charlie feels hurt and rebellious. He is looking for someone to blame. Still in a state of uncertainty, Charlie finally decides to go home.

A week has passed since Elizabeth's unexpected death. The days have been filled with loneliness and emptiness for Charlie. He is like a dormant volcano ready to come alive again. Something is growing in his heart, something mysterious.

When Sunday arrives, he drives to the cemetery once again. Elizabeth's headstone is supposed to be there by now. He wants to see it. When Charlie gets there, he is happy to see that the headstone has been placed on her grave. He manages a short smile as he reads the inscription.

ELIZABETH THOMAS DELANEY
BORN OCTOBER 17, 1947
DIED JULY 13, 1987
FOR I AM IN DOUBT NO MORE FOR
I AM WITH THE LORD

Charlie looks beside Elizabeth's grave and sees Karen's headstone. A tear runs down his face when he reads the inscription.

KAREN THOMAS DELANEY
BORN SEPTEMBER 10, 1967
DIED JUNE 6, 1987
THE LOVE OF MY LIFE REMAINS IN MY VIRGIN HEART

In the center of Karen's white headstone, there is a beautiful angel standing alone. The angel's hands are locked together as if she stands waiting for someone. It is a beautiful headstone. There is also an angel in the center of Elizabeth's headstone. The angel has her head up and her arms open as if she is flying up to heaven.

The sight of the gravestones standing side by side gives Charlie a peculiar feeling. He sits down on the ground and looks at the two monuments with pride. He thinks back to when he first met Karen, at Little Tony's pizza place. Charlie laughs as he remembers the first time he talked to Elizabeth. He sits there and remembers how happy these two special women made him.

As Charlie is thinking, a powerful thought enters his mind like a flash of lightning. He realizes Elizabeth never would have needed this operation if she hadn't been burdened by the loss of her husband, Colonel Alan Thomas. He sees a vision of the major drinking and then giving the order to fire on the colonel's plane. His hate for Major Lester Cain now becomes more dramatic.

Charlie glances over at Karen's headstone. He smiles briefly before his expression turns into a sad frown. He sees visions of Karen as a little girl, the images of Karen growing up without her daddy. This thought gives the hate growing in Charlie's heart more zeal. Charlie says to himself, "If Karen's daddy hadn't died in Vietnam, she might still be alive today. Her father would have been at the wedding, which would have altered the time we left."

Charlie gets up and begins to walk. His mind aches with the thought of how both his wives had to suffer all these years because of one drunken individual, Major Lester Cain. As Charlie walks around the cemetery, trying to figure things out in his head, he runs up against another headstone. When Charlie reads the inscription, his heart begins to beat fast.

DEBORAH LYNN SWANSON
BORN MARCH 28, 1961
DIED JUNE 14, 1987
I SHALL NOT BE SAD ANY LONGER FOR I AM NOW
WITH THE LORD THY GOD

Charlie lies down on the ground and begins to remember an earlier time in his life, an innocent time—a time when he and Dee used to talk together on the school bus, a time when he was too shy to tell Dee how he felt about her. He remembers her gorgeous blond hair, soft and shiny. Her eyes were as green as brilliant cut emeralds. He reminisces about how important she was to him during that tender, innocent time early in his life. But most of all, he remembers the last day of school of ninth grade, the day he received his first kiss. He remembers that day as if it were yesterday. He can almost feel Dee's young, soft, tender lips pressing up against his previously untouched mouth. That was a time when the world stopped.

He thinks she would be alive today if he hadn't seen her that day at the mall, the day he was trying to pick out an engagement ring for Karen. If he hadn't gone to the nightclub where she worked, they never would have been intimate that night. He had given her encouragement that night and then rejected her, tearing her heart apart. Charlie recalls how desperate she was when he told her that he was going to marry Karen.

Charlie takes another look at the headstone before breaking down. He puts his hands over his face to cover up the tears of sorrow. He lies there for several minutes before he gets control of himself. He cries out, "Why, God? Why did she have to die too?" Charlie's voice is loud and demanding. His voice cracks as he cries out again, "Why did you have to take all three of them away from me? You have taken everything away from me. Why, God? Why are you testing me this way?"

Charlie wipes his face and gets up from the ground. As he walks away from Dee's grave, he remembers what the corporal said: "Don't blame God for the bad things that happen in your life. Blame the ones who are responsible." Then it dawns on Charlie. He says quietly to himself, "If Karen's father were still alive, none of these bad things would have happened. Karen and Elizabeth wouldn't have suffered all these years. Karen and I probably would have been married at a different church. Elizabeth never would have had that operation. I never would have had that fight with Karen about staying over with me that night. Her daddy would have kicked my ass good if she did. I never would have gone to see Dee that night. She too would still be alive if Karen's father hadn't died in Vietnam. I see everything clearly now. I see what I must do."

Charlie's life has purpose once again. He must settle the score with the man who took Colonel Alan Thomas's life, a man whom Charlie has never seen, a man who, directly and indirectly, caused suffering to the ones Charlie loved so dearly. Because of the actions of this one individual, the three most important women in his life besides his mother died. A powerful force establishes itself in Charlie's soul. The man must be confronted and dealt with. He rushes home to design his plan of battle.

# Chapter 4
## SOMEONE TO BLAME

Charlie continues to take his lithium religiously. Every single day, he thanks God for bringing this medication into his life. Charlie doesn't resent God for the tragedies he has suffered. He has someone else to blame.

Charlie looks at the adversity he has faced as a test of his faith. He is determined to strengthen his faith, not weaken it. An injustice has been done, and he is ready to correct it. Charlie feels that this is his mission; he must do it.

Charlie visits his psychologist on Monday morning and tells the doctor about his problems. The psychologist treats Charlie as if he is just another face. He gives advice like a rubber stamp, exactly what he tells everyone else. He tells Charlie to get involved with other people and forget about the things that are important to him. Charlie disagrees with him on nearly everything he suggests. He treats Charlie not as an individual, but just as another patient. Charlie decides not to go see the psychologist anymore. Now he understands why people call them shrinks. Charlie only needs the psychologist to prescribe the lithium.

After leaving the doctor's office, a disappointed Charlie pays Mr. Bowman a visit. As he walks through the door, Nancy Walker throws up her hand and waves at him but continues to talk on the phone. Charlie, carrying a small briefcase, waves back. After Nancy hangs up the phone, she says, "Hello, Charlie. How are you doing?" Her happy face cheers him up a little bit.

Charlie replies, "I am doing pretty good, I guess. Is Mr. Bowman busy?"

"Just a minute, Charlie, and I'll go see." Nancy gets up and disappears down the hallway. She returns a minute later and gives him another friendly smile before saying, "Charlie, Mr. Bowman is quite busy right now. He is talking to three people in Chicago on the conference line. He said it would be at least an hour before he's finished."

Disappointed but determined, Charlie says, "I'll wait." He walks over to a chair and sits down. As Charlie waits, he thinks about his mission in great detail. Corporal Spencer's words repeat in his mind: Cain "never got punished for this act." Charlie also recalls the way Elizabeth felt about taking vengeful action against him. She would be disappointed if he went out and killed this man. Charlie knows in his heart he can't do that. Killing is wrong. Charlie tries to think of a plan to punish Major Cain. As Charlie thinks, something else the corporal said flashes through his mind, something about how Major Cain was hurt by an attack on his pride. This gives Charlie an idea.

More than an hour later, Mr. Bowman walks out of his office. He looks surprised to see Charlie still there. He gives Mrs. Walker a stern look, and she puts up her hands and says, "I told him it would be an hour before you could see him."

Charlie gets up and walks over to Mr. Bowman and shakes his hand.

Mr. Bowman says, "Charlie, I was just on my way to lunch."

Charlie says, "It won't take five minutes to tell you what I want you to do."

Mr. Bowman hesitates and then asks Charlie into his office.

Once in Mr. Bowman's office, Charlie opens his briefcase and takes out a file.

Mr. Bowman says, "Charlie, I was just thinking about you the other day. I was reading the obituary column in the newspaper and saw the name of a woman. Let's see … I think her name was Elizabeth Delaney. I read she passed away. Was she related to you?"

Charlie suspects that Mr. Bowman already knows the answer because the obituary said, "Surviving is her husband Charlie Delaney." Charlie glances up at Mr. Bowman and says, "Yes, she was my wife."

Mr. Bowman looks confused. "How did she …"

Charlie answers without even hearing his entire question. "She was having a triple bypass operation. Remember my telling you about that?

She had an allergic reaction to one of the anesthesia drugs. She died before the operation even got started."

Mr. Bowman shakes his head in sadness. He kindly says, "My friend, you sure have had a bad year. You have had your share of problems."

Charlie doesn't waste any time. "I want you to locate somebody, or should I say some people." Charlie places a piece of paper on Mr. Bowman's desk. "This is the main character I want to find. His name is Lester Cain."

Mr. Bowman reads Charlie's notes, which go into quite a lot of detail. Charlie wants to know everything, from where the man lives and works to the things he does in his spare time and the places where he drinks. Charlie wants answers to a complete questionnaire regarding the man's habits and practices—all the important functions of his life.

As Mr. Bowman reads, Charlie places another piece of paper on his desk. "After you finish with the first request, I want you to do some research on this man's daughter. I don't know her name or anything informative about her. All I know is that she is around nineteen or twenty years old. This paper lists the information I want you to find out about her and her activities."

Mr. Bowman slides the first sheet of paper aside and glances at the second one. There are questions about where the woman works, where she hangs out, and a host of other things. Mr. Bowman begins to shake his head. He knows this is going to take a lot of investigating.

After reading the information, he slides the pages aside and says, "Charlie, this is going to be a very time-consuming project. I will have to go out in the field to gather this kind of information." Mr. Bowman picks up the first page and reads the location: Lynchburg, Tennessee. He continues, "For me to gather this information, I will have to travel personally to Lynchburg. I will need to bring along several assistants to help cover the territory. This might cost a—"

"There is one other thing I want you to find out," Charlie says before he can finish.

Mr. Bowman listens with great care.

"I want you to record for me all the industrial real estate property that is for sale in a twenty-mile radius of where Lester Cain lives."

Mr. Bowman looks flabbergasted. "Why on God's green earth do you want to—"

"Also, I don't want to be bothered with any questions. I am the only one who needs to know why I want these things." Charlie hands Mr. Bowman a page providing a detailed description of what he wants. The instructions tell Mr. Bowman to draw maps of all roads in the area, including all the area restaurants, gas stations, housing developments, and so on.

Mr. Bowman looks at this paper and shakes his head with disbelief. He tosses it aside and says, "Charlie, you are asking me to give you a detailed description of this man's complete environment. This work will take weeks."

Charlie gives Mr. Bowman a strong, stern look, which then transforms into a lonesome grin. Charlie calmly says, "You have three days."

Mr. Bowman stands up and cries, "Are you crazy? I can't do all this in just three days! Charlie, you are asking me to scout out an area like a general would scout out a territory he was fixing to invade."

Charlie smiles gladly upon hearing this.

"And furthermore," Mr. Bowman continues, "this will cost you a fortune! I would have to charge you—"

Mr. Bowman stops talking when Charlie suddenly takes out a large, thick, yellow envelope from his briefcase. He has seen envelopes like this one many times throughout the years.

Charlie casually tosses the envelope on the desk. "Here you go, Mr. Bowman. There are three thousand dollars in that envelope. It is all yours. I want you to gather all the information you can that is outlined in those three documents. Today is Monday. You should be through investigating by Friday. I will be back here next Monday afternoon at three o'clock for your report. If the three thousand dollars isn't enough, I will be glad to compensate you for the balance. Don't let money interfere with your accomplishing your objective. Do we have an understanding?"

Mr. Bowman remains silent for a moment, dazed at Charlie's unusual behavior. "Sure, Charlie. I will have everything done by next Monday."

Charlie smiles, turns, and leaves the office without saying another word.

As the week goes by, Charlie finally works up the courage to call his boss and tell him the news about Elizabeth's death, but to Charlie's surprise, his boss already knows. He read about it in the newspaper just as Mr. Bowman did. Charlie asks his boss if he can take the rest of the month off. He tells him he has some unfinished business to tend to. His boss understands the grief he must be going through, so he grants Charlie's request without giving it a second thought. He tells him to report back to work Monday, August 3. He jokingly tells Charlie to please not get married anymore this year. He can't afford to be without him much longer.

After talking to his boss, Charlie feels like a lion again. The only obstacle he had to worry about was getting back to work, but now nothing will stop him from carrying out his mission. He grins with determination and resolution. He eagerly waits for Monday afternoon to come.

When Monday does come, Charlie is ready to go. The car is packed with everything he will need. He plays with Little Charlie right up until two o'clock and then takes his little dog to stay with Wayne Scott while he is away.

Charlie arrives at Mr. Bowman's office at exactly three o'clock. Mr. Bowman greets him just as he walks in the door. He smiles happily, shaking Charlie's hand firmly.

He says, "Come on back to my office, Charlie. I want to show you what I have."

Charlie eagerly walks with Mr. Bowman to his office.

"Please sit down, Charlie. I have exactly what you want."

Charlie takes a seat and prepares to listen to Mr. Bowman's report with great interest.

Mr. Bowman tells Charlie where Lester Cain lives, where he works, the hours he works, and a great deal of other things about him. He works for Kimble Real Estate Corporation and has been working there for thirteen years. He is now fifty-two years old.

Mr. Bowman gives Charlie the report on Cain's daughter as well. Her name is Dolores Cain. She is nineteen years old, and she works at the K+N Newsstand at a local shopping mall. The report gives the address of the shop, the hours she works, and of course, a photograph of what she looks like today as well as other items. Charlie is happy with what he sees.

Charlie smiles gladly as he browses through the report. He looks up at Mr. Bowman and says softly, "Well done! Well done!"

Mr. Bowman says, "I'm not finished yet, Charlie." He takes out another report. Handing it to Charlie, he says, "I hope this will be to your liking."

Charlie opens the report and sees maps of roads and descriptions of real estate properties—where they are located and how much they cost. It is a complete, detailed description of a twenty-mile radius, just like Charlie wanted. Charlie is pleased with the reports.

As Charlie gazes at the real estate maps, Mr. Bowman says, "Charlie, if you turn to the very back, there is a photograph of Lester Cain."

Charlie grows nervous as he prepares himself to look at this man's face for the very first time. He pulls out the 8x10 glossy color photograph and frowns. The image is just what Corporal Spencer said it would be. He looks similar to the Italian dictator Mussolini, except he has hair. Charlie briefly studies the face and then puts the photograph back into the folder.

Charlie asks, "Was the three thousand dollars enough to cover all your expenses?"

Mr. Bowman looks stunned. He then smiles intriguingly. "Yes, Charlie. The amount took care of everything. I hope this information is of some use to you."

Charlie replies, "Oh, it will be of great use to me. You don't know how happy and pleased I am with this. I don't know how I could ever repay you, Mr. Bowman."

"You have paid me in full, Charlie. I am glad this is to your liking. Just please don't do anything that will get you into any trouble."

Charlie gives Mr. Bowman a wry smile. "I'll be very careful."

Not knowing exactly what Charlie means by that remark, Mr. Bowman simply replies, "As I was making my investigation, I met this man."

Charlie sits down and says, "You did! Tell me, what do you think of him?"

Mr. Bowman laughs and says, "I have never met such a nasty-talking, arrogant, mean spirited man in all my life. He takes the award for being the biggest asshole I have ever met. Charlie, you be careful at whatever you are planning. He isn't someone you want to be friends with. One of the fellows I brought along with me to help in the investigation found out that Lester Cain has killed several people. He also has several girls working for him, if you know what I mean."

Charlie nods.

"He also has a small-time gambling racket set up. One of his former clients didn't pay up on a football game, so Cain had some of his thugs pay him a visit. Charlie, they broke both his legs. That is just one who didn't pay up."

Charlie grows concerned as Mr. Bowman continues.

"Our source also told us that one fellow won a lot of money from Mr. Cain in a football bet. But he didn't live long enough to collect his winnings. This man is not someone you want to mess around with, Charlie. He is a very bad dude!" The stern look on Mr. Bowman's face tells it all.

Charlie gives Mr. Bowman a delightful smile, and Mr. Bowman looks puzzled in response. "What you just said has given me more encouragement and strength than I had before coming here today," Charlie says. "I am glad I know what I am up against now." Charlie reaches in his coat pocket and tosses Mr. Bowman a yellow envelope. Charlie doesn't wait for him to open it. He gets up and says, "For a job well done, here is another three thousand dollars." Charlie doesn't wait for a response. He opens the door and leaves a dumbfounded Mr. Bowman.

Charlie happily drives to a printing establishment and places an order for a set of business cards. Charlie writes down his name, the company name Steven's Knitting Inc., and the business address, phone number, and logo. He provides accurate and truthful information, even the business phone number. He gives the order to the clerk at the counter.

The man says, "Yes, sir, Mr. Delaney. How many cards would you like printed up?"

"As small a number as possible."

"The smallest order is one thousand cards, and they are twenty-one dollars and fifty cents."

Charlie shakes his head and says, "Okay. That will be fine. When will they be ready?"

"You can pick them up tomorrow."

Charlie quickly replies, "I want them today! I want them in an hour!" Charlie stares at the clerk sternly. He pulls out his wallet and slams a hundred-dollar bill down on the counter hard.

The man quickly picks it up and says, "Yes, sir, Mr. Delaney. Your cards will be ready in an hour."

With a satisfied smile, Charlie says, "Fine. I'll just take a seat and wait."

The clerk brings the cards to him as soon as they are finished. "Here you go, Mr. Delaney."

Charlie doesn't say anything. He takes a small handful of cards from the top of the pile and tosses the others in the trash can. The bewildered store clerk shakes his head. Charlie puts the cards in his shirt pocket, nods to the clerk, wishes him a good day, and leaves.

Charlie then drives to a liquor store. He tells the clerk there that he wants a fifth of Jack Daniel's Black Label. The man hurries to retrieve the bottle of whiskey, and Charlie checks out. Outside, Charlie opens the bottle and pours half of the amber-colored liquid on the ground. Charlie then opens the trunk of his red Mustang and places the half-empty bottle of whiskey in a black duffel bag containing two cameras and other numerous items.

Closing the trunk, Charlie gets in the car and drives away as though he is on a schedule. He goes by Elizabeth's, Karen's, and Dee's graves one last time. He touches their headstones and says a prayer for each of them. He doesn't sit down or rest. He stands as he stares down at their graves, mesmerized by the fact that they are all gone. He says to them, "I am leaving tomorrow to punish the one who has caused you all so much pain. I love you all. Please prepare a place for me, for we will all be together again someday."

Charlie drives himself home in a lonely state. As soon as he arrives home, he hurries to take his lithium. He takes his medication automatically now. But every time he swallows the small capsules, he remembers how depressed life would be without them.

He eats a sandwich and then studies the contents of the three reports. He designs his battle plan down to the last detail. After Charlie is satisfied with what he has read, he goes to bed. Tomorrow morning the attack will begin! May God be with him.

The next morning, Charlie maps out how long it will take him to drive to the location. He leaves his house early. As he drives, he thinks about the order in which he wants to carry out the parts of his plan. His first objective is to get a room, a place to set up his headquarters.

After he arrives in Lynchburg, Tennessee, it takes Charlie only about thirty minutes to find the major's house. He drives by it slowly but doesn't stop. He just wants to make sure he knows where it is when the time is right.

Charlie gets a room at a nearby hotel, the Pine Tree Inn. When checking in, he doesn't think to give a false name or anything that might be deceptive. Charlie has devised his strategy very carefully, so he doesn't use any deceptive tactics as he carries out his plan. Charlie wants everything to be done as truthfully as possible. How the battle is fought is just as important as how it is won. There must be honor in battle.

After unloading all of his cargo in his room, Charlie gets ready to visit the shopping mall. He knows Dolores will be getting off work at four o'clock. He hurries so he won't miss her.

Charlie has no problem finding the shopping mall. Everything is laid out for him on the maps. He walks around the mall until he finds the K+N Newsstand. He walks by it the first time without looking inside. The second time Charlie walks by, he notices Dolores standing behind the counter. A nervous energy fills him when he sees the familiar face. Charlie decides to wait until all the other customers have left. Soon, the newsstand is empty. He then makes his move. He walks in and smiles at the young girl.

Charlie says, "Hello there, young lady."

The girl puts her hand up to her face in a timid way and says, "Hello." She is wearing black oval-framed glasses. Her hair is brown and very short. The style of her hair resembles a round, fluffy ball of steel wool. She has thin lips, a flat chest, and a plain face. With her chubby figure, she is as sexy as a Canadian moose wearing a bikini. The only thing she has going for her is her eyes. They are a soft blue and have a delicate beauty all to their own. But when she smiles, that beauty is dissolved by the view of her crooked teeth. They are as white as butter. Charlie uses this only feature of hers to his advantage.

Charlie asks, "So what's your name?"

The girl replies, "My name is Dolores. What's yours?"

"My name is Charlie, Charlie Delaney."

Dolores doesn't say anything. Charlie can tell she is very shy.

He asks, "Do you have any reading material on the Beatles or Led Zeppelin? They are my favorites."

Dolores excitedly says, "Really? They are my favorite groups too. Let me see what I can find."

While Charlie waits, Dolores finds Charlie a couple of books and a few magazines on the two rock groups. As she finally hands him the reading materials, he gazes at her eyes and says, "Oh my, you have blue eyes, don't you?"

Dolores smiles shyly and nods her head.

He continues, "Blue is my favorite color."

"It's my favorite color too. Isn't that funny? What did you say your name was again?"

Charlie reaches out his hand and gently shakes hers. "Charlie Delaney. You can just call me Charlie."

"Okay, Charlie. You can call me Dolores."

Charlie gives her a smooth, enticing grin. "Fine. So do you live around here?"

"Yeah. I live about twenty minutes from here. Do you live around here?"

Charlie pulls out one of his business cards and hands it to her. He says, "No, I don't live around here. I am out here to do some business. Here is my card."

Dolores reads the card and says, "Steven's Knitting."

Charlie responds, "That's right. I am in the textile business. I am scouting out the territory around here. I hope to find something out here that might be worthwhile for my interests. My company is thinking about building another manufacturing plant. You wouldn't happen to know any reliable realtors in this area, would you?"

Dolores grins like an opossum. "Just so happens my daddy is in the real estate business."

In a surprised voice Charlie replies, "Really? I would like to meet your father sometime."

She excitedly replies, "I would be glad to introduce you to my daddy."

Charlie grins contentedly and says, "I'll tell you what, how would you like to have dinner with me tonight? I know I have only just met you, but I sure would like to treat you to dinner and a movie."

Dolores doesn't hesitate one second. "Yes. I would like that." Dolores quickly draws Charlie a map to where she lives.

Charlie takes the map along with the merchandise he has just purchased and places them in the bag. "I will pick you up about seven o'clock. Will that be all right?"

Dolores smiles excitedly again and says, "That will be just fine. I'll be ready then."

Charlie nods his head, turns, and walks away. He is content with himself; everything went smoothly.

Charlie goes back to his hotel room and reads the reports again. As he plans what he will do when he finally meets the man he hates, something Corporal Spencer said enters Charlie's mind: "If you let hate take control of your life, then you are destined to destroy yourself." Charlie remembers these words sternly. He tells himself, "*No matter what I do, I must not kill this man with my hands. I must not commit any sin that will prevent me from seeing Elizabeth, Karen, and Dee in heaven. I must do this in a way in which I don't destroy myself.*"

Before too long, six thirty arrives, and Charlie gets back into his car. As Charlie turns onto the road where the major lives, a nervous energy fills his soul. He pulls into the driveway, stops the car, and gets out. He walks nervously toward the house, eager to finally meet this man. Charlie has everything planned out to the last detail. As he gets closer to the door, Dolores suddenly comes out of the house.

Charlie is surprised. He wanted to go in and meet the major. Charlie gives Dolores a puzzled look.

She says, "Come on, Charlie. Let's go."

Charlie tries to persuade Dolores to let him meet her parents. "The movie doesn't start until nine o'clock. I thought maybe I could meet your folks for a little while."

Dolores pays him no mind. She says, "Daddy has a friend over, and Mama is busy. So let's go." Dolores takes Charlie by the hand and pulls him to the car. Charlie gazes up at the house one last time before they leave.

Charlie is stuck taking Dolores out for dinner and a movie. He pretends to be interested in Dolores's conversation, but his mind is still on meeting her father. He asks her a few questions about her parents so that it won't seem strange when he knows so much about Major Cain in a future conversation.

Dolores orders one of the most expensive items on the menu but eats only half of it. Her conversation is boring and drab, but to keep her interested in him, Charlie pretends he is enjoying himself.

Charlie takes her to a movie after their meal. Of the four movies playing, only one is rated PG. Charlie picks that one, but Dolores persuades him to see one of the R-rated films. They go in together and find seats about halfway down. Charlie always likes to sit on the end, and Dolores follows like a puppy on a leash. He sits down, and Dolores follows. Charlie hopes like hell there won't be a lot of nudity in the film. He doesn't want it to give Dolores any ideas. He can tell by the way she talked at the restaurant that she is eager for a relationship. She's probably never had one in her life.

Just as Charlie feared, the movie hasn't been playing thirty minutes before a slender, attractive woman starts undressing. She doesn't stop until she is fully naked. Charlie feels uneasy as her large breasts fill the screen. As the woman talks and moves around, her black, woolly triangle is exposed totally for all to see. The view of her naked body, along with the provocative dialogue, apparently begins to stimulate Dolores. As the camera pans over the attractive, slender brunette's body, Dolores reaches over and holds Charlie's hand warmly. Charlie sits there nervously, feeling very uneasy as Dolores's head rests upon his chest and shoulders. She lets out a long feminine moan as the woman in the film crawls into bed with a naked man.

Dolores snuggles up closer to Charlie and rubs his hand. As the man and woman in the film make out, Dolores whispers to Charlie, "That sure does look like fun."

Charlie, not knowing what to do, says, "I sure am thirsty. Would you like something to drink?"

Dolores looks up with a dazed expression and says, "Huh? No. I'm fine."

Charlie quickly gets up and leaves the auditorium. He walks to the concession stand and buys himself a Coke. He takes his time returning. Charlie opens the door to the auditorium and peeks up at the screen—the love scene is over. He wishes this evening were over. Charlie realizes he will have to wait until tomorrow to meet with the major.

Charlie walks back to his seat and sits down. Dolores gives him a stern, negative look. Charlie thinks, *She is pissed off at me now. She feels like I've rejected her. She is probably feeling like an ass now for saying what she said earlier. If I don't do something, she will take her frustration out on me. I must make her feel that I still like her.*

Charlie leans over and whispers, "Did I miss anything?"

Dolores gives Charlie a quick "Nope."

Charlie whispers, "If that brunette had your soft blue eyes, I believe I would have gotten my Coke later." This brings a smile to Dolores's face. Charlie then pulls out two Milky Way candy bars and hands one of them to Dolores. "Here, I thought you might like this."

Dolores's eyes light up like a Christmas tree. She thanks Charlie sincerely. This is something Charlie always did when he dated Karen. He liked to surprise her with a candy bar halfway through a movie. Karen always did enjoy this simple little treat from him. It added something special to their relationship—not the candy bar, but the thought of giving her one.

Having accepted the candy bar like a proposal of marriage, Dolores gobbles it down. She once again reaches over and holds Charlie's hand. Charlie is relieved that Dolores isn't upset with him now. He doesn't want to do anything that will prevent him from meeting the major. He will make any sacrifices he has to, even if that means holding hands with the man's ugly daughter. They watch the movie to its end. There are a few more nude scenes, but Charlie just sits and lets Dolores hold his hand anyway.

After the movie, Charlie walks Dolores to his car. She holds on to him as if glued to his body. Once they are inside the car, Charlie says, "I guess I should take you home now."

Just as Charlie starts the car, Dolores says, "I have a better idea. Why don't we go over to your place for a while?"

Charlie hesitates before saying, "I have been up since early this morning. I need to get some rest now. How about if I come over and see you tomorrow?"

Dolores, looking delighted, eagerly replies, "Yes! Yes! I mean, that will be fine, Charlie. About what time will you be coming over?"

Charlie takes a moment to think and then answers, "How about five o'clock?"

"Okay. That sounds fine."

Now that Charlie has set the stage for tomorrow, he takes Dolores home without delay. When Charlie arrives at Dolores's house, he walks her to the door.

Dolores turns to Charlie and says, "Charlie, I had a wonderful time. I really did enjoy the movie, didn't you?"

Charlie stutters a couple of words before saying, "It was a very interesting movie. I will say that for it."

Dolores looks up at Charlie and closes her eyes. She clearly wants him to kiss her good night.

Charlie thinks fast and says, "I would kiss you good night, but since this is our first date, I won't."

Dolores replies, "I don't care if you do, Charlie." She closes her eyes again.

"Oh, I don't want you to think I am being too forward or anything. Well, I guess I will see you tomorrow."

Disappointed, Dolores politely says, "Okay, Charlie. See you then."

Charlie turns and begins to walk away. He quickly turns back around and says, "See if your father and mother will be home tomorrow. I would like to meet both of them."

Dolores nods. "Okay, Charlie. I'll make sure they're both home tomorrow."

Charlie smiles happily as he walks back to the car. He leaves satisfied that everything turned out okay tonight. He is pleased with himself.

The next day is Wednesday. Charlie spends most of the morning rereading the data reports on the major. He studies the real estate maps like a general in a war zone. Charlie focuses on how much the properties are selling for and who the realtors are. He focuses especially on the properties being sold by the Kimble Real Estate Company, the company that Major Cain works for, plus the properties owned by Lester Cain.

At noon, Charlie decides to leave his hotel room. He wants to drive around the area and check out a few things before confronting Major Lester Cain. He says a little prayer before leaving and then walks out to his car.

Charlie arrives at the Cain residence at 4:40 p.m. after checking out one of the items in his game plan. He feels unusually nervous when he arrives. When he gets out of the car, he has butterflies in his stomach, and his legs feel like rubber. He walks up to the front door slowly because his feet feel as if they are caught in quicksand. It takes all of his nerve to make this short walk. Thoughts of turning around and saying "to hell with it" enter Charlie's mind. The only thing that keeps him moving forward is the vision of Elizabeth's, Karen's, and Dee's headstones at the graveyard. They are all dead now, and Major Lester Cain is alive and well and living in a nice house, without any care for the suffering he has caused.

Charlie remembers seeing a picture of Karen when she was five years old at her birthday party. Her daddy couldn't be there to add to her happiness. He thought of Elizabeth, struggling to raise Karen on her own. And he thought of Dee, the first girl he ever kissed, lying in her grave because of the various circumstances that had brought him here.

This man must be punished for his actions! Charlie will refrain from going ahead with his plan only if the major repents for what he did that hot, humid day in Southeast Asia. That is the only way Charlie will forgive him. Charlie will give him an opportunity to repent, but if he doesn't, his soul will be in jeopardy of being damned for eternity.

Charlie knocks on the door, and Dolores answers it, an excited look on her face. "Come on in, Charlie. I have been waiting for you." She grabs Charlie's hand and pulls him into the house. She leads him into the living room where a woman is sitting.

Charlie says, "Hello there."

Dolores then introduces Charlie to her mother. "Mama, this is the guy I have been telling you about. His name is Charlie Delaney. Charlie, this is my mama."

Mrs. Cain smiles happily at Charlie. She is probably glad to see that such a handsome man has come to court her daughter. She invites Charlie to sit down. "Could I get you something to drink—tea or coffee?"

Charlie answers, "Some iced tea would be nice."

As Mrs. Cain leaves the room to get the refreshments, Charlie looks around the living room with awe. Everything looks modern and very expensive. The room is filled with exquisite furnishings. There is a large ivory carving sitting on the mantle that must be worth thousands of dollars. All of the furniture and fixtures are of the highest quality. Charlie thinks, *Selling real estate didn't buy all of this stuff.* Charlie recalls the report, which stated that the major had girls working for him and operated a gambling establishment. The house's furnishings tell Charlie that the major's crooked lifestyle has paid off very well for him.

As Mrs. Cain comes back into the room with the iced tea, Charlie asks, "Isn't Mr. Cain here?"

She says, "Yes, he is. He is having a business meeting with a couple of his buddies in the conference room."

Charlie disappointedly sits back and takes a sip of his iced tea. He worries that he won't have a chance to meet the major. Dolores and her mother talk openly with Charlie, and the atmosphere becomes irksome for him.

Back in the conference room, Lester Cain is discussing business and other matters with two of his associates. He sits at his desk counting the money his two associates have brought him.

One of the two men drinks a full shot of whiskey straight down. He asks Lester, "Is all the money there?"

Lester grins. "Yep. I never knew making money could be so easy. I never thought farmers could be so stupid. Just as soon as they get their money for their crops, they can't wait to give it to me for a bet on a ball game. I can't wait for football season."

The first man takes a drink from his glass and says, "How are the girls making out?"

Lester lets out a hearty laugh. "Don't have enough to go around. Now that the farmers are getting money for their crops, demand is greater than supply. I talked to a buddy of mine in Vegas, though. He is sending me five more whores next week so I can keep up with demand. After a month or so, the farmers won't have any money left. Then I will send the girls back."

They all laugh with delight.

The first man says, "It will be good to have a few new faces around here. Did your buddy tell you anything about them?"

Lester smiles a dirty, nasty smile. "Yes, he did. He told me they are all young, stupid, attractive, and very talented. I believe he said they all are in their early twenties or younger."

The three men laugh and continue to drink their whiskey.

Lester gets up with an intoxicated grin and walks over to the liquor cabinet. He turns around and says, "Fellows, I have wanted to break out this bottle of cognac for ages. I think I will break it out now with two of my best friends."

The major serves each of his two associates a glass of cognac. They drink down the first glasses immediately, and the major quickly serves them again. He grins at them proudly. "You fellows are the greatest. I want to propose a toast. To the three most important things in life: money, women, and power."

The three men hold their glasses high in the air, laugh a lusty laugh, and then drink down the amber-colored liquid. The men continue drinking and laughing until they hear a knock on the door.

A woman's voice says, "Lester, may I enter?"

The second man whispers to the major, "I like the way you have your wife trained."

The three men laugh as the major says, "What is it?"

Lester's wife says through the door, "Dolores's new boyfriend is here. She wants you to meet him. Will you be coming out soon?"

After a moment, Lester shouts, "Yes, I'll be out there shortly! Now go away!"

The first man says, "My wife would have just opened the door and walked in."

The major grins fiendishly and says, "The last time that woman opened that door and walked in without my giving her permission, she learned to regret it. I stripped her down to her bare ass and got out my long wooden paddle. I made her ass red as a stop sign. Believe me, she will never enter this room again unless she has my clear permission. I promise you that."

Both men laugh heartily.

"Yeah, fellows, if you ever have a problem with your wives, all you need to do is strip them down to their bare ass and then make it red! They will be good as gold after that."

The two men snicker with delight as Lester, looking proud, downs another drink.

The first man says, "So who is Dolores's new boyfriend?"

The major puts the money he has collected in the safe and says, "I don't know him. Dolores came home after work Tuesday saying that she was in love. She was in love. She has finally met Mr. Right. You know, all that stuff."

The first man says, "I'm glad she found somebody she likes. Have they dated any?"

Lester says, "Yeah. They went out last night for dinner and a movie. All day long she has been talking about how wonderful he is."

The first man asks, "So what's his name, Lester?"

The major turns to his friend and says, "How can I forget it, as many times as Dolores has said it these last two days? His name is Charlie. Charlie Delaney."

The two men stand up. The second man says, "Lester, we must be leaving now. We just came over to bring you the money."

"Well, I am glad you did."

The first man says, "I hope everything works out with Dolores and her new fellow."

The major shakes their hands. "I sure would like to have some grandkids to spend some of this money on," he says, chuckling.

The second man says, "Well, maybe everything will work out with them. If you want him as a son-in-law, all you have to do is sweeten the pot with money. Money will make a man do anything. Money is what makes the world go around."

Lester smiles proudly as he replies, "Yeah, I know that. I definitely know that."

The major opens the back door. As the two men exit the house, the second man turns and says, "Hey, Lester, let me know when the new girls arrive. I want to try them out before everybody else does."

The major says, "You will have to wait till I am through with them first. Then I will give you a call."

All three men laugh, and the associates head toward their car.

Lester locks the back door, puts away the cognac, and then leaves the conference room to join the others in the living room.

When the major enters the living room, Charlie sees Lester Cain's face in person for the first time. The atmosphere in the room is filled with a sense of mystery. Charlie's long-awaited day has finally come. He jumps up from his seat as Dolores introduces her father to him.

"Daddy, this is the fellow I have been telling you about. His name is Charlie Delaney. Charlie, this is my daddy."

Charlie smiles gladly as he holds out his hand. Lester does likewise. Charlie shakes his hand with a firm grip. He says excitedly, "I sure have been wanting to meet with you, Mr. Cain."

Lester says, "Well, it's good to meet you too. Please sit down." The two men sit down, Charlie on the couch and Lester in his chair. Dolores sits down next to Charlie as her mother sits in another chair beside the major.

Charlie doesn't waste any time striking up a conversation with the major. "Your wife and daughter have been telling me you were in the Marine Corps."

Lester grins. "Yes, that's right. I was in the Marine Corps for eighteen years. When I left, I was a major."

As soon as the words leave Lester's mouth, Charlie feigns an impressed expression and says, "Wow! A major! That sounds great! I always said if I ever went into the service, I would want to be a marine."

This visibly excites the major. He begins to take a liking to Charlie, right off. Lester says, "So tell me, Mr. Delaney—"

"Oh, please, call me Charlie."

The major begins again. "Okay. So tell me, Charlie. What do you do for a living?"

Charlie pulls out his business card and hands it to the major. "I am in textiles. I am here to scout out this area."

The major reads the business card with admiration. He then says, "You mean you might be looking for another location for this Steven's Knitting company?"

Charlie replies, "Let's just say that I am looking over a lot of different real estate properties to see if they would be suitable for our future expansions."

The major looks intrigued when he hears that Charlie is looking for real estate. He asks, "How big a property is your company looking for?"

Charlie says, "The property we have now is on a five-acre lot. More than likely we will need at least that much."

The major quickly says, "I know of a piece of property that you might be interested in. It is over on the south side of Lynchburg, a property owned by Tom Gilmore. It is zoned for industrial use and—"

"Oh," Charlie says, interrupting him, "you mean the seven-point-eight acres on Davis Boulevard, priced at seventy-eight thousand dollars."

The major looks impressed. He replies, "Yeah, that's right."

Charlie continues, "That piece of property wouldn't be suitable for three reasons: First, a lot of the property is too hilly; we would want something flatter. The flatter the property is, the less it would cost to build a plant there. The second reason is the location. The location should be right off a main road, near a highway. This is for our trucks coming and going. The closer to a main highway, the better."

The major marvels at Charlie as he listens.

"The third reason is price. The property is really only worth fifty thousand seven hundred dollars."

The major, now completely invested in this conversation, responds, "It sounds like you have really done your homework, Charlie. You are quite right about the price; ten thousand an acre does sound like quite a lot for that property."

Dolores, getting bored with this talk, says, "Charlie, how would you like to go up to my room?"

Charlie looks back and forth between Dolores and the major and says, "If you don't mind, Dolores, I would rather just sit here and talk with your father, if that's all right with you."

Dolores frowns and says, "Okay, Charlie."

The major clearly enjoys hearing Charlie talk like that to Dolores. "Charlie, I like you. You sound like you have a good head on your shoulders. I like that in a young man."

Charlie is delighted to see that the major has taken a liking to him. The two continue to talk about other real estate matters for an hour.

Mrs. Cain walks into the kitchen; Dolores follows her. Disappointed at not receiving enough attention from Charlie, Dolores says, "Mama, I wish Daddy would go somewhere. He has been talking to Charlie long enough."

Mrs. Cain, seeing the disappointment on her daughter's face, says, "Dolores, you are lucky that your father has taken such a liking to your new boyfriend. I'll tell you what—why don't you and I run to the grocery store and buy some steaks for dinner?"

Dolores is confused. "You mean, leave while Charlie is still here? Mama, don't you think that would discourage him?"

Her mother smiles at her and says, "No. I don't think it will discourage him at all. We won't be gone for more than thirty minutes. He will still be here when we get back. What do you say?"

Dolores reluctantly agrees with her mother, and they walk back into the living room. Dolores sits down beside Charlie and says, "Charlie, Mama and I are going to the store to get some steaks for dinner. I won't go if you don't want me to."

Charlie replies, "I think that's an excellent idea. How long do you think you will be?"

Dolores quickly answers, "Not more than thirty minutes."

Charlie glances down at his watch and says, "That will be just fine. You go ahead with your mother, and I'll just stay here and talk with you father."

Lester smiles contentedly as Dolores and her mother prepare to leave. Before leaving, Dolores picks up her handbag and walks over and kisses Charlie on the cheek. Charlie responds with a cheerful grin. She says with a frown, "Now don't you leave before I get back. We will be back in thirty minutes. Okay?"

Charlie doesn't answer her question. He simply says, "Just make sure you drive carefully, Dolores." Charlie turns to Mrs. Cain and waves good-bye. He says, "It sure was good to meet you. Don't let anyone pick Dolores up at the market."

She laughs before saying, "Okay, Charlie. I won't. Come on, Dolores. Let's go."

Dolores waves at Charlie one last time. She looks sad and innocent. "Bye," she softly says as she walks out the door with her mother.

Charlie's blood turns to ice water as he realizes he is now alone with his enemy for the first time. He stares at the major's red face and says, "So tell me … would you mind if I call you Major?"

Lester looks uncertainly at Charlie. "No, I don't mind."

Charlie nods. "So tell me, Major, how long did you serve in Vietnam?"

The major answers without hesitation. "Oh, I guess I served about six years."

Appearing fascinated, Charlie says, "I guess you saw a lot of action over there."

The major nods.

Charlie asks, "Everybody I've ever talked to who went over there had something they regretted doing. You don't have to tell me, but do you have any regrets about your time in Vietnam?"

The major pauses for a moment and says abruptly, "No. I have no regrets whatsoever. Everything I did over there was for my country. I don't feel I have any regrets for what I did over there in the least."

Charlie scrutinizes the way the major talks. He shows no remorse in his face or his words. Charlie continues to listen, hoping for a change, as the major goes on.

"The only thing I do regret," the major says, causing Charlie to hold his breath, "is that we didn't pulverize the North Vietnamese Army. We could have spearheaded straight to Hanoi, and the war would have been over in less than a month. If Johnson wasn't such a wimp, we would have won that war without any problem."

Charlie is disappointed that the major shows no sorrow for his actions at Chu Lai. He now realizes he must carry out his plan. He studies the major but does so carefully. He doesn't want to behave in a way that might lead the major to question his intentions. Charlie suspects that this man has forgotten all about that day he gave the order to shoot down Colonel Alan Thomas. He decides to hurry with his plan before Dolores and her mother return from the market. He especially doesn't want to sit down and eat at this man's table.

Charlie throws his plan into action. "Major, are you familiar with the property on Forest Manor? The eight-point-three-acre lot owned by William Miller, or should I say owned by the estate of William Miller? I am interested in that lot."

The major smiles contentedly. He knows that property well—because he owns a half interest in it.

Three months before William Miller died, Lester gave him ten thousand dollars in cash so that he could pay off some outstanding debt. Lester had his attorneys draw up an agreement with Mr. Miller that would entitle Lester to one-half interest in this piece of property at William Miller's death. The major knew Miller would not live much longer. He had terminal cancer and was undergoing chemotherapy treatments. Lester used Miller's illness to swindle him out of a very expensive piece of property. Because of the good location and quality of the land, this property could sell for as high as twenty thousand dollars an acre or more! The only drawback now is that the entire piece of property must be sold before Lester can receive anything. Since the other beneficiaries of Mr. Miller's estate, his three children, were outraged at discovering they were cozened out of their rightful entitlement at the reading of the will, Lester is more than eager to unload this piece of real estate before any lawsuits are filed against him.

The major says nonchalantly to Charlie, "So, you say you are interested in that piece of property?"

Charlie says, "That piece of property would be ideal for another textile plant. It is about the best prospect I have found so far."

This excites the major tremendously. Charlie studies his face like an astronomer studies the planets, trying to figure out Lester's thoughts. Charlie sees greed pollute the major's red face as he contemplates making a quick, easy profit.

The major smiles at Charlie and says, "The price for that property is around $166,000."

Charlie nods and smiles back. "Yes, that's right."

The major grins before saying, "How would you like to make a handsome profit for yourself, Charlie?"

Charlie focuses his attention directly on the major.

The major's voice gets soft and quiet. "You see, Charlie, I just so happen to own a half interest in that property. I am eager to sell it because of the family who owns the other half."

Charlie strives to look surprised and interested.

"I'll be up-front with you, Charlie. The property can't be sold for under 75 percent of the appraiser's estimate without the consent of the owners. And believe me, they aren't going to budge. We aren't speaking to each other these days."

Charlie doesn't ask any questions. He just continues to listen with a sparkle in his eyes.

The major gets up and walks over to the liquor cabinet. He asks Charlie, "Would you like a whiskey?"

Charlie replies, "No, thank you."

The major fixes himself a drink and hurries back over. He looks directly at Charlie and resumes speaking in a very soft tone. "That property can't be sold for under 125,000. That is the lowest price." The major takes a long swig from his drink as Charlie listens with apparent interest.

Lester continues, "Charlie, if your company wants to purchase that specific piece of property at 125,000, I can arrange for it to be done. Your company will have an asset worth $166,000. That means your company will have already made over $40,000 in appreciation on the land. Then build a factory on it. Who knows what it would be worth then?"

Charlie smiles enticingly before saying, "You asked how I would like to make a handsome profit for myself. Explain that, Major."

The major drinks from his glass and smiles. He stares at Charlie with a look of drunken avarice. "Charlie, this is the deal. If you can persuade your company to buy that piece of property at $125,000, I will give you ten thousand in cash."

Charlie widens his eyes and smiles to show Lester that this idea for making a quick profit appeals to him.

Lester continues, "No taxes to be paid. No IRS to bother you. I will give you the money in cash privately the day after the transaction takes place. I give you my word. How does that sound?"

Charlie looks excited and says, "Let me go back to my hotel room and make a few phone calls."

The major's happy face turns sour. He frowns as he says, "Now? You want to leave now? What about dinner? Dolores will be furious at me if you aren't here when they get back."

Charlie enjoys seeing the major upset and disappointed but doesn't let it show in his face. Charlie says, "I don't mean to be rude, but this is more important than dinner. It's not every day I get a chance to make ten thousand dollars so easily. I must leave now to make some phone calls."

The major looks disoriented as Charlie stands up. Charlie, excited now that he has a reason to leave, says, "Tell Dolores that I am sorry about dinner, but something very important came up. I know you can explain it to her."

The major, now wishing he hadn't said anything, says, "Maybe you could wait till after dinner. How far is your hotel from here?"

Not thinking, Charlie says, "My hotel isn't far at all. It's only four or five miles away."

The major quickly asks, "What's the name of it?"

Charlie doesn't want to answer this question. Nervous energy builds as the major waits for an answer. Finally, Charlie says, "I am staying at the Pine Tree Inn." He realizes he shouldn't have revealed this, but he had no choice; he doesn't want to make the major suspicious. His inner spirit is activated now by his first mistake.

Charlie glances at his watch and notices that twenty-two minutes have passed since Dolores and her mother left. He walks over to the major, shakes his hand firmly, and says, "I must leave now, but … I'll tell you what …"

The major stares at Charlie attentively.

"How would you like to play a game of golf?"

A long pause fills the room. The major finally answers, "Well, I guess so."

Immediately, Charlie says, "Excellent! Do you know where the Mountain Hills Golf Course is?"

The major nods. "Yes, I do."

Charlie quickly says, "I talked to the owner just today. He said tomorrow is Ladies' Day at the golf course. He told me if I could get there early, he would let me and anyone accompanying me tee off first. And with all those women playing, we won't be rushed or bothered—a perfect setting for us to understand each other better, a place where we won't be bothered."

The major scratches his head and says, "Okay. Sounds all right to me."

Charlie shakes the major's hand firmly and says excitedly, "I believe tomorrow we will work out everything I came here for."

The major smiles contentedly as he says, "Do you really think so?"

Charlie stares into the major's excited eyes. "Yes. I think tomorrow you and I will come to an understanding that will change both of our lives."

The major shows a stunned, bemused look and then laughs happily at Charlie. "Well, I hope we do too."

Charlie walks to the door and opens it. He glances at his watch. It has already been twenty-eight minutes since Dolores and her mother left. Charlie knows he needs to hurry before she comes back and interferes with his leaving. He turns to the major and says, "So I will see you at Mountain Hills tomorrow morning … say, eight o'clock sharp."

The major's face shows despair at Charlie's leaving. He knows he is going to catch hell from Dolores. "Yes, I will be there at eight o'clock sharp. But couldn't you wait until after dinner to leave? Dolores is really going to be sore at me if you aren't here when they get back."

Charlie smiles at him. He knows the major is going to be held responsible for his leaving, and he enjoys the thought of the major being bitched at because of his departure. "I know she might be disappointed, but just tell her I had to make an important phone call. She will understand." Charlie gives the major one last look and then turns and walks out of the house and toward his car. He leaves without seeing Dolores or her mother.

Five minutes later, Dolores and her mother drive up. Dolores immediately notices that Charlie's bright-red Mustang isn't there. She runs into the house and yells, "Daddy! Where is Charlie?"

Lester tries to explain why Charlie had to leave, but his daughter begins to cry as her mother enters the room.

Dolores screams at her father, "You said something to make him leave! It's all your fault he left!"

Dolores cries more profusely as her mother tries to calm her down. "Honey, please don't act this way. He will come back."

Lester says, "That's right, dear. He will be back. Charlie and I are playing golf tomorrow morning. I like him, dear. I didn't say anything to him to get him to leave. I tried to get him to stay for dinner, but he said he had to make a phone call. I gave him a very good offer on a piece of land and—"

Dolores cries, "I don't care about your stupid land deals!" Her crying begins to make her stutter. She acts wild as she continues to shout in a disturbed manner. "I love him! I love Charlie! And you had to ruin everything. I hate you! I hate you, Daddy! It's all your fault! He won't ever come back."

The major feels awful. He didn't think Dolores would react so angrily. The only thing in his life that is precious to him is his daughter. He has always spoiled her by giving her everything she ever wanted, but now he can't give her what she wants. He feels guilty and heartbroken. Hearing her speak to him like this is like a knife cutting away at his soul. He feels worse than he has felt in a long time. He tries to convince her that he will have Charlie over for dinner tomorrow, but she still behaves in a mean-spirited way toward him.

He says gently to Dolores, "Sweetheart, I didn't know you felt so strongly toward this young man. I promise you he will come to dinner tomorrow. Okay?"

Still crying, Dolores says, "He'd better come back tomorrow, or I will never speak to you again! I mean that! He left because of what you said to him. And I will never forgive you as long as I live if you don't bring him back here tomorrow!" She turns and storms to her room. At her door, she turns around one last time and says, "Daddy, how could you ruin my life by letting him leave? How could you?" She slams the door to her room.

The major just stands there heartbroken as he listens to his daughter crying. He walks away until his wife stops his sad walk.

She stares coldly at Lester as she says, "I didn't know she felt so strongly about him. You just better bring Charlie over for dinner tomorrow, or Dolores will be furious for months. You know how long she stays mad if she doesn't get her way. She will expect to see him tomorrow night for dinner now that you promised her."

Gruffly, the major says, "He will come to dinner tomorrow. I'll make damn sure he does. I will make damn sure!"

Charlie arrives at his hotel. He can't believe how well things are going. He feels like a million bucks. But there is one thing bothering him, like a thorn in his side. He told the major exactly where he is staying. This mistake plagues Charlie's mind.

After entering his room, Charlie takes one look at the telephone and picks it up. He does make a phone call after all, just as he told the major he would. He calls Wayne Scott to check up on Little Charlie. Wayne tells him that his little basset hound is doing fine. Charlie is happy to hear Wayne's voice. He needs to feel that there is someone there to talk to.

After Charlie finishes talking with Wayne, he studies tomorrow's plan. Earlier that day, he rented the golf clubs and paid the cart and green fees at the Mountain Hill Golf Course. He is ready for tomorrow. The weather report calls for sunny skies and warm sunshine. All Charlie needs is for the major to show up. Charlie has everything worked out.

Charlie tries to concentrate on tomorrow's plan, but worry over having told the major where he is staying continues to surge through him like an electrical current. Charlie knows he can't stay here. He must relocate, right now!

Charlie jumps off the bed, gathers all of his stuff, and hurries to the car. He drives twenty miles to another motel. He gets a room at the Chasten Motel and signs in as William Delaney. Since Charlie's middle name is William, he isn't falsifying anything. He is signing his true name.

Charlie unloads all of his stuff and then lies back and rests for about an hour. He then reconsiders being dishonest about where he is staying. *Maybe this isn't such a good idea*, he thinks. He thinks for a while and then decides to spend the night back at the Pine Tree Inn.

Charlie stops off for a burger at a fast food place before returning to his room. He feels confident as he parks his little red Mustang. Then he spots something hanging on the door to his room. A rush of horror floods Charlie. He looks around to see if anybody is there. He gets out of his car with caution. His legs shake as he approaches the door. His terror is fully realized when he sees that the note is signed by Major Lester Cain.

Charlie stuffs the note in his pocket, hurries into his room, and quickly locks the door. Once inside, Charlie walks around the room in a nervous fit. His hands begin to shake at the realization that the major came here. He pours himself a glass of water and drinks it quickly. He then gets himself another one. After he has settled down a little bit, he sits on the bed, takes the note out of his pocket, and carefully reads it.

Dear Mr. Delaney,

My daughter was furious with me because you left before she came back. I came by to see if you would stop by and reaffirm to her that you didn't leave because of something I might have said to you. I don't like to see my daughter angry at me this way. I hope you will make up this rude act to my daughter. I will see you at the Mountain Hills Golf Course tomorrow at eight sharp! Don't be late!

Lester Cain

P.S. Where have you been? I have waited almost an hour!

Charlie collapses on his bed with fright. He knows that the major is mad at him now. He thinks out loud, "My gosh! What if I had stayed at the Chasten Motel? I never would have seen this note! The major would have brought this note up tomorrow, and then he would have realized I didn't stay here. He would have become suspicious. Who knows what would have taken place then? He would have caught me in a lie. Boy, am I glad I was truthful about where I was staying. That one deceptive thing would have been the end for me. Just one white lie would have meant curtains for me and my game plan."

Charlie lies back on his bed with grave concern. The thought of packing up everything and aborting the mission enters his mind. His thoughts are filled with images of terrible things that have not happened. They rush into his mind like a flood.

As Charlie thinks, a vision of Corporal Spencer telling his story comes to his mind. He sees the weary, depressed face of the corporal very clearly now. He doesn't want to end up like the corporal, so he makes himself think positively.

Charlie picks up the black duffel bag and lays it on the bed. He takes out the half-full bottle of Jack Daniel's' Black Label whiskey. Charlie knows that if he quits now, he might end up like the corporal. The major might do some probing and come looking for him. Charlie would have to live with a troubled, worried mind for the rest of his life, wondering if the major will one day knock on his door. Now that his daughter has taken a special liking to Charlie, the major would have an extra incentive to come looking for him. Charlie knows that he can't quit now. He has gone too far to back down. He presses on.

The true force of Charlie's inner character starts to take control of his negative thoughts. He doesn't let the negative forces persuade him to quit. Charlie battles the enemy from within with strength and courage. He pushes the negative thoughts aside and tries to focus clearly on what is really taking place.

Charlie's fright begins to die down some. He thinks, *The major isn't going to come back tonight, so don't panic, Charlie ole boy.* He reminds himself that this man caused the suffering of Karen and Elizabeth. Dee is in her grave too because of the indirect actions of this man. Charlie quietly tells himself, "I will not yield! If it costs me my life,

I will gladly give it just to see that this man is punished. I don't have anything significant in my life to go back to anyway." He knows that if he doesn't finish what he's started, he will hate himself. He will feel that he let down Elizabeth, Karen, and Dee. *I must not let these stupid negative thoughts take hold and persuade me to be a quitter,* he decides. *I must not trick myself into stopping now. I must finish my mission. I will finish my mission!*

Determined, Charlie gets up from his bed and walks to the table where he left his bags. He takes out the photographs of Dolores and the major. He looks at them until he isn't afraid of their faces anymore. Charlie then gets an idea. He says to himself, "Hmm. Since Dolores seems to have a strong liking for me, maybe I can use that to my advantage and make my original plan even better." Charlie thinks about his new plan. He redesigns it to give it an extra kick, working on it until late in the night. He has key phrases he wants to say and backup ideas to use if everything doesn't fall into place.

Charlie draws a few signs with a Magic Marker and carefully places them in his black duffel bag, along with a few other things he will need for tomorrow. He has everything ready. He sets the alarm clock to go off at six o'clock. He cuts the lights and then takes off his clothes. As he lies in the strange bed, he remembers how wonderful it was to reach over and touch Elizabeth's soft, warm, loving body. His heart aches for her loving touch now. He yearns for her fragrant scent to arouse his senses, but he knows he will never feel her feminine touch again. His actions tomorrow will be primarily for Elizabeth, the one woman with whom he became bonded through his love, not just his lust. He remembers how happy she made him feel. The memories he made with her give him strength and determination to carry on with the plan. He eagerly waits for tomorrow to come.

The sound of the alarm clock comes early for Charlie and brings him to his feet immediately. He hurries and takes a shower. He dresses in shorts and a T-shirt. He puts all his cargo back into his car and leaves the room empty except for a sign that hangs from the overhead light.

Charlie drives straight to the golf course. A nervous energy fills his stomach as he makes the long drive. He picked this golf course because it is so far away from the major's house. He didn't want the course to be a local hangout of his. Charlie has everything worked out in his head, but he knows that everything doesn't always go as planned. He has backup plans if the main plan doesn't work out.

Charlie's thoughts are of Elizabeth as he drives up to the clubhouse. He arrives there at 7:30 a.m. Carrying the black duffel bag, he heads for the front door of the clubhouse. After walking in, Charlie spots the man behind the counter with whom he spoke yesterday. Charlie walks over to him and says, "Hello there, Barney. Have you got my clubs ready?"

Barney smiles gladly. "Yes, sir, Mr. Delaney." His voice is strong and deep. "When you told me yesterday that you had an important game you wanted to play today, I thought I would let you use my clubs instead of just the rentals. Since you are paying twenty dollars to rent a set of clubs, I thought you should have a nicer set." Barney hands his golf clubs over to Charlie.

Charlie's eyes light up. He says, "Oh yes! These clubs will do just fine. You have a nice set of clubs, Barney."

Barney grins. "Yes, they are a nice set. I hope you do well with them today, Mr. Delaney." Barney pauses before saying, "This must be some golf game you have scheduled for today, Mr. Delaney. I don't think I have ever had anybody come in here a day ahead and pay for the green fee and cart fee, rent my clubs, plus give me a tip just to tee off. Most people just wait until the day they play, just in case they don't make it in."

Charlie gives Barney a self-assured smile as he is handed the keys to the golf cart. Charlie's self-esteem begins to come alive; he is enjoying every minute. He is in a happy frame of mind and is in complete control of everything. He waits patiently for the major's arrival.

At exactly eight o'clock, the major walks through the door. He spots Charlie right away sitting at a table. Charlie gives the major a wry smile as he begins to walk toward his table.

The major is wearing shorts, a T-shirt, and golf shoes. He has a cap on his head that reads, "USMC Looking for a Few Good Men," in all caps. The major looks at Charlie with a peculiar stare and appears to be a little disoriented this morning. He frowns at Charlie as he says, "I just thought you would like to know that my daughter isn't speaking to me this morning."

Charlie smiles at the major anyway and says, "Please, Major, sit down."

The major sits down, but he still stares at Charlie with a rough expression. The look he gives Charlie is chilling, but Charlie is enjoying it. The major asks, "Didn't you get my note I taped to your door last night?"

Charlie, cool as a cucumber, looks directly at the major with a smirk on his lips and says, "Yes, I read your note. I didn't know Dolores had such a crush on me. She is a nice girl. Don't worry. I'll make it up to her."

The major quickly asks, "When? I promised her that you would come for dinner tonight."

Charlie replies exuberantly, "That's sound like a terrific idea! I gladly accept." Charlie doesn't bat an eye while he speaks. His nonchalant behavior seems to relax the major, but he notices the major still isn't completely happy. "I hope you aren't angry at me. The last thing in the world I want is for you to be angry at me."

The major speaks the words Charlie was hoping to hear. "No, I ain't mad. I just don't like to see my daughter mad at me. She is my baby girl."

With a happy expression Charlie says, "I understand. You are just looking out for her best interests. Any good father would act the same way. She is lucky to have a father as concerned as you are."

The major cracks a smile and quickly says, "You're absolutely right, Charlie. Kids these days don't appreciate anything you do for them."

Charlie responds, "You're right, major. They expect everything to be given to them like money grows on trees."

"You're absolutely right again, Charlie."

Before the major has time to say anything else, Charlie announces, "After reading your note last night, I got the feeling you were pretty angry with me … you know, the part about being rude for leaving."

The major is silent for a moment and then says, "Oh, that. Well, Charlie, don't—"

"So I went ahead and paid for our golf game. Everything is on me."

The major smiles contentedly. He pulls out cash to try to pay Charlie for the game, but Charlie says, "You just put that money back in your pocket. This game is on me. This is my way to make up for last night. That's the way I want it."

The major puts his money back in his billfold and asks, "Are you are coming to dinner tonight?"

Charlie grins heartily and says, "Yes, I will come over for dinner, and I'll tell you what—I'll bring Dolores a dozen red roses when I come, just to make up for last night."

The major produces a giant smile and says, "Charlie ole boy, you are all right. Now let's see how you hit a golf ball." The two men get up and walk toward the door in a happy state of mind.

Charlie walks out to the golf cart with his black duffel bag in one hand and his clubs in the other. He puts them both in the back of the cart and says, "Hey, Major. We'll just drive over to your car to get your clubs."

The major nods in agreement. "Okay, Charlie."

The two men jump into the golf cart, and the major shows Charlie where his car is. Since there are only two other vehicles in the parking lot, it isn't hard to find.

The major gets out of the golf cart and opens the trunk of his black Lincoln Continental to get his clubs. Charlie thinks, *Gosh. That sure is a big car. I wonder how many tricks his girls had to make and how many farmers lost their crop money to buy him such a car.*

The major displays a proud look when he spots Charlie staring at his car. "What do you think, Charlie?"

He replies, "Nice car."

"Would you believe that this car cost thirty thousand dollars?"

Charlie nods as the major fastens his clubs in the golf cart.

"Okay, Charlie. I'm in. To the first hole, my good man." The major speaks with a happy, clear, friendly voice. He is in good spirits now. Charlie pays close attention to the major's facial expression at all times. This is how he figures him out. It gives him the added advantage he needs.

Charlie stops the cart at the first hole. The two men take out their drivers and head for the tee. The major swings his club a few times to warm up. He gives Charlie a shit-eating grin and asks, "Do you want to make a bet on the game?"

Charlie thinks for a second and says, "How about a six-pack, just for the first nine holes?"

The major quickly agrees. "You will probably wear me out, Charlie. I usually hit in the high eighties. What do you usually hit? And be honest."

Charlie swings his club and says, "The last time I played, I finished in the nineties, but I had a good time."

The major puts his ball on the tee, takes a few practice swings, and then hits the ball high and straight.

"Wow!" Charlie says. "Nice shot, Major! Right down the middle of the fairway."

The major looks proud. Charlie walks up and places his ball on the tee. He takes a couple of practice swings and strikes the ball solidly. The ball goes straight at first and then begins to fade away to the right. It wasn't a good shot. Charlie turns his head and watches a distasteful, haughty grin form on the major's face. The major clearly feels superior to Charlie now. Charlie enjoys knowing that the major is feeling this way. He says, "I know I should hold my club in, but when I remember, it's too late."

"Maybe we should have made it two six-packs," the major says with a snicker. "No mind, Charlie. I thought you were going to drive it three hundred yards, straightaway." The two men walk back to the golf cart, and Charlie drives them to his ball.

Charlie takes out his three iron and whacks away at the ball. It gets close to the major's ball when it does finally stop rolling. Charlie remarks, "I don't play golf just to get the ball in the hole. I play golf to get to know the person I'm playing with. I enjoy learning about people as I play."

The major says, "You know, Charlie, that's a good way to be, but I would concentrate more on putting the ball in the hole unless you don't mind losing."

Charlie shrugs off the comment as he drives up to their balls. "So tell me, Major, how long have you been in the real estate business?"

"Ever since I got back from Vietnam."

Charlie keeps asking questions to get the major to say a key word that Charlie wants to hear. Charlie focuses on that key word, so that he can use it to learn other things he wants to know about.

Charlie asks, "I guess you gave orders over there that meant life or death?"

The major gives him a negative look as he replies, "Yeah. Why do you ask?"

Feeling that he is rubbing the major wrong, Charlie decides to talk about other things besides Vietnam, at least for now. He senses that the major doesn't like talking about Vietnam.

Charlie takes out his four iron and hits the ball close to the fringe of the green.

The major eagerly walks to his ball. He uses his four iron also and pops the ball straight up. It bounces and then rolls up on the green. The major jumps for joy when he sees his ball lying on the green.

Charlie watches the major's awful proud expression. His red face glows with an appalling, disdainful look. Charlie's stomach almost turns over as he hears Lester say, "Well, I'm there in two, Charlie ole boy. And you're close to the fringe on three."

Charlie just smiles gladly for the major, to boost up his ego a little more. "Yes, siree. That was a nice shot, Major. Right up there on the green."

Lester shows a happy look of accomplishment as they both hop into the golf cart and drive to the green. Charlie hunts for his nine iron and putter. After finding them, he walks to his ball. The major walks beside him carrying only his putter.

Charlie looks around and notices it is going to be a beautiful day. Not a cloud in the sky. The sun is shining on the warm, green Tennessee landscape, but soon it will be hot. The golf course has its own special feel of excitement. The grass is well mowed and trimmed. The trees on the sides of the fairways and in the background provide a peaceful and pleasant view. The landscape gives a sense of a new, crisp, cheery adventure ready to happen, and Charlie feels a tingle of excitement.

Charlie chips the ball onto the green and then continues to study the major. He carefully watches as Lester gently strikes the ball with his putter. The ball stops short of the hole, and the major curses loudly and obnoxiously. After the major calms down, he putts the ball into the hole. He cries out, "A damn par! All I got was a damn par!"

Charlie, not saying anything, studies how Lester is reacting to missing his birdie putt. He realizes how irritated he becomes when he doesn't get his way. Charlie putts twice before his ball goes into the hole, getting him a double bogey.

When Charlie gets back to the golf cart, Lester has already recorded their score on the scorecard. He doesn't waste anytime bragging about his accomplishment. "Hey, Charlie. You're going to have to do better than that if you plan on beating me."

Charlie smiles a suave, cool smile. He stares at Lester's repugnant red face and says, "This is just the first hole. Before it's over, I will beat you like you have never been beaten before. I guarantee it!"

The major laughs wholeheartedly as they drive over to the second tee.

Charlie and the major take out their drivers and walk over to the tee together. Lester tees up. He drives his ball straight into the woods and immediately has a fit.

Charlie says, "Go ahead and hit another one, Major. You can take a mulligan if you want too."

Lester doesn't hesitate in placing another ball on the tee. He smiles at Charlie and says, "Thanks, Charlie. You are all right." The major swings his club and hits the ball down the center. It stops right at the edge of the fairway—a fairly good shot. He smiles that proud, repugnant grin of his again as he says, "Not bad, not bad at all. I am glad you reminded me of using a mulligan, Charlie ole boy. You know, most people only use them on the first hole."

Charlie doesn't say anything. He just smiles now that Lester is happy again. He wants to keep him happy. Charlie holds his breath as he walks up and places his ball on the tee. He strikes the ball with a little less force than last time. He manages to hit it straight but not as far as Lester.

The major bellows, "Hey, Charlie, if you plan on beating me, you're going to have to put your whole heart in it."

Charlie walks over to him and says, "I'll have to remember that."

Charlie and Lester drive to where their balls are lying. The major says, "Oh, by the way, Charlie, how are we making out on our business deal?"

"It's too early to say now, but before the day is out, everything will be said and done."

Lester looks glad to hear this. "Fine, fine. I hope we can settle this deal as soon as possible. I hope it doesn't linger on for weeks and weeks."

Stopping the cart, Charlie says, "I would say before our golf game is over, the final touches will have already been put into place."

The major, acting surprised, says, "Really? You sound as if you know what you are talking about, Charlie. I like you, Charlie. You seem to know how to handle things."

Charlie just sits there contentedly as the major prepares to hit his ball again.

The men continue to play their game with high spirits. Charlie keeps boosting Lester's ego every now and then with exuberant cheers and compliments. He never lets him stay upset very long. Charlie puts out the flames of anger and shrinks the boulders of frustration every time the major hits the golf ball poorly. Lester eats up Charlie's praise like a hog eating slop. Charlie feels out the major's inner weaknesses and studies the man with determination. Charlie doesn't talk about anything that he thinks might make Lester feel touchy or uncomfortable. Charlie lets the major feel superior to him all during the game, using praise and compliments to increase his trust in him. He is fattening him up like a turkey for Thanksgiving.

As Charlie and Lester drive up to the ninth hole, Charlie is three strokes behind. The major has been bragging on himself almost every hole.

Lester addresses his ball with his driver with a powerful swing. The ball takes off fast toward the right and makes a splash into a little pond there. A powerful force inside Charlie's mind urges him to laugh and ridicule the major about his shot. Hearing the major brag on himself so much has given Charlie a strong urge to laugh back. But Charlie stays in complete control of himself. He doesn't unbridle his tongue even though he wants to very badly. He just holds it in and doesn't say a single mocking word.

Charlie places his ball on the tee and strikes it at an angle toward the left. He doesn't want to make the same mistake the major did. The ball doesn't go a great distance, but it does land near the middle of the fairway. It was a good, safe shot.

Charlie drives Lester down to the pond, where the major grumbles as he throws out another ball. He strikes it with fury with his three iron. As Lester watches his ball fly through the air, Charlie studies how nasty the major's character is. With all his bragging and all his profanity, Charlie realizes that Lester Cain is just a rotten individual right down to the core. He is simply a nasty, vulgar man.

Charlie drives them up to their balls. Charlie makes a fairly good shot up the fairway, but Lester still has a problem hitting his. He slices it to the right and into a bunker. Charlie wants to put his fingers in his ears so as not to hear the vulgar language, but he doesn't.

Charlie makes his third shot. It lands on the green. The major swings his sand wedge, but the ball doesn't make it out of the trap. He then pulverizes it and sends the ball flying into the woods. Charlie adds all the strokes plus the two-shot penalty for losing a ball in the pond. Lester is laying a seven and is fit to be tied. Charlie keeps quiet so as not to anger him as he chips onto the green. Now the major is laying eight. Charlie putts twice before sinking the hole. Lester double-putts his ball before it finally goes into the hole. He ends up with a ten.

Charlie and Lester walk back to the cart. As they walk, Charlie asks, "What did you get, Major?"

Lester grunts, "Eight! A damn eight! What did you get?"

Charlie, not wanting to say anything out of place, says, "I got a six." He really got a five, and Lester really got a ten, but Charlie wants the major to win their little bet. He wants to make him happy.

After hearing that Charlie was only two strokes better on this last hole, Lester quickly realizes that he has won the first nine holes by one stroke. His nasty expression is replaced with a joyous grin. Charlie looks over the scorecard and says, "Major, it looks like I owe you a six-pack."

Lester says with enthusiasm, "Well, Charlie ole boy, let's go to the clubhouse. I am thirsty."

Charlie drives them to the clubhouse. The golf course is starting to fill with ladies now. Charlie looks at his watch; it is 10:25 a.m. Charlie and Lester sit down in the bar area, and Charlie calls out to Barney, "Let's have a couple of beers over here." Charlie pays for the beers and for a six-pack and then takes the two beers over to the table and sits down with the major. Charlie says joyfully, "Here you go, Major. This one is on me. Your six-pack will be on ice for the back nine. Is that okay with you?"

This makes Lester happier than a fat rat in a cheese factory. He smiles exuberantly and says, "Charlie ole boy, you are the nicest fellow I have met in a long time. The world needs more men just like you, son."

"Well, thank you, Major. I try to be."

Lester takes a long swig of his beer and says, "Enough with this Major bit. From here on, I want you to call me Lester."

Charlie gives the major a surprised look and says, "Okay, Lester." The two men drink their beer and talk openly and freely.

After they've both had a couple more drinks, Lester has forgotten all about those two strokes he didn't add on. He is guzzling down the beer like someone who really has beaten Charlie. As the major becomes intoxicated, he looks over to Charlie and says, "Charlie ole boy, I hope you and Dolores hit it off. I wouldn't mind having you as my son-in-law."

Charlie beams with delight when he hears this. "I am glad you think so, Lester. I have an idea!"

The major excitedly asks, "What?"

"How would you like for me to call Dolores at work and surprise her? She will get a big kick out of hearing that I am with you, playing golf."

The major raises his bottle of beer and with a big smile on his face says, "That would be great! That would just make my day, Charlie ole boy."

Charlie gets up and says, "Stay right here while I make the call. I have her work phone number right here." Charlie pulls a scrap of paper from his pocket and shows the number to the major before he leaves.

Charlie looks over at Barney and says, "Hey, Barney. Bring another beer to Lester while I use your phone." Charlie throws him a couple of bucks, which Barney quickly pockets.

Charlie is gone for about ten minutes to make his call. When he returns, he sits down next to the major with a big smile. "Well, I had a lovely talk with your daughter. Everything is set between you and her and me now."

This adds more bliss to the major's already jubilant frame of mind. The major's attitude, thanks to the alcohol, is at its height now. He is feeling loose as a goose. His ego is inflated. He is happy that his daughter isn't mad at him anymore. The carefree feeling of intoxication gives Lester Cain a sensation of being in paradise. Lester is now vulnerable to anything Charlie might subject him to. He is the fruit ready to be picked.

Charlie turns up his beer and takes a long swig. He then says in a confident manner, "Well, Lester, are you about ready to play the back nine?"

The major says kindly, "Let me go to the bathroom first." Lester stands and gives him a salute as Charlie happily stands to leave the clubhouse, heading for the golf cart. Before he leaves, he tells Barney to give the six-pack to Lester.

Barney smiles and says, "Yes, sir, Mr. Delaney. I will surely do that."

While Charlie is waiting, he feels a robust energy flood his soul. He just can't believe how well everything is going. All he has to do is brag on the major a little, hold his tongue, and zero in on what he wants to hear, he tells himself. Charlie looks around and notices quite a few women are playing today, all different types of women—young ones, older ones, and even some very attractive ones. Charlie sees them all heading for the first hole. It will be a while before any of them catch up to where he and the major will be, if they catch up at all.

The major comes outside with an open beer in one hand and his six-pack in the other. The six-pack is in a black plastic garbage bag with ice in it. Smiling from ear to ear, Lester says, "Okay, Charlie ole boy, let's hit it … Wait!"

Charlie stops the cart suddenly. "What's the matter, Lester?"

Lester turns to Charlie and says with a slur, "I wanna drive. You drove the first nine holes. I wanna drive the last nine."

Charlie smiles as he gets out. The two men exchange places. The major then drives them to the tenth hole.

Lester gets out his club, tee, and ball and then proceeds to tee up. Charlie takes his driver and knocks Lester's ball off his tee. "What are you doing?" Charlie says. "If my memory serves me right, I won the last hole."

The major, remembering this, says, "Oh yeah. That's right. I am in such a habit of going first I almost forgot that you won the last hole. Go ahead, Charlie ole boy. Go ahead."

Charlie puts his ball on the tee and, without taking any practice swings, addresses the ball straight down the fairway.

The major is impressed. "Nice shot, Charlie ole boy."

Charlie turns to the major and says, "Lester, that shot is how I interpret life."

The major looks confused. "How do you mean?"

With a blank expression, Charlie says, "When you travel down the path of life, always focus down the center. Don't stray to the left or the right but stay right down the middle. And when you find that you have stopped in the rough or a difficult place, always try to get back in the center. It's a great deal harder to get yourself out of the hazards and obstacles than it is to discipline your mind and body to journey down the straight and narrow path."

The major gives Charlie a somewhat meaningful look but doesn't say anything. Charlie turns and walks back to the golf cart. Lester drinks down the rest of his beer and simply hits his ball. The two men continue their game without much conversation.

Charlie studies the golf course layout on the back of the scorecard. Now that he is riding on the passenger side instead of driving, he has a better angle from which to study the major's face—his key element in figuring out what Lester is thinking.

The major drives the cart as though he owns the world. He talks wildly and flippantly about all the material wealth he has acquired over the years, and he implies that he has acquired this wealth because of his expertise in the real estate business. Lester shows great enjoyment in bragging to Charlie about how he has become such a successful businessman. Charlie doesn't talk much; he mainly listens to the major and watches him drink his beer with a gleam in his eye.

As they play, the major frequently offers Charlie one of his beers, but Charlie refuses them. Charlie has something else on his mind, something that he doesn't want to numb with alcohol. At the sixteenth hole, the major drives the golf cart up to the tee and stops. Charlie is losing by five strokes. Lester reaches back and pulls out another beer from his plastic sack of melting ice. He cracks open the ice-cold beer and says cheerily, "Hey, Charlie ole boy, there is one beer left, and I want you to have it."

Charlie gazes at the intoxicated fifty-two-year-old man with a look of domination and says, "Well … all right, Lester." Charlie reaches in the plastic sack and pulls out the frosty beverage. He places it in the cart's cup holder, unopened.

The hole is a short par three, so the two men pull out their nine irons. The major goes first. He strikes the ball hard and swift. The ball goes up high into the sky and lands just short of the green. Lester bellows, "Damn! I teed up too high. I got too much loft. Damn!"

Charlie, hearing this, tees his ball up only half as much as the major did. Charlie lines up the ball straight with the flag and swings his club with strength and determination. The ball leaves the tee on an upward climb with a sweeping *whoosh*. The ball lands right on the green and stops dead where it landed, only three feet away from the hole.

Lester lets out a cheer. "Nice shot, Charlie ole boy! Just think, if it wasn't for me, you wouldn't have made that shot."

Charlie grins at the major and says, "If it wasn't for you, I wouldn't be here at all." Charlie laughs, and the major looks at him curiously.

The two men hop into the golf cart and begin to drive to the green. Charlie pops the top of the ice-cold beer and begins guzzling it. By the time Lester stops the cart, Charlie has finished it. Charlie mashes the can abruptly with his right hand. The sound of the aluminum being crushed draws the major's attention. Charlie hurls the can into the air and into a nearby trash can.

The major says with a slight slur, "You sure drank that beer fast. I didn't know you could drink beer like that."

Charlie gives the major a wry smile and says, "There are a whole lot of things about me you don't know about."

The major just laughs as he gets out of the cart to fetch his pitching wedge and putter. He walks over to his ball and chips it on the green. He then putts the ball carelessly and misses. He goes on to putt it in for a bogey four. Charlie casually walks to his ball with his putter resting on his shoulder. He easily taps the ball in for a birdie.

Lester starts to laugh. He yells out, "Hey, Charlie ole boy, even with that birdie you are still losing by three strokes." The major laughs loudly and haughtily as Charlie walks back to the cart.

Charlie gives him a determined look as he says, "This next hole is where I rise up and beat you."

The major gives a dumb, intoxicating, shit-eating grin before he laughs out loud. He drives them to the next hole. Upon arrival, Lester turns the scorecard over and studies the layout of the seventeenth hole. It is a long par-five hole. There is a circle around the number 17, but Lester doesn't pay it any mind. He gets out of the cart and happily walks over to get his driver from his bag.

Charlie carefully watches how the major walks to the tee. He is slightly tipsy now but not too much. Charlie grabs his driver and follows right behind the major toward the tee.

Lester puts his ball on the tee and makes like he is going first. Charlie gives him a stern look and says, "Hey! What do you think you're doing?"

The major realizes his mistake, picks up his ball, and says, "I did it again. Sorry about that, Charlie ole boy. I guess I wasn't thinking again. Go ahead, Charlie."

Charlie gives the major a blank, empty expression. "You know, Lester, a friend of mine recently told me about a man who was absentminded for one brief moment. He told me that because of this man's thoughtless action and aggressive behavior, a tragedy resulted. And a lot of people had to suffer because of it."

Charlie places his ball on his tee as the major listens. Charlie stares back at Lester with the same blank expression. "This man's thinking was impaired by the consumption of whiskey. This man, with the help of the alcohol, caused the death of a very important and much loved man."

The major remarks, "That's terrible, Charlie. Did they find the man and prosecute him for the incident?"

Charlie takes a few practice swings with his driver and replies, "Yeah, they found him, but because he had clout and was a military man, he didn't have to answer for his crime. He was let go without even having to go to trial."

The major, showing a little emotion, says, "That's the way our sorry judicial system works. They don't attempt to prosecute criminals like they ought to. It sounds like the guy who did this crime should have been horsewhipped and then shot."

Having studied the major carefully as he spoke these words, Charlie turns and addresses his golf ball with force and fury, driving the ball straight down the fairway.

Lester shouts, "Wow! What a shot! That was the longest drive you have made all day. See what happens when you put your heart into it? Nice shot, Charlie."

Charlie responds, "It's amazing what you can do when you set your mind to it."

The major laughs as he tees up his ball. "With a shot like that, one might think you have been sandbagging all day just to give me the impression you don't know what you're doing."

Charlie replies boldly, "Oh, but you are wrong, Lester. I know exactly what I'm doing."

Lester looks gleefully at Charlie as he tees up his ball. Charlie watches the major with detestation as he hits his golf ball with a powerful strike. The ball flies into the air with great speed and direction. It travels down the fairway to the left and stops in the vicinity of Charlie's ball.

The major doesn't waste any time showing Charlie a proud look. Charlie gives the major another blank, empty expression.

"So what do you think of my shot, Charlie ole boy?"

Charlie hesitates at first and then says, "I think it has landed left of mine. I believe we have finally arrived at the same place and point in our game."

"Except one thing, Charlie ole boy—I am three strokes behind you." Lester laughs as he gives Charlie an intoxicated, proud look.

"You might be winning by three strokes, but I am on the verge of taking over."

Lester laughs again as they walk back to the cart.

Charlie looks at the major carefully as he puts away his driver. Solemnly, he says, "Remember when I told you about the man who got away with causing another man to die unnecessarily?"

"Yeah, I remember."

"That man never saw all the heartache and suffering because he never saw this man's family trying to survive without him. Let me ask you something, Major."

"Go ahead, Charlie."

"Let's say someone was responsible for the death of, say, your father-in-law and you saw how your wife and mother-in-law had to suffer throughout the years because of one man's absentminded, muddled act." The major and Charlie sit down in the cart, with the major still listening to Charlie as he begins to drive off. "And then one day you encounter this man. And you know what he did because of the overwhelming evidence against him. You know, without a shadow of a doubt."

The major listens to Charlie in a carefree manner. He drives slowly so that he can hear him more clearly.

"But this man has completely forgotten all about this incident for which he was responsible. He has lived quite comfortably throughout the years while your wife and mother-in-law have had to live with hardship and depression. Tell me then, Major, what would you do if you caught up with this man?"

The major smiles deviously and says, "Killing this man would be too easy. I would first torture him a little with the help of a few buddies of mine. Then, after I tortured him a few hours, I would take him to a remote area where nobody could hear his screams."

Charlie gets angry as he hears the major's response. These evil words begin to activate the volcano in Charlie's soul.

The major continues, "I would tie this man to a small tree and pour a five-gallon container of gasoline on him. I would then ignite him with a torch and delightfully watch him burn to ashes."

Charlie is appalled by the major's words. They have almost arrived at the location of the two golf balls when Charlie says, "Mr. Cain, the man who told me who this man was … is Philip Spencer."

The major stops the cart abruptly. His happy face turns into a concerned one. "Who?"

Charlie turns to the major and stares at him with a look of hate. "My friend's name is Philip Spencer. You might know him as Corporal Spencer of the United States Marine Corps. He told me you are this man, Major." Charlie reaches over and removes the key from the golf cart. And so it begins!

The major looks at Charlie with fright and panic. He says, "What in hell would you be talking to him for? Why … what … when did you …? Don't pay any attention to him, Charlie. He is a liar and a disgrace to the uniform of the Marine Corps."

Charlie smiles wryly and says, "He told me you gave the order to fire at a United States Air Force colonel, which resulted in his death."

Now getting jumpy, Lester says, "That's a lie! Don't believe what he told you, Charlie. He is nothing but a damn liar!"

Charlie gets out of the cart and walks around to where the major is sitting. Lester shows more panic, and his face becomes angry as he says, "What the hell is going on here? What the hell?"

Charlie jerks the major out of the cart, slaps him in the face, and then throws him on the ground. "You are the one!" he shouts. "You are the one who gave the order that killed Colonel Alan Thomas!"

The major begins to shake with fright. He jumps up from the ground and begins throwing punches. Charlie ducks two of his swings before striking the major across the face, hard. This knocks the major down. Charlie strides over and picks the terrified drunk up off the ground. He throws three hard shots to the major's gut. Charlie then opens his right and left hands and begins to slap the major repeatedly. Time after time after time, Charlie slaps Lester harshly in the face.

The major falls to the ground again and cries out, "Stop! Stop!" The fifty-two-year-old man is no match for Charlie's youthful strength.

Now that Charlie has administered the softening-up process and put fear into his soul, he goes ahead with his plan without delay. Charlie's voice is loud and forceful. "Let me tell you who Alan Thomas was, you drunken coward! He was the father of my first wife! She had to grow up without her daddy being there to help raise her. She was denied a daddy because of you!" Charlie angrily points his finger at the major.

The major pleads, "It was an accident!"

Charlie shouts, "Shut up!" He walks back to the golf cart and retrieves the black duffel bag he has been carrying all along. They are right in the middle of open ground with nobody in sight.

Lester jumps up and attempts to run away. Charlie hurries after him with agility and quickness and brings him down from behind. Charlie gets on top of him and slaps him around a few more times. He then drags him back to the golf cart and the black duffel bag.

Charlie bellows, "Don't you try that again, you stupid imbecile! Do you understand me?"

Lester, shaking from his drunken stupor, says, "Yes … yes … I understand."

Charlie says with authority, "Just to make sure, I want you to take off your shoes and socks, right now!" Charlie's harsh voice leads the major to remove them quickly.

Charlie walks over to the duffel bag and takes out a microcassette recorder. He turns it on and then pulls out two cameras, a 35mm camera and a Polaroid. Charlie puts the 35mm camera around his neck and keeps the Polaroid in his hand.

Charlie looks down at the major and says, "Get up, you drunken slob. Get up!"

The major hurries to his feet.

Charlie bellows, "Now tell me what you were about to say, something about an accident."

His voice cracking, the major says, "It was an accident; I didn't know he was one of ours."

Charlie looks up to the sky and cries out, "Elizabeth! Can you see me, Elizabeth? I have found the man who killed Alan. He has just confessed to me. Can you hear me, Elizabeth? Don't worry. I will make sure he gets punished for what he did."

The major looks at Charlie as if he's crazy. He pleads, "Please, Charlie, it was just a mistake. I didn't know it was Red Man. I never would have given that order if I had known. Please believe me."

Charlie snarls at the pitiful old man. "Oh, I believe you all right, you dirty, rotten killer. Do you know who Elizabeth is, Lieutenant?"

Lester asks, "Lieutenant? Are you all right, Charlie?"

Charlie screams, "Am I all right? You are the one who is shaking like a leaf. I am just fine, Lieutenant. That's right! Lieutenant! I just demoted you to lieutenant."

Lester's expression becomes more terrified as Charlie screams.

"I said, do you know who Elizabeth is?"

Lester shakes his head.

"She was my wife. She was my wonderful wife." Charlie's face is full of emotion and anger and hate now. "She was also Colonel Alan Thomas's wife—you know, the man you had killed over in Nam, at Chu Lai!

"You see, Lieutenant, you don't need to die before you stand for Judgment Day—because your Judgment Day has arrived today!" Charlie takes a picture with the 35mm camera. "For killing Colonel Alan Thomas, I command you to take off you shirt and shorts, right now!"

Lester begins to take off his shirt slowly.

Charlie bellows, "Faster, you swine! Faster! If those clothes aren't off in one minute, I am going to come over there, crawl on top of you, and hit your slimy, nasty face until you can't see straight. So move it, Lieutenant!"

Lester hurries frantically to remove his shirt and shorts. They are off in less than thirty seconds, just like Charlie ordered.

After Lester has removed his clothes, Charlie announces, "You see, you dirty killer, I came all the way from North Carolina to settle this score with you. My wife Elizabeth developed a serious heart ailment because of you. She experienced hardships and worried tremendously because of the doubt she had about her former husband. She thought he was a POW all those seventeen years. You see, Lieutenant, the air force lied to her about his unfortunate death. She was only thirty-nine years old when she died a couple weeks ago. And she died because of your drunken ass, Sergeant!"

Lester looks at Charlie with a scared, curious look.

"That's right. Sergeant. I have just demoted you again." Charlie smirks and then resumes yelling. "Okay, Sergeant, throw those clothes over here, and remember, if you raise your hand to me, I will be all over you like black on molasses! Do you understand me, Sergeant?"

Lester quickly answers, "Yes, Charlie. I understand." He throws the garments to where Charlie is standing. Lester is now standing in only his underwear. Charlie takes another couple of snapshots with the 35mm camera and one with the Polaroid as Lester stands there disgraced.

Charlie says, "There is another person whose life was tarnished by your stupid act. That person is Corporal Philip Spencer. His life was ruined by the dishonorable discharge he got, because of the wicked plot you conceived to destroy him."

Lester shakes with fear as he listens. Charlie reaches in the black duffel bag and pulls out the half-full bottle of Jack Daniel's Black Label whiskey. He tosses it to Lester. Charlie bellows, "Does this look familiar, Sergeant?" He doesn't wait for an answer. "This is what you poured out after you killed the colonel. I guess you didn't want to get caught drinking on duty, or maybe you just wanted to destroy the evidence. So tell me, Sergeant, did you devise a plan to destroy the reputation of Corporal Philip Spencer? Did you do this because he told your superiors about seeing you drinking on duty?"

Lester confesses in a scared voice, "Yes. I planned the—"

"Speak up, Sergeant! My little recorder can't pick up your wimpy voice."

Lester shakes as he says in a louder voice, "Yes. I am responsible for having Corporal Spencer dishonorably discharged from the marines. I arranged it. I did it." Lester Cain is in tears now. His shame and humility have reached an all-time high.

Charlie shouts, "Okay, Corporal. I want you to drink the entire bottle now. Yes, that's right, I have demoted you once again. I want you to have what you missed out on then."

Lester takes a short swallow.

Charlie yells, "I said I want you to drink the entire bottle! So drink it, you good-for-nothing drunk!"

The newly born corporal begins to drink the amber liquid faster. Some of it runs down his face as his whole body shakes and quivers, but he does finish the entire bottle.

As Lester drinks the whiskey, Charlie takes a couple of snapshots of him with the Polaroid camera and flips these photos over to him. Charlie takes a couple more with the 35mm. Charlie then reaches into the black duffel bag once more and takes out three small signs, each with a different statement written on it:

I gave the order that killed Colonel Alan Thomas.

I destroyed Philip Spencer's military reputation.

I am a pimp, a drunk, a hoodlum, and a gambling boss.

Charlie makes Lester hold each sign up as he takes his picture. He takes one of each sign with the Polaroid, which he throws to Lester, and then several with the 35mm. Charlie makes him hold the bottle up to his lips while he takes the pictures. It is here that a yellow stain appears on Lester's underwear.

After he is through with the signs, Charlie says, "Now, Private, I want you to stand on one foot. That's right! I have demoted you all the way down to a private. Do it!"

Lester does what Charlie says without question. Charlie laughs as he continues to take pictures. Charlie gives Lester a mean look as he says, "Oh, by the way, Lester ole boy, you know that phone conversation I had with your ugly daughter?"

Lester glares at him.

Charlie continues, "I told her it was all your fault I didn't have dinner with her last night. I told her it was because of you that I will never see her again. When you get home tonight, she is really going to hate you. She may never speak to you again."

Lester gets bold and says, "I'll kill you for this! I swear on my mother's grave, I will kill you for this!"

Charlie removes the 35mm camera from around his neck and walks over to Private Cain. Lester tries to fight once again with Charlie, and Charlie strikes him in the face repeatedly. Charlie brings him down and gets on top of him and says, "Privates don't make threats to their commanding officers. This is what they get when they do." Charlie slaps Lester across his face hard, time after time after time. This goes on for several minutes.

Charlie then orders him back to the golf cart. Lester does exactly as Charlie says, hurrying back as Charlie walks over to where the black duffel bag is lying. Charlie pulls out a can of yellow spray paint and yells, "Okay, Lester ole boy. Now drop those drawers, and I mean right now!"

Lester pleads, "Please, Charlie, don't make me do that."

"Shut up, you big sissy," Charlie snaps. "Now do what I told you to do! Pull off your underwear and toss them over here. Right now!"

Lester slowly pulls off his underwear and tosses them in the pile with his other clothes.

Charlie laughs outrageously as he stares at his completely naked private. "Private, you look plumb ridiculous. I don't think I have ever seen anybody look more stupid than you do. Ha!"

Lester's face is full of humiliation and shame.

"You know, you are out of uniform now," Charlie informs him. "Do you know what happens to privates who are out of uniform?"

Lester doesn't say anything. He just stands there naked as a jaybird with a terrified look on his face. He notices the can of spray paint and begins to tremble. He shakes like Elvis Presley in 1968.

*He is all shook up!* Charlie thinks with a laugh. Charlie walks over to Lester and says, "Turn around, you worthless drunk. The penalty for being out of uniform is this." Lester turns around, and Charlie shakes the can and sprays a yellow streak down Lester's back. He sprays it again and again. Lester just stands there, without saying a word.

Charlie asks, "Tell me, Private, how many whores do you have working for you? How many daughters of other men do you have prostituting for you?"

Lester begins to cry and blubber in response.

After Charlie is finished spraying Lester's back with the yellow paint, he walks back to the duffel bag and puts everything back inside, except the Polaroid camera. He yells out, "So tell me, Private, how many young girls do you use as whores to make you rich?" Charlie takes a snapshot of Lester as the man cries and stands there naked. He throws the naked picture of Lester over at him. Charlie continues to take more pictures of Lester while he stands naked, until the cartridge's last picture has been taken, ten altogether.

Charlie puts the Polaroid camera back into the black duffel bag and returns the bag to the golf cart. He gathers Lester's clothes and puts them on the golf cart too.

Lester becomes panicked and anxiously says, "You aren't going to take my clothes away. Please don't do this to me, Charlie."

Charlie bellows back, "Shut up, you pitiful piece of shit! You came into this world with nothing, and I shall leave you in this world with nothing."

Lester falls to his knees and begins to cry and beg desperately. His whining voice cracks as he says, "Please don't leave me here without any clothes. It is a long way to the clubhouse."

Charlie snaps back, "How many mothers and fathers have cried because their daughters became whores? How many thousands of dollars did you make from their disgraceful and shameful acts? How many farmers lost their hard-earned crop money because of your gambling organization? How much heartache have you caused? You are the lowest form of life."

Lester is hysterical now. Charlie looks up to the sky and cries out, "Look, Elizabeth! Look at the man who has caused you so much grief. Look at him now, Elizabeth. I have punished him good, my love. He knows what it feels like to experience the shame of his hidden past. He feels the burning fire of shame from his self-inflicted sinful life. Can you see me, Elizabeth? Can you hear me?"

Lester looks up at Charlie talking to the sky. He sobs more tears of shame and despair. Charlie, still looking up, says, "Can you see me, Karen? Can you hear me? I have punished the man who killed your daddy. He has felt the pain you suffered. I love you, Karen. I love you."

Charlie walks over to the kneeling, crying man and says, "Just want you to know something, Private. I am going to send the United States Marine Corps and the air force complete documentation on what went on here, complete with pictures and the recording of your confessions. They will know what you did to Colonel Thomas and to Philip Spencer. You will be hearing from them soon. Then they can punish you again for your past sinful life, you worthless, pitiful piece of shit! Soon your whole life will be exposed to the world, you evil man."

Lester cries out, "No, Charlie! Please don't do that!"

Charlie snaps back, "Shut up, you whining heap of shit! Now, after the military has received the report, I am going to send these pictures to your wife and daughter."

Lester cries out more desperately in his hysterical drunken state, "No, no, no! Please don't send them those pictures! Please don't!"

Not yielding to Lester's pleas, Charlie says, "Then, you low-life scum of the earth, I am going to mail a copy of these pictures and recording to the *National Query* magazine. They really enjoy printing up stories about such matters. You will be famous all over the country, Lester. Your name and face will be in millions of households."

Lester crawls over to Charlie and looks up to him in a pitiful state.

He begs pathetically, "Charlie, I will give you one hundred thousand dollars if you will give me my clothes back and promise not to do these things."

Charlie laughs. "Do you think you can buy your way out of this? Money can't buy you out of everything, or don't you know that?"

Lester pleads, "I will give you two hundred thousand dollars. Please don't do these things."

Charlie gazes down at the pathetic-looking man and says, "I told you, you piteous piece of shit, money isn't going to get you out of this. Money doesn't rule the world. It never has. The only ones who think it does are scum like you who latch onto it to perpetuate evil. Money has enticed you to use people as if they were nothing more than worthless pieces of flesh."

Charlie turns and looks away from Lester. He notices a group of women golfers standing up at the seventeenth tee. He hurries to get into the cart. Lester, seeing the lady golfers, jumps up and tries to convince Charlie one more time. Charlie gets out of the golf cart and walks over to Lester. He gives him a punch in the gut and pushes him to the ground. "You'd better gather up your ten photographs before those ladies get down here. You wouldn't want them to get an early preview." Charlie laughs out loud as Lester scrambles for the photographs.

Charlie gets in the golf cart and puts the key back in the ignition. He tosses Lester's wallet and the keys to his car in Lester's direction. "Here you go, crybaby. I wouldn't want you to think I was robbing you," Charlie says, laughing.

Lester looks at Charlie in a state of shock. He grabs up his wallet and car keys from the ground.

Charlie says, "Oh, by the way, Lester ole boy, tell your ugly daughter Dolores that I won't be having dinner with her tonight. You can tell her that I will be busy sending off some pictures. I know you can explain it to her, Lester ole boy. And one more thing, Lester ole boy—would you tell her something for me?" Charlie pauses as Lester stands up quietly. "Tell her that her breath stinks real bad. She might want to try a different mouthwash." Chuckling, Charlie starts the golf cart and drives off, leaving Lester Cain naked and completely dumbfounded.

The golfers at the seventeenth tee are making their second shots when one of the four ladies spots a naked man at the edge of the fairway, about one hundred yards away.

"Lordy be! I don't believe it! I just don't believe it," says one of the ladies.

"What's the matter, Kathy?" asks her friend Kay.

Kathy points as she says, "Kay, there is a man down there."

"So what's the big deal about that?"

Kathy announces excitedly, "But the man is naked!"

Kay spots the man walking on the edge off the fairway. She too reacts with disbelief. "I see him! My Lord! You're right, Kathy. He doesn't have any clothes on! Let's go tell Eleanor about this. She will get a big kick out of seeing him." The two ladies laugh as they run over to Eleanor.

Kay cries out, "Eleanor! Eleanor! Come here. Kathy and I want to show you something."

Eleanor's curiosity is piqued by Kay's enthusiasm. She walks over to Kay and Kathy and says, "Yes? What is it?"

Kay points her finger at the man and says, "Look down there! There is a man walking down there, and he ain't got no clothes on!"

Eleanor sees him, and her mouth falls open. She says, "Glory be to Jesus! I ain't never in my life …" Eleanor turns to Kathy and says, "I don't believe it. That man is walking stark-naked in the middle of the day right out where God and everybody can see him. I can see now that this man needs the help of the Lord."

Kathy, Kay, and Eleanor are joined by Amy. Amy says, "What's going on? Have any of you seen my ball?"

Kay laughs. "No, I haven't seen your ball, but I've seen a naked man walking around down there." Kay points in the direction of the man.

When Amy sees him, her face turns red as a stop sign. "Oh my gosh! That man doesn't have any clothes on."

Eleanor says, "I can tell that man is troubled. Jesus once said, 'I was naked, and you clothed me.' Ladies, we have a mission to do for the Lord. We must lead this man in the direction of salvation."

Amy asks, "What about our golf game? We are only two holes away from finishing."

Eleanor responds, "Which is more important, Amy? This stupid game or leading this man to the path of righteousness?"

Kathy says, "Eleanor is right. I am tired of hitting this stupid little ball anyway. You hit it; then you chase after it. You hit it; then you chase after it. I would rather chase after that naked man."

The three other women give Kathy a peculiar look.

Kathy quickly says, "I mean, chase after him for the Lord."

Eleanor says boldly, "Ladies, to your carts! We have a mission to do for the Lord." The four women hop into their golf carts. Eleanor points at the man and cries, "Charge!" The four women proceed to drive toward the stranger as fast as their carts will take them.

Lester turns around and spots the two golf carts approaching him. He tries to walk faster, but without shoes on, he doesn't gain much ground. The ladies keep driving until they close in on him about halfway through the seventeenth hole.

He hears one woman tell the driver of her cart to drive right up to him, which she does. The woman who seems to be in charge calls out, "Hey, mister. Can I ask you a simple question? Why don't you have any clothes on? Has somebody done something to you?"

Lester turns around, trying to hide his private parts from the four women. He is completely humiliated. "No! Nobody has done anything to me. Leave me alone!"

A woman from the second cart says, "Then you ought to be ashamed of yourself, walking around without any clothes on."

The first cart's driver asks, "Hey, what's that yellow streak down your back supposed to mean? You aren't one of those druggies, are you?"

Lester bellows, "No! Will you ladies please go away and leave me alone?" Lester keeps walking as the four ladies creep along beside him in their golf carts.

The woman in charge says, "You look like you are troubled by something, mister. My name is Eleanor. My friends here are Amy, Kathy, and Kay," she says, pointing to them in turn. "Have you ever met Jesus?"

Lester replies angrily, "Are you crazy? Go away and leave me alone!"

Kay says, "Is she crazy? You are the one walking around with a yellow stripe on your back, stark-naked in the middle of the day." The other ladies laugh as they stare at Lester's wrinkled white butt.

This adds fuel to the fire of Lester's humiliation. He tries to walk faster, but the sticks and rocks slow down his pace.

Eleanor calls out, "Mister, don't you think it is time you met Jesus? He will bring you peace and happiness. He can lead you to the right road of salvation."

Kay blurts out, "He can even lead you to the road to J.C. Penney."

All the ladies roar with laughter. Even Eleanor has to take a few moments to get control of herself. She reminds the girls, "Now, ladies, we must behave like good Christian ladies are supposed to act. Remember, we are on a mission for the Lord."

Lester keeps walking as the ladies keep driving.

Eleanor says, "If you knew the Lord, you wouldn't be walking around lost or naked. Did you know he died for your sins, mister?"

Lester thinks, *I wish I was dead. I will kill him for this. I will kill Charlie for this.*

Eleanor keeps up with Lester. She keeps asking him questions, but Lester doesn't respond. The other ladies seem to be taking great enjoyment and amusement from the experience as they tag along and listen to Eleanor trying to win Lester's soul.

"If you knew Jesus, you wouldn't be in the position you're in now. Maybe you need to live your life for Jesus instead of for yourself. What do you think?"

Lester turns around and says, "I don't need you! I don't need Jesus! I don't need anything. Now leave me alone!"

Kay bellows, "You do need something all right, a pair of Fruit of the Looms." The ladies roar with laughter as Lester's face gets redder.

This keeps up until Lester passes the seventeenth green and walks onto the eighteenth tee. Eleanor continues to do most of the talking as the other ladies do most of the laughing.

Lester keeps on walking but at a slow pace. He walks until he is halfway up the eighteenth hole. It is a par four, so it won't take long now for him to reach his car. He can see the clubhouse. He continues to walk as the ladies snicker behind him.

Eleanor doesn't give up on Lester's soul. She says, "What are you going do when you get up there to the clubhouse? There are dozens of other ladies there. Are you going to expose yourself to them too? Jesus wouldn't want you to do that."

Lester turns around and stares at Eleanor. He covers his privates with one hand while he holds on to the pictures, his car keys, and his wallet with the other. Lester looks at Eleanor with desperation and despair. He says meekly, "Please give me something to cover myself with."

Eleanor smiles gladly and says, "I can see the Lord is working on you now. Jesus is talking to your heart. If you accept Him now, you will never have to walk down this path again. You don't want to travel down this road again, do you?"

Lester says, "No, I don't. Now will you give me something to cover myself?"

Eleanor asks, "Do you accept Jesus as your personal savior?"

Lester says modestly, "Okay, okay. I accept him. Now will you please give me something to cover myself with?"

Eleanor jumps out of the golf cart with jubilation. The other ladies just sit and watch with amusement as Eleanor says, "I have brought another lost soul to Jesus! Hallelujah!"

The three other ladies open their eyes wide as they and Lester realize what Eleanor is doing: she is starting to unbutton her blouse. Kathy yells, "What on God's green earth are you doing, Eleanor?"

Eleanor, looking quaint with spice in her eyes, replies, "This man needs to be clothed, so I am doing what Jesus would want me to. I am giving him my blouse."

The ladies continue to watch wide-eyed as Eleanor removes her blouse, exposing her small white bra to Lester. Eleanor says as she hands Lester her blouse, "I just want you to know, mister, that no matter what you do after you leave here, Jesus is the only man who died for your sins. If you really trust and believe in him, that will prevent you from burning in hell for your sinful life. You can know you will go and be welcomed into heaven when you die."

Lester looks at Eleanor with kindness and understanding as he thinks about what she just said.

Eleanor says with vigor, "Here, I give you my blouse in the name of Jesus."

Lester covers himself with the garment and begins walking again.

Looking down at her white bra with a carefree expression, Eleanor says, "I have done what my Lord wanted me to do. Amy, to the clubhouse."

When Lester gets close to the clubhouse, he is noticed first by a small group of ladies. They gather around like a pack of curious spectators, but with Eleanor's blouse wrapped around his waist, Lester makes it to his car without much more attention.

Lester finds his underwear, shoes, socks, shorts, and shirt lying on the hood of his car. His golf clubs are propped up against the back of the trunk. He quickly puts his clothes on as women begin to gather. Some of the ladies call their friends over to view the partially naked man getting dressed. A few spectators really get an eyeful, but most of the women just look on with curiosity and amazement, and some look angry about seeing the odd attraction.

Eleanor gets most of the attention when she comes riding up shirtless, with her chest stuck out like she is Joan of Arc. Her exposed white bra becomes an instrument of diversion while Lester hurries to finish dressing.

After Lester is dressed, he casts the blouse aside on the pavement like a piece of useless garbage and climbs into the car. He reaches under the seat and pulls out a .44 Magnum handgun. Everything Eleanor said to Lester earlier, he has tossed aside, just like her blouse.

He starts his car and heads straight for Charlie's hotel room in a rush. As Lester drives, he remembers Eleanor's words: "I just want you to know, mister, that no matter what you do after you leave here, Jesus is the only man who died for your sins. If you really trust and believe in him, that will prevent you from burning in hell for your sinful life. You can know you will go and be welcomed into heaven when you die." Lester smiles deviously as he cuddles his gun. He says out loud, "Those women were all crazy, especially that old woman who took off her blouse. She gave it to me because she thought Jesus would have wanted her to. Stupid females! Wait till I get my hands on that Charlie

Delaney. I'm going to blow his goddamn head off. I'm going to blow his ass to hell and back."

When Lester reaches the Pine Tree Inn, he runs straight to Charlie's room and knocks the door open with his body. He rushes into the room and looks around. He finds only a sign hanging from the overhead light:

You didn't think I would come back here, did you? You will never see me again. The world will soon learn of your hidden past. The shame will burn like fire!


Sincerely,


Charlie Delaney


P.S. You also have bad breath.

Lester stares at the sign with rage. Furious, he looks around the room, hoping to find something that might tell him where Charlie is. He doesn't find anything. He tears the sign up into small pieces and then leaves the room in a hysterical rage.

He doesn't know where to go or what to do. The alcohol has brought on a terrible hangover. Lester decides to go home. As he drives, he breaks down and begins to cry. He cries out to himself, "Soon everybody will find out. How can I live with myself when all this shit comes out?" He pulls off the road to finish his sobbing. He looks over and spots the Polaroid pictures lying on the floorboard. He bends over and picks them up. Once he begins looking at the humiliating pictures of himself, he begins to cry again, uncontrollably. He cries for more than an hour until, finally, he gets control of himself. He drives home.

Charlie drives to the Chasten Motel after leaving the golf course. He pulls his car around to a spot where nobody can see it from the main road. He quickly unloads all of the cargo from his car to his room and locks the door behind him. He falls on the bed, exhausted. He says out loud, "Well, Charlie ole boy, I am proud of you. You have done it. Now you must wait. The battle has been fought, but the war isn't over yet."

Charlie has made arrangements for the manager not to tell anybody he is staying there. He told him not to let any maids knock on his door for anything. A newspaper is to be dropped at his doorstep at exactly 9:00 a.m. and an evening newspaper at 6:00 p.m. Charlie slid the manager an extra forty bucks just to make sure everything would be done as he instructed. He lies on his bed and waits.

Lester drives his car up his driveway and parks it. He stuffs the pictures down his shirt. He quickly walks to the front door and goes inside. He goes to his special room and puts the pictures in a safe and then pours himself a stiff drink.

He sits and drinks until four thirty in the afternoon, when he hears the front door open. He hears footsteps coming closer and closer until the door is flung open. Standing in the doorway is Dolores. She stares at her father with a vicious look. She bellows, "Daddy! You … you … you lying, inhuman monster! How could you? How could you ruin my life and then lie about it to me?"

Lester, showing a worried, concern look, says softly, "Honey, please understand. I haven't lied to you. You know what that Charlie Delaney did to me today? He—"

"Don't start your lying again. Charlie called me at work and told me that you would tell me an outrageous story when I got home today. So don't lie to me, Daddy!"

Lester's pain and anxiety increase, and a couple of tears begin to trickle down his aged cheek.

Dolores too begins to cry, but not for him. Softly, she says, "Daddy, I'm not a very pretty girl. I didn't have any boys ask me out while I was in school. They didn't ask me out because I'm ugly."

Lester tries to speak, but Dolores doesn't let him. "Then along comes somebody like Charlie. I fell in love with him the moment I laid eyes on him. He was the man I always wanted to marry. Then you go and ruin my life!"

"I am not ruining your life!" Lester insists.

Dolores yells back, "When he called me today at work, he said the reason he didn't stay for dinner last night was because of you! He said because of you! So don't lie to me."

Lester yells back with fury, "I'm not lying to you! I haven't been lying to you!"

Dolores says bitterly, "Don't yell at me! Mama had to take your shit all these years, but I'm not going to take it."

Growing more anxious, Lester asks, "What are you talking about? I have given your mother this house and everything she has."

A rebellious Dolores says, "You are lying again. You have been mean to Mama. I have heard you call her those awful names. She told me about the time a couple of years ago when she entered this precious little room of yours."

Lester snaps back, "Shut up! I don't want to hear your mouth anymore."

Dolores smiles wryly. "Oh, but you are going to hear it. Mama told me she entered this stupid room without your permission. She told me that you stripped her down to her bare ass, and then you beat her with a paddle."

Lester furiously bellows, "She is lying! Damn it! She is a goddamn liar!"

Dolores says softly through her tears, "That just proves you lied to me about Charlie, Daddy. You wouldn't admit you're wrong if God Himself were in this room. I hate you, Daddy! I hate you! I hate you! I hate you!" Dolores turns and leaves the room, slamming the door behind her.

Lester puts his head down on the desk and cries like a child. He remains in his private room for ten minutes. Finally, he gets up and walks into the living room. The house is as empty as his soul. He walks out to his car, reaches under the seat, and pulls out the .44 Magnum. He takes it back with him into the house and walks back into his private room once more. He gathers the Polaroid pictures and goes out the back entrance of the room. He walks until he is directly behind his house, near the woods. He takes out his lighter and burns the pictures, one by one, until they are all destroyed. He starts to cry again. His hand shakes as he puts the barrel of the large gun deep inside his mouth. He pulls the hammer back and pulls the trigger, ending his life with a horrendously loud explosion.

Back in his rented room, Charlie is still lying on his bed. He looks out the window once in a while just to see what's out there. He finds it hard to rest. He feels like a soldier of Vietnam lying and waiting for something to happen. The time goes by slowly for Charlie. He continues to remain there on the field of battle in a war of the unknown.

Several hours later, it begins to get dark. Charlie feels more secure now that his car is covered by the darkness of the night. Charlie manages to fall asleep for a short period, but he is awakened every time a car door slams in the parking lot. He tells himself to be strong and not to let this unknown fear overwhelm him. He is ready for anything bad that might happen now. Charlie has executed his battle plan courageously and gallantly, but now he must continue to wait to learn the final outcome.

While Charlie sleeps, he feels strange forces of evil trying to penetrate his mind and soul. He struggles with this eerie force that feels so real in the room. Charlie wakes up again after only an hour or so of sleep. Charlie wrestles with this evil force all night. He sits up in his bed and says out loud, "Dear God in heaven, what evil presence has entered my room? Please cast this evil presence out." Charlie gets up and walks over to a chair. He stares at the walls of his room like they are the walls of a prison cell. He whispers to himself, "I believe I could live a hundred years if I could just get through this night." He doesn't try to go back to sleep. He doesn't want to experience any more of the evil dreams and thoughts plaguing him. He spends the rest of the night, until morning finally comes, reading the Bible.

Charlie waits for the newspaper to be dropped at his doorstep at exactly 9:00 a.m. When he sees the manager drop off the paper himself, he opens the door and picks it up. Back in his room, he looks over every page but doesn't read what he was hoping to see.

Around eleven o'clock Charlie calls and orders a pizza from one of the restaurants whose advertisements are near the phone. The pizza arrives forty minutes later. After Charlie has eaten a great deal of the pizza, he lies down on the bed and falls asleep.

Charlie awakes at 6:00 p.m. when he hears the afternoon paper being dropped at his doorstep. Charlie eagerly jumps up from the bed and retrieves the newspaper in a rush. He flips through the paper quickly, searching for something very specific. He looks over every page until he finds what he is looking for:

**Local Businessman Commits Suicide in Backyard of His House**

Lester Cain, a local realtor, shot himself yesterday afternoon around six o'clock. The suicide was possibly related to a fight he had with a family member earlier in the day. The family reported to the police that Mr. Cain has had a problem with alcohol for a great many years. It was reported that he was wandering around the Mountain Hills Golf Course Thursday without clothes. At the time of Mr. Cain's death, there was a large amount of alcohol in his blood. The local authorities said there will be no investigation into the matter.

Charlie flips to the obituary section just to make sure. There he reads Lester's obituary, which states that Mr. Cain is survived by his wife Sharon, his daughter Dolores, and his son Jimmy.

Charlie feels an enormously pleasant sense of relief. He knew that if Lester didn't take his own life, he would be after Charlie all the days of his life. Charlie risked everything to see that his mission was completed. Charlie's assumption paid off. He has won the war.

An evil man had to be stopped from hurting others. God's mission for Charlie has been accomplished. God worked through him in a very mysterious way, Charlie feels. Charlie overcame his fears and hardships. He knows that if he had inflicted any serious physical pain on the major, he too would have had to answer for it someday. Charlie executed the plan of battle not to inflict pain and suffering, but to expose the sins of Lester's past. Lester Cain then turned the cannons of death on himself and inflicted the mortal wound that would end his evil life by his own hand.

Relieved by the outcome, Charlie says to himself, "The battle has been fought. The enemy has been defeated. The war has been won. My mission has been completed. Time to go home. Yes, time to go home."

# Chapter 5
## THE OLD MAN RETURNS

Charlie arrives ho me Friday night. He feels a strong, powerful force inside himself as he unloads his car. It hits him all at once; a pleasant, mysterious feeling fills him with a glorious joy. He stops unloading and sits down. Charlie can hear Elizabeth's laughter and joyous voice deep inside his head. Charlie remembers all the happy moments he shared with her while he experiences this mysterious sensation. The trancelike episode lasts less than five minutes before it vanishes. Grabbing the last of the cargo, Charlie walks into the house. He goes straight to his bedroom and sleeps a restful, tranquil sleep.

The next day, Charlie drives over to his friend Wayne Scott's house to pick up Little Charlie. Charlie tries to pay Wayne something for keeping his little friend, but Wayne doesn't accept any money. Charlie and Little Charlie happily go home. Charlie pulls his car into the driveway and begins again to experience another glorious sensation. The force runs through him like an electrical current. This time he hears Karen's happy-sounding voice inside his head. The voice is soft and true. The sound of laughter and the delicate splendor of Karen's lovely-sounding utterances put Charlie into another sensual trance. This wonderful, pleasant feeling, like the first one he had, lasts less than five minutes.

Charlie plays with Little Charlie happily all day long. His mind projects happy visions of the times he spent with Karen. Charlie has no worried thoughts. He feels as carefree as Little Charlie does. The whole day is filled with joy for him, and all of his thoughts are happy, positive ones. He remembers how wonderful and spectacular it felt to be in love. After a peaceful day of playing with his little basset hound,

Charlie retires to bed. He sleeps the most serene, tranquil sleep he has ever had in his life. He doesn't wake until late in the morning.

As soon as Charlie wakes up, he is compelled to view a photograph of Dee. He goes to his closet and looks for his tenth-grade yearbook. Charlie looks and looks until he finally finds it. He frantically flips through the pages until he locates Dee's sweet, smiling photograph. Another wonderful sensation erupts throughout Charlie's inner self. He smiles a happy, glorious smile as the pleasant memories of her overwhelm him.

Charlie relives how it felt when he was just a young lad again. He remembers the first day he saw Dee. He remembers how it felt when her soft, tender, innocent lips pressed up against his on that day long ago, when he experienced his very first kiss. Charlie also remembers the silly arguments he made up because of his immature jealousy over her. Charlie lies back down on his bed and laughs out loud as he recollects those times he had with his first love. Charlie cries tears of joy as his youth flashes before his eyes. As Charlie remembers those innocent times, he cries tears for the love that he had for Dee but forgot as the years went by. Like the trance he experienced yesterday and the one he felt the day before, this one also lasts less than five minutes. Afterward, Charlie gets up and looks around the room. He realizes what just took place. He felt Dee's presence inside his own soul. His thoughts just now were the thoughts he had back then. He spends the whole day reminiscing about those times he had with his first true love.

As Sunday comes to a close, Charlie prepares himself for bed. He puts Little Charlie up and then lies down in his bed and falls into a deep sleep very quickly. Charlie begins to dream a quite extraordinary dream: He is walking down a road. He feels like he is fourteen years old again. The road is easy to walk on. Charlie keeps walking until the road begins to get wider. He notices Dee standing by the road. She looks as if she too is fourteen years old. She urges him to stay on the right side of the road, so Charlie does what she asks. Just then, the road he is on begins to divide into two separate roads. The road to the right is narrow and rocky. The road to the left looks wide and smooth. Up above, Charlie then see's that this wide road becomes black and scary. Charlie can't view the right side of the road because it is blocked by Dee's innocent looking face. Charlie continues to walk on the narrow road looking at Dee's face right above him. He does this until Dee is no longer in sight.

As Charlie continues forward, the road he is walking becomes very narrow, so narrow that it eventually becomes a path. The other road has branched off and disappeared from sight. Charlie struggles up this path for eight miles, feeling the terrible bouts of sadness and depression he suffered during those eight empty years of his life, after his mother's death. The path gets so narrow that it becomes difficult to travel, but he manages to keep moving forward but at a slower pace. Looking ahead, Charlie sees the other road again, which rendezvous with the path he is on. Charlie continues to walk. He keeps his eyes focused on the crossroads as he gets nearer.

Standing in front of Charlie near the crossroads is Karen. She is waving at him. Her luscious, long, red hair and radiant eyes of blue are tantalizing to Charlie as he gets closer. She is wearing a beautiful white gown. Her face glows with excitement as she makes eye contact with Charlie. Karen holds his hand and comforts him as they move down the new path to the left. The path grows wider as Karen walks along with Charlie. Her beautiful figure blocks the view of the other road. No words are spoken. Soon, there is an obstacle on the path. Charlie turns to view the obstacle and sees himself. He turns back to Karen, but she has left him.

Charlie yells out, "Karen! Karen! Where have you gone?" Charlie turns around in a circle as he calls out her name. She is nowhere to be seen. The other road to the right is in plain sight for Charlie now. It is filled with an appealing glitter of lusts and enticements. The flat, wide road draws Charlie's attention. Paved with gold, it stretches over alluring hills of temptations and worldly pleasures, but Charlie sees that the end of this road is black and smoky. Charlie turns and notices that the obstacle that was in his original path has destroyed part of the road. Charlie will have to leap over the small hole or go around it if he is to continue his journey. Charlie turns his head and gazes over at the other road again. He decides not to jump over the little hole, but to walk around it. By doing so he steps onto the other road. He continues to walk on the enticing, pleasurable road even after he passes the hole. He looks over to the road on the left with a feeling of guilt but continues to journey on this pleasurable road on the right. Charlie turns around and looks behind himself. He doesn't see either of the two roads. Charlie quickly turns back around and continues to walk but at a slower pace. Then a strange cold wind strikes him in the face. He feels and hears the wind blow harder and harder as he continues to walk on the right road.

Charlie realizes that this road is not the road he should be on. He keeps his eye on the other road so that it will not go out of his view. With every step Charlie makes, he knows he is traveling on the wrong road, but he doesn't seem to care because of how pleasant the road is to travel on. He reasons that if he ever wants to go back, he can—because he sees how easy it would be to walk back over to the other road at any time he chooses.

Just ahead, the two roads begin to divide. Charlie hears the agonizing cries of Karen. Charlie quickly hurries over to the other road where Karen is standing. He reaches out his hand for Karen to take, but she doesn't take it. Her face tells him that she is angry and upset.

"Karen, take my hand. Please, take my hand, Karen."

She doesn't say anything, and she doesn't take his hand, but she does walk along with Charlie. She doesn't allow Charlie to walk in the center of the path, only on the edge. As Charlie struggles to keep up with Karen, Dee comes up and takes his right hand. She tugs on him, encouraging him to come back to the other road. Her face is full of seduction as she laughs with a strenuous tone. When Dee pulls on Charlie's arm, Karen takes hold of Charlie's left hand. The threesome walk together down the two roads. One of Charlie's feet strikes the road where Karen walks, and the other foot strikes the road where Dee walks. They all three walk together until the two roads begin to separate.

A strong, brief wind blows into their faces. It strikes all three with a dark, cold bite. They all continue to walk until the two roads begin to branch off and separate. Charlie is pulled by both Dee and Karen, one wanting to go one way, while the other wants to go the other way. Charlie then releases Dee's hand. She falls to the ground and dies. Karen pulls Charlie to the center of the left path now. As Charlie walks along the path, Karen turns to him and shows him her loving, innocent, smiling face. As they walk, another brisk wind strikes her in the face. It blows her heavenly red hair assertively. She smiles once more at Charlie and then releases his hand, falls to the ground, and dies.

Charlie stops walking and turns around to view Karen, but when he does, he doesn't see anything, not even the path. He turns back around and continues his journey. The road on the right branches off and disappears. Charlie doesn't walk far on the rocky path he is on before he spots Elizabeth standing in a white wedding gown, waiting for him. She takes him by the hand, and they walk down the path together. The path gets smoother and easier to walk on. The walk is pleasant and enjoyable. Charlie can see a glorious, bright white light up ahead.

Elizabeth smiles seductively at Charlie as he asks, "Elizabeth? Elizabeth? Where are we going?"

She doesn't answer. Her white wedding gown begins to change color. As they get closer to the white light, Charlie glances over and notices that Elizabeth's white gown has turned completely to gold. Then another brisk wind begins to blow. Charlie looks up and sees the sky of good and evil. The side he is traveling on is blue and clear, but the other side is dark and turbulent, with a wicked sense of evil and death. The wind blows coldly and strikes Elizabeth's face. She turns her head slightly sideways as she stares at Charlie's face with a look of love and devotion. She releases his hand and closes her eyes. She falls to the ground abruptly and dies.

Charlie stops and looks around, but she isn't there anymore. He turns back to the road and sees the magnificent white light more clearly now. It isn't far from where he is standing, so he continues to walk down the road without delay. As Charlie continues his journey, he sees that the path on which he is traveling overlaps the other path. Charlie stops walking where the two roads overlap each other.

Charlie looks up, and to his amazement he sees three angels flying toward him. He isn't afraid, for he can tell they are truly angels because they are coming from the bright white light. Charlie gazes up at the features of the angels. He notices that they have the faces of children. None of the three angels have a navel. All with boy faces and golden curly hair they seem to be fascinated with Charlie. The angel on the left is playing a violin. The angel on the right is playing a guitar. The angel flying in the center is playing a flute. None of the three angels speak as they look down at Charlie with humble, passive expressions. They all play pleasant-sounding music from their instruments as they fly effortlessly over Charlie's head.

The angel playing the flute points down the road with his instrument. He gives Charlie the understanding that it is all right to travel down the road. Charlie begins to walk down the path carefully. He makes sure not to step on the road that isn't part of his road. As Charlie cautiously walks, he feels an evil presence near him. The three angels continue to follow Charlie on this part of his journey.

As Charlie walks, he sees Lester Cain dancing with three demons up ahead. They don't see Charlie, even though he is plainly in their sight. Charlie continues to walk as the three demons encircle Lester Cain. Lester is laughing a laugh of power and intoxication. The three demons dance a jig around him. Charlie continues to walk until he is right in front of them. Charlie then sees what they are dancing for: they are dancing around hundreds of graves. These three demons block the view of the graves as they encircle Lester. Lester's face is filled with lust, power, and pride. Charlie understands that these are the graves of people who have died because of Lester. Charlie impulsively picks up a stone and hurls it at Lester. The stone strikes him in the head. Lester falls on the black ground and dies.

All three of the demons turn around and see Charlie for the first time. They look at Charlie with horror and fright. They scurry away quickly and disappear in a flash, as if terrified of him. Charlie keeps walking through the dark area until the path he is on branches off and leads to the side where the sky is blue and clear. The two roads separate at this point. Charlie sees that he is very close to the bright white light now. He gets a wonderful sensation as he gets closer. He will soon be upon it.

As Charlie continues to walk, he glances back to the other road. Charlie then gets a fright—he sees him! Charlie sees the Old Man again! The Old Man is looking down at a grave, Lester Cain's grave. His long, curly, blondish hair hangs down to his shoulders, just like Charlie remembers it. He has a dark, sad frown upon his face. As Charlie looks at him, the Old Man looks up and stares directly at him, and a jolt as fear rushes through Charlie's soul. The Old Man with a wicked, stern face continues to glare at him. Charlie quickly turns his head away and sees that the three angels are right above his head. They are motioning him to follow them. They are all playing music with an upbeat rhythm.

Charlie takes three steps and then cautiously turns around. Charlie gets a horrifying rush when he sees that the Old Man is standing right behind him! His face is full of evil and wickedness. The fright Charlie experiences is so powerful that it wakes him from his sleep immediately! Charlie jumps up from his bed. He looks around his room and realizes that he has had a dream. He rushes to the bathroom to wash his face. He is deeply shaken by the dream. Charlie remembers everything that happened in the dream. It felt so real. Charlie feels like it wasn't a dream at all, but an event that really happened.

Charlie spends the rest of the week working around the house. He goes over to Elizabeth's house to make sure everything is in order and takes care of all the loose ends that have accumulated. After Charlie finishes, he gets into his car to drive back home. As soon as he drives away from Elizabeth's house, a car that was sitting next to the curb begins to follow him. Charlie turns onto his street, and the other car turns onto it as well. The car pulls up next to a curb right before Charlie pulls into his driveway. It is like the driver of the car knew where Charlie was going to stop.

Charlie glances out the window from time to time to see if the car is still there. This bothers Charlie. The longer the car sits out there the more anxious Charlie becomes. The car stays there for twenty-five minutes before leaving. When the car leaves Charlie soon forgets about the matter.

Soon, Sunday arrives again. Charlie wakes up late in the morning. He eats breakfast and then eagerly prepares to go to the cemetery. He decides to take Little Charlie along with him this time, just to keep him company. Having picked up three dozen red roses at the florist yesterday for the graves of his three loves, Charlie places the flowers in the backseat of the little red Mustang and Little Charlie in the front seat. Charlie gazes up to the sky and notices that it looks like it is going to be a beautiful day. He has a strange feeling as he gets into the car, like he is being watched.

Charlie looks over at Little Charlie and says, "Okay, little guy, I want you to behave yourself today. I want you to be a good little basset hound today because we're going to pay our respects to Dee, Elizabeth, and Karen. You remember Karen, don't you, little guy?" Charlie rubs Little Charlie's long ears and smiles happily at his sad-looking face.

Charlie starts the engine and backs out of his driveway. Just as he pulls away from his house, the car that followed him before pulls out from a curb and begins following him once again. The car keeps a lengthy distance from Charlie in order not to be noticed. Charlie doesn't notice the car following him at all.

Charlie arrives at the Shiloh Cemetery shortly thereafter. There are a few cars driving around and a few people walking around the large cemetery. Charlie drives up close to Elizabeth and Karen's graves and parks. He gets out of the car and walks around to the other side to let Little Charlie out and then reaches inside and retrieves two of the three bundles of roses. As he walks to Elizabeth's and Karen's graves, Charlie looks up to the sky and notices a large, dark cloud over to his left. The cloud is low and black and separate from the blue sky right over his head. Charlie begins to remember the dream he had the other night as he walks up to Karen's grave. The thought of the dream diminishes as he places the red roses near her headstone.

Charlie says, "How have you been, Karen? I brought Little Charlie with me today. You know, he sure has missed you. I know you know by now that I punished the man who took your daddy away from you. I thought I would bring you some roses today. I hope you are happy up there in heaven, Karen. I just want you to know that I still love you. I hope you and Dee are best of friends by now." A single tear runs down his cheek as he looks at her headstone with quiet emotion.

Charlie places the other bundle of roses near Elizabeth's headstone. He looks down at her grave and says, "Hello, Elizabeth. I brought you some roses too. I felt your presence the other day. I know it was you. I can't begin to tell you how much I have missed you. You better have a place ready for me when I join you. I brought Little Charlie with me today—you know, Mr. Ears. He has missed you too. I love you, Elizabeth; I love you so very much." Charlie sits down on the ground and looks over the two graves with serenity. Charlie hugs Little Charlie as he gazes at the headstones. He sits there with Little Charlie for about ten minutes before he gets up from the ground.

He walks back over to his car and reaches in the backseat to get the last bunch of roses. As he grabs them with his right hand, one of the thorns plunges into his finger. Charlie recoils from the sharp pain of the thorn and uses his left hand to carefully take the dozen roses out of the car instead. He senses something odd and looks up toward the sky. The black cloud above is moving over to block the sun. Everything begins to get dark as the cloud moves. Charlie gets an eerie feeling as the dark cloud covers the sun completely. Charlie looks around and spots Little Charlie wandering off into the woods.

Quickly, he yells out, "Little Charlie! Little Charlie! Come here, puppy. Come here, boy."

Little Charlie hears his master's voice and comes running back to him. Charlie kneels down and rubs his little friend's head and says, "Now don't you run off anymore today, Little Charlie. You are all I have left in the whole world." Just then, the dark cloud is overcome by the light of the sun. Everything gets brighter. The pair proceeds to walk over to Dee's grave now.

There, Charlie places the roses near her headstone and says, "Hello there, Dee. I'm sorry I haven't been by here lately. I've had some business to attend. I hope you aren't mad at me. I brought you some roses. I hope you like them. I hope you are getting along with Karen by now. I know you two will be the best of friends. I sure have missed you. I really mean it. I think about you all the time. I just want you to know that I love you. I have loved you ever since I laid eyes on you for the first time. I hope you are happy up there in heaven. Whenever I get there, I will be looking for you, so you prepare a place for me. Okay?" Charlie stands over the grave for only a few minutes before he notices a bench just right across from Dee's grave. He walks over to it and sits down. Little Charlie follows right behind him.

As Charlie sits there staring at Dee's headstone, the dark cloud overhead once again blocks the sun. The atmosphere of the cemetery grows dark and gloomy. Charlie pays it no mind until he sees a figure in the distance walking toward him. The person is too far away for Charlie to see who it is, but Charlie keeps his eyes focused on the unknown figure.

As the figure gets closer, Little Charlie begins to growl. Charlie glances down and watches his little basset hound behave in a most unusual manner. The puppy is growling like there is something wrong, or another dog is nearby. Something definitely is bothering Little Charlie. Charlie keeps an eye on the walking figure. As the person gets closer and closer, Charlie can finally make out his features, and a jolt of shock runs through him. He can't believe it! His blood turns to ice when he realizes who it is. It's him! It's the Old Man! He has returned once again. Charlie sits still, full of fright and anger, as the Old Man approaches him.

Little Charlie growls spookily at the oncoming figure. The Old Man doesn't look any different than he did when he spoke to a fifteen-year-Old Charlie. His long, curly, blond hair still dangles down to his shoulders. His eyes are a beady blue and filled with mischief. He is holding a strange-looking cane. He grins deviously as he stops walking. Little Charlie begins to bark even more furiously at him.

The Old Man says in a frightful voice, "Keep that dog away from me! Keep him away from me!"

Charlie quickly picks up Little Charlie and holds him in his lap. Charlie stares angrily at the Old Man. He says, "Who are you, Old Man? And don't you lie to me! Tell me your name."

The Old Man sits down on the ground right in front of Charlie and gazes up at him with a devious smirk, with a look of evil. He clings to his cane with authority. He smiles as he speaks. "Hello, Charrrlieee. Don't you know who I am? Don't you remember me, Charrrlieee?" The voice of the Old Man is like that of a man, like that of a woman, and with an unique accent from some far away land. The words he speaks are crystal clear. Charlie hears every syllable of every word with clarity of perfection.

Charlie, holding his little basset hound securely in his arms, says, "Yeah, I remember you. You are the one who killed my daddy. I remember you all right. You tricked me. You tricked me into believing that there was nothing wrong in fishing up there on that bank." Charlie gives the Old Man a mean stare as he continues. "Who are you, Old Man? What is your name?"

The Old Man looks at Charlie with a proud expression and says, "My real name is Lucifer, but you might know me as Satan, the devil!"

Horror rushes through Charlie's soul. Holding Little Charlie tighter, he says, "Why have you come here? Why did you kill my daddy? What are doing on this planet?"

Lucifer looks at Charlie with a fiendish grin and says, "I have come to see you on behalf of one of my most dedicated followers. He was buried last week. You know him. His name was Lester Cain. You killed him, Charlie."

Though full of fright and trepidation, Charlie shows no outward fear. He says in a strong voice, "I didn't kill him, Lucifer. He killed himself. He killed himself because he couldn't admit to all of his sinful ways. I guess you could say he was a lot like you."

Lucifer gazes up at Charlie and laughs a short baleful laugh. He speaks once again in that cold, clear voice. His accent is unique and bizarre. "Yes, I guess you could say he was like me. When I heard of the news of his death, I became very angry. You see, Charlie, he wasn't supposed to die then. You interfered with what was to happen."

Charlie, feeling bold, says sarcastically, "Well, Lucifer, I hope I didn't ruin your day, but if I did, I can live with that."

Lucifer snarls at Charlie and says, "Oh, but Charlie, that's why I am here today. You see, Charlie, you are going to die today. I know you are. I have everything arranged for you to be killed today. I have come to see you die."

Charlie interrupts in an angry, loud voice. "You lie!" Lucifer laughs deviously as Charlie angrily bellows, "That's all you do—lie! Lie, lie, lie!"

Lucifer quickly responds, "No, Charlie. I deceive. That is the only power I have on this planet—the power to deceive."

Charlie, staring at Lucifer's face angrily, asks, "Why do you deceive, Lucifer?"

Lucifer pauses before saying, "Why don't you call me Satan instead of Lucifer? 'Satan' scares people more effectively. I can administer my plan better when people are afraid of me."

Charlie says boldly again, "Well, I'm not scared of you, Lucifer! Answer my question. Why do you deceive?"

Lucifer fiendishly smirks and says, "Well, Charlie, since you are going to die today anyway, I guess it wouldn't hurt any by telling you."

Charlie sits back and listens.

"You see, Charlie, He"—Lucifer looks up to the sky—"and I had this little quarrel about how to rule the universe. He didn't want to do things my way, so I decided to take over and run things my way. We had this little quarrel."

Charlie listens with great anticipation but is mindful of whom he is listening to.

"After He wouldn't let me do things my way, I decided to just take over the entire kingdom. Everything would have worked out just fine if Michael hadn't ruined things. I hate Michael! I've paid him back over the centuries by destroying his society of man, but that's another story. Michael is a lot like you, Charlie. If you hadn't ruined things with Lester Cain, I would have won many more souls for my army, many more. I have been wanting you dead for a long time. I shall finally get my wish. You must pay a price for what you have done!"

Listening to this has filled Charlie with fury and outrage. "What makes you so sure you will get your wish, Lucifer?"

Lucifer laughs halfheartedly and says, "Because I have deceived someone into carrying out my plan. You see, Charlie ole boy, I can deceive anyone into doing my work for me."

Charlie stares at him in silence.

"I have deceived mothers into destroying the souls of their own children. I have deceived fathers into making their own children slaves, slaves to do others' toil. I have even tricked them into paying to have their own children's souls destroyed." The evil man laughs as he studies Charlie's expression. "I have even deceived grandparents into partaking in the destruction of their own grandchildren's souls. I have deceived the highest religious leaders and the highest political leaders in order to bring war and destruction into the world. The religious leaders were the easiest to deceive because they thought they were doing His work." Lucifer once again looks up at the sky.

Charlie frowns at Lucifer gazing up to the heavens. "What did you mean when you said you need souls for your army?"

Lucifer, looking at Charlie with a blank expression, says, "That's right, Charlie. I need all the souls I can get before Armageddon comes. That's when I shall lead my army into battle and regain what is mine."

"What is yours?" Charlie says. "You will never regain something that was never yours in the first place. You will never lead anyone into battle, you coward."

Lucifer laughs frivolously. "Everything has been worked out and discussed. If I can deceive enough of humankind to conquer this world for me"—Lucifer looks up to the sky again—"then He will have to destroy it. When He does, that's when I will order all of my warriors to invade His kingdom. I will then capture Him and take over."

Charlie glares at Lucifer, angry and disgusted.

"You see, Charlie, He and I discussed this matter in great detail a long time ago. One time I almost took control of all of His kingdom. He had no alternative but to accept my terms. I had control of five of the seven levels that make up His kingdom. I would not relinquish one level until I had an agreement with Him."

Charlie says, "What agreement was that?"

Lucifer smiles deviously and says, "You don't need to know everything, Charlie. All I will tell you is I need souls for my army, and the only way I can get them is by deceiving humankind into committing acts that they will one day fail to acknowledge, even when those acts are shown to them when they stand before His judgment." This time Lucifer looks up to the sky with a frown. He turns back to Charlie and says, "They will then rebel against Him and join my army willingly." Lucifer laughs fiendishly.

With anger in his face and voice, Charlie shouts, "You will never get enough souls to overcome God's kingdom. Never!"

Lucifer smiles a long, evil smile, exhibiting pride and conceit. "When I arrived in this world, I had one-third of His angels with me. They are all still with me, and they will always be with me, no matter what happens. If I can get them to follow me, I can get anybody to follow me. As long as humankind can be deceived, I will continue to win over their souls."

Charlie notices that as Lucifer talks, he keeps a viselike hold on his cane. Charlie sees something on it. "Hey, what's that?" Charlie points at the cane. "There, on your cane, it looks like a switch of some type."

Lucifer turns the cane in his hand so that the switch isn't visible. "Don't worry about that, Charlie. You don't need to know about that. It isn't something you would understand anyway."

Charlie, thinking about other things, says, "Why did you kill my daddy?"

Lucifer laughs happily. His piercing blue eyes stare right through Charlie as he says, "You see, Charlie, I set that trap for you. You were the one who was supposed to have died that day." Lucifer glares at Charlie with a sinister smile.

"Why did you want me to die? Why me?"

Lucifer, still smiling, says, "Because I knew you were going to save that little girl." His smile disappears.

"What little girl?"

Lucifer says with a frown, "You remember that little girl you saved from that dog?"

Charlie thinks for a moment and says, "Oh yeah, that vicious dog. Yeah, I remember now. I saved a little baby girl from that monster. You wanted me dead so I wouldn't save her? Why?"

Lucifer tightens his grip on his cane He speaks with a voice of vengeance. "Because that little girl will one day create a device that will cure every known virus and disease in the world. Because of that device, she will save millions and millions of people. And you are the one responsible for allowing it to happen! She was supposed to have died that day. That was the agreement He and I made." Lucifer gazes up to the heavens once again. "You interfered with what was supposed to happen. You, Michael, you!"

Charlie smiles gladly as he says, "Well, what do you know? What kind of device will she develop?"

Lucifer hesitates for a moment and then says, "Well, Charlie, since you are going to die today anyway, I don't think it will harm anything to tell you. She will invent a special type of laser light. This laser light will kill every type of virus and disease there is—not the heat of the light but the light itself."

Charlie asks, "You mean this laser light will also cure cancer?"

Lucifer frowns sadly as he says, "Yes, it will even cure this. It was not supposed to come into being! But now that her guardian angels are around her, there is nothing I can do to stop it. She will create this instrument of light. That's why I wanted to get you first, but your father interfered."

Charlie snarls at Lucifer. He asks, "Did you have anything to do with the death of my mama?"

Lucifer smiles gaily as he says, "She prevented you from rebelling against Him." Lucifer looks up toward the sky once more with vengeance in his eye. "Also, since the little girl lived, someone had to die in her place. Therefore, I had Sara destroyed first."

Charlie gets very angry. His face is full of hate. He says vengefully, "I ought to kill you right here and now."

Lucifer laughs freely. "You can't kill me. There are things about me you don't know or understand. I am an angel. I can't be killed. I will always stand the test of time. Even He couldn't kill me." Lucifer looks up at the sky and then quickly back at Charlie.

Charlie angrily says, "There were three women in my life. They—"

Lucifer interrupts Charlie abruptly. "Deborah Swanson, or should I say Dee. Then there was Karen Thomas and her mother, Elizabeth. They all too had to be destroyed. They prevented you from rebelling against Him. They all three infected your heart with love. That stupid love prevented you from taking out your natural human emotions on Him. Plus, I wanted to pay you back for interfering with what should have happened." Lucifer glares at Charlie as he holds his cane.

Charlie, now angrier than ever, tries to control his emotions. He studies the situation quickly and realizes he can't kill him, so he tries to figure out another way to get him. "Lucifer, tell me something."

Lucifer smiles again deviously and says, "Yes, Charrrlieee."

"How do you deceive? How can you enter a man's mind and trick him into doing something wrong?"

Lucifer stares at Charlie with his beady blues eyes. He then holds up his cane proudly. His clear voice gets very soft. "Charlie, I can deceive only when the person who is about to be deceived allows me to. He or she must first do something that will be shameful if exposed. I will help him or her with this act through temptation. Then when the first sin is committed, I begin to set up shop in that person's heart. When the person starts to cover up his or her wrongdoing that allows me to begin the deception process. He or she then can deceive others who are ignorant of the person's sinful act. I use peoples self-pride as a key element to encourage the deceptive process to multiply. But first they must commit that first sin."

Charlie is listening attentively.

"But the key weapon I have to deceive humankind is this." Lucifer raises his walking cane over his head. He exhibits pride as Charlie stares at the cane.

Charlie laughs then says flippantly, "Your key weapon is a stick? You think you are going to conquer the world—excuse me, the universe—with a stick. You make me laugh." Charlie laughs again as Lucifer gets very angry.

"Stop! Stop laughing at me! Don't you dare laugh at me! I am the master of the universe! Stop your laughing!"

Charlie stops laughing only to say, "How is that stupid stick supposed to help you deceive? I believe you are trying to deceive me now."

Lucifer, with a face full of fury, says, "This is not a stick! This is my scepter. This scepter gives me all the information I need to know about any individual. It feeds me knowledge that I may use to plant seeds of false thoughts in their minds. My scepter can even tell me an individual's weaknesses. With it I can tempt them with temporary pleasures that will be irresistible and very shameful if exposed. I can deceive anybody with this scepter. I can even deceive Him." Lucifer stares at the sky again.

He looks back at Charlie with self-assurance and says, "When He casts His eyes on sin for the first time, that's when I will order my angels to attack His kingdom. He has to only look upon sin one time, and then I will have the power to control Him. I will take over His kingdom. That's why I have so many followers, Charlie. It's just one single and simple thing that has to take place before I take over His kingdom and then the entire universe. It's just a matter of time before He exposes Himself to sin. He will have to expose himself to sin when I conquer this world. I almost did, you know."

Charlie, disturbed by what he is hearing, asks, "When did you almost conquer this world?"

Lucifer smiles at Charlie and says, "He came before you were born, Charlie—my son Adolf. He almost conquered this world for me. He failed because he attacked Joseph Stalin, the one who gave him his scepter."

Charlie feels confused as Lucifer continues.

"It was Stalin who gave my son Adolf the authority to invade the country of Poland. It was he who gave Adolf his assurance of power. I tried to prevent Adolf from invading Stalin's country."

Charlie asks, "How did you do that?"

"I deceived one of Adolf's Reich ministers into flying into Scotland and exposing the plan so that the battle wouldn't take place. But Adolf was already set in his ways. He was determined to rise up and conquer the one who gave him his authority."

Charlie listens with intense scrutiny and asks, "Who gave you your scepter, Lucifer?"

Lucifer gives Charlie a quick look, turns his head to the sky once more, and says, "He allowed me to have it."

Charlie quickly says, "Then why are you trying to rise up against God? He gave you, or allowed you to have, that scepter. You just said if Adolf had not invaded Stalin's country, he would have won. Aren't you just like Adolf?"

Lucifer becomes angry. "That's not the same thing. I am Lucifer! I am perfect in every way. I am the most beautiful of all the angels. I can do anything! I am God!"

Charlie angrily says, "You aren't anything but a rebellious, lying, deceiving murderer. You haven't got the power to pour piss out of a boot. I don't even think you have a scepter. I think you made up the whole story."

"I do have a scepter!" Lucifer shouts.

Charlie responds, "Then show it to me. All I see is a walking cane, a walking cane with a switch on it. Don't try hiding it from me, Lucifer. I see the switch. If you are who you claim to be, then show me what the scepter looks like."

Lucifer stares at Charlie with a devious grin. "The only way I can show you the scepter is to show you what I look like in my original form. I won't ever let my scepter free from my grip. As soon as I release my scepter, it would be taken away from me."

Charlie stares at Lucifer and without blinking an eye says, "Well then, show me what you really look like, Lucifer."

Lucifer looks back at him silently for a single second and then shows Charlie a delightful smile, giving Charlie the impression that this is what Lucifer has been waiting for all along.

Lucifer pleasantly says, "Okay, Charlie. I will show you myself and my scepter, but only for a brief moment since you are going to die today anyway." Just then, Lucifer turns the cane around, rubs the switch a few times, and then flips it. A tear in the universe appears and shows a doorway. Lucifer walks to the side of this doorway, and the Old Man turns into a young being of astonishing glamour and spectacular beauty. He stands there holding his scepter in his original beautiful form. The scepter is about three feet long, and it looks as if it is composed of gold and platinum, with diamonds covering it, for the device glimmers and dazzles with an array of lights, unlike anything of this world. It has a keyboard of tiny buttons and switches up and down the back. Charlie looks at Lucifer standing there with a breastplate of gold covering his chest. The name Lucifer is etched on the top of this gold plate. His eyes are the purest blue color Charlie has ever seen. His hair is the color of the morning sun, yellow with the texture of spun gold. The yellow strands of hair curl around his head like swirls of interwoven charisma. His complexion is pure white. When the vision first began his face shows a look like that of an innocent, playful child with a somewhat retarded, feebleminded facial features with pudgy cheeks. As Charlie views the spectacle Lucifer's face and body begin to age right before his eyes! Lucifer's face ages until he looks like a forty-year-old man. The transformation takes less than two minutes.

As Charlie gazes at this sight, he begins to feel a closeness to him. He feels compassion and a strange liking for him because of the tranquil appearance of his alluring face.

Lucifer says softly, "See here, Charlie. The scepter is off." Lucifer shows Charlie the scepter with the switch off. "There is no deception present now. This is what I really look like."

Charlie marvels at the sight. His mind is overwhelmed by the view.

Lucifer continues in a soft, mellow tone. "I have been around since the earth revolved around its nucleus the six hundred and sixty-sixth time. Charlie, I am over four billion earth years old." Although Lucifer's outside appearance has changed dramatically, his voice hasn't changed any. It still has the sound of a man's voice and woman's voice blended together. His words are precise and crystal clear. Charlie hears every syllable of every word he speaks.

As Charlie marvels at the sight of him, Lucifer says, "You see, Charlie, I am the most beautiful angel."

Charlie stands and walks over to the doorway. He is still holding Little Charlie in his arms as he approaches.

Lucifer continues speaking in a soft voice. "Join me now, Charlie. I will give you a high place in my kingdom."

Charlie begins to be enticed and drawn in by the spectacle before him. Then Little Charlie begins to bark at Lucifer.

Looking at the dog, Lucifer says, "Charlie, you asked to see me in my true state. It was your decision to view me in this way." He gives a short laugh. "Now that you have seen me, do I look like someone who would do any wrong?"

Charlie, in a daze, answers quietly. "No."

Lucifer smiles gladly and says, "So prove your allegiance to me and strangle to death that dog you're holding."

Little Charlie is still barking his frail, innocent-sounding yelps. He looks up at Charlie with his sad brown eyes. His long floppy ears and innocent face turned sideways arouse Charlie's consciousness. Charlie is standing there in a state of confusion when he hears Lucifer speak once again.

"Charlie, take that dog by his neck and squeeze hard against his throat. Kill him, Charlie. Strangle him now and then walk through the doorway!"

Charlie continues standing there as though he is in a trance. The view of Lucifer has bewildered him. The sight of his face has intoxicated his mind. He doesn't know what to do. Just then, Little Charlie starts to move around in Charlie's arms. He manages to get loose and jump to the ground. Little Charlie runs over to where Lucifer is standing and begins barking at him. He isn't afraid of Lucifer. He barks as hard as he can. Lucifer quickly flips up one of the switches on the scepter. The true image of Lucifer disappears. The tear in the universe also vanishes. Lucifer once again appears as the Old Man. Little Charlie continues to bark as hard as he can. He then runs over and tries to bite at Lucifer's heels.

Lucifer screams, "Get away! Get away! Get that dog away from me!"

Charlie, now seeing Lucifer as he is, says to him, "Look at you now, Lucifer."

Lucifer tries to fight off Little Charlie with his cane. His face is full of terror as Little Charlie barks and bites at his heels.

Charlie says sarcastically, "Look at you now, you coward, master of heaven and master of the universe. Ha! You are terrified of a three-month-old basset hound puppy. Ha! You're a phony, Lucifer! You are nothing but a dried-up piece of wood ready to be burned in the everlasting furnace of fire. Go get him, Little Charlie! Go get him, little dog."

Little Charlie harasses him until Lucifer frightfully shouts, "Keep that dog away from me! You will soon pay. My angel of death will soon come and end your life." Lucifer looks down at Little Charlie and screams, "Back away! Back away from me, you stupid canine!"

Little Charlie continues his barking and harassing without stopping. He isn't afraid of Lucifer in the least. He isn't afraid of anybody who tries to harm Charlie because Little Charlie loves his human friend more than anything and because Little Charlie is a basset hound.

Charlie watches the Old Man run away into the woods. Charlie yells, "Little Charlie! Come here, boy! Come here, boy!"

Little Charlie comes running back as fast as his short, wobbly legs will carry him. Charlie picks up his little basset hound and hugs him as he has never hugged him before.

Charlie says, "Little Charlie, you saved me from the devil! He wanted me to kill you so you wouldn't rescue me. But I couldn't ever harm you, you long-eared basset hound. I love you, Little Charlie. I love you, puppy! I love you so much." Charlie wraps Little Charlie in his arms and cuddles him. He kisses him many times as the little dog excitedly licks Charlie's face.

Charlie carries the puppy back over to the bench and sits down. He sits back and thinks about what just happened. He feels strange about being exposed to all of this. He has a special feeling in his heart as he holds Little Charlie in his arms. Twenty minutes after the Old Man disappeared into the woods, Charlie decides to leave and go home.

He rubs his little friend's head and says, "Little Charlie, I guess we ought to head for home now." He is about to reach over and pick up Little Charlie when a loud shot is heard throughout the cemetery.

A bullet plunges through the bench where Charlie is sitting and enters his back. Pieces of wood splinter up into the air as the bullet shatters the back of the bench. Charlie falls to the ground and closes his eyes for the last time.

His body does not move, and Little Charlie becomes frightened. The pup begins licking Charlie's face repeatedly in hope of reviving his master. Sirens begin to sound only minutes after the loud explosion of the rifle. Soon, police and an ambulance arrive on the scene. They find Charlie William Delaney dead on the ground. His lifeless body lies still where it fell. Little Charlie doesn't leave his friend. He remains there until the police and paramedics remove Charlie's lifeless body from the ground.

It was determined that Charlie Delaney died from a single .30-caliber rifle bullet through his back. Charlie Delaney was only twenty-six years old when he died. The police found the man who shot him less than thirty minutes after the incident took place. The car that the assailant was driving was spotted by a man who had heard about the shooting on a police scanner. A rifle found in the backseat checked out as the one that had killed Charlie Delaney. The name of the man the police arrested was Steve Johnson.

# EPILOGUE

A POEM FOR CHARLIE
There was once a fellow named Charlie Delaney
His intentions were true, his character was too
He was truly a simple man
At an early age is where his story began

He found a dog one day, a mutt from the streets
Near home with good intentions in his heart
Only to find regret and defeat
From his mother and father they pulled them apart

As a result he grew up sad
A withdrawn lifestyle he had
A hurting boy with an unknown pain
He kept to himself his purity remained

He met his first love at a tender age of fourteen
The touch of her lips for the first time were felt at fifteen
His young heart accepted the new experience with coy
They would part for a season, but his heart ached with joy

His father would die, his mother would follow
But a little girl's life would be saved in between
His first love disappeared, nowhere to be seen
And his life would seem empty and hollow

Eight years would pass, this lonesome man

Until he met another girl, his love would burn
He fought his rival, he made his stand
He won her love, and she won his in return


Her love was true, her age was young
A conflict of interest prevailed that she was to overcome
Death would soon follow this maiden of red hair
She married her man but died a virgin, it was a nightmare

Charlie soon fell in love with the mother of the second
His appetite for her love, her mature flesh beckoned
They experienced each other totally with the pleasures about
Her lust craved his flesh, but in time her heart wore out

Soon, she would die and leave Charlie alone
He would do God's mission that had already been sewn
His heart did ached as a test of faith would procure
The mission would be completed soon in the future

Then one day the Devil would pay Charlie a visit
He talked to Charlie, about on the ground he would sit
He came to see Charlie die
Deception would be his power, and he would lie

He showed Charlie his scepter, his instrument of deception
For he showed Charlie himself, there would be no exception
He told him he was an angel that had been ousted
But Charlie wasn't aware his soul too would be tested

The lure was strong, the lure was real
The archangel Lucifer, his soul he was trying to steal
Charlie watched as his mind became weak
There was one who present, and he was meek

The sound of the Basset Hound, whose bark was so frail
The tranquil sound would move like a ship at full sail

His innocent bark would interrupt the Devil's plan
Lucifer's end would be near, when the pup's feet did land


He barked and barked with fury and fright
The view of fear in Lucifer's face was surely a great sight
Lucifer acting scared turns his scepter back on
He disappeared into the woods, and he was gone

Charlie loved his friend who came to this rescue
A friend he was, for a Basset hound's love is true
But the little dog didn't care for recognition
He loved Charlie under any condition

But shortly a rival from Charlie's past would come
His prolong hate would not succumb
He hid in the bushes this murderous man
He took Charlie's life, then like a coward, he ran

Charlie has gone to be with his mother, and his three loves
Like an angel, Charlie flew to heaven like a white dove
The Devil accomplished this by deceiving mankind again
The man responsible for his death will plead he was insane

Charlie Delaney lived a simple life
Which he didn't live in strife
He briefly experienced the love that only a woman can show
He left this world; to a happier place he did go

To the reader, I hope you have enjoyed for I must leave
There is happiness for Charlie now, for this you can believe
Charlie has gone to be with his loves, and there were three
This ends the saga of the Three Loves of Charlie Delaney

Written by:

# Joey W. Kiser